Pat,
Best q les

MW00914634

The
Ovary
WARS

MIKE HOGAN

the Peppertree Press
Sarasota, Florida

For information regarding permission,
call 941-922-2662 or contact us at our website:
www.peppertreepublishing.com or write to:
the Peppertree Press, LLC.
Attention: Publisher
1269 First Street, Suite 7
Sarasota, Florida 34236

ISBN: 978-1-936051-84-7

Library of Congress Number: 2010921787

Printed in the U.S.A.

Printed March 2010

CHAPTER 1

"Come on, Mrs. Martin, pushhh, pushhh. That's it. Push. You're almost there Mrs. Martin. Come on. Push. Push." Everybody in the room seemed to be yelling at her. The pain was excruciating, and she felt like her entire abdomen was exploding. She just couldn't do any more. "Pushhh. Pushhh. Good. Good. That's it Mrs. Martin. Push. Here it comes. Good. The baby is out. 10:03 AM. It's a girl! Mrs. Martin, it's a girl, a nice healthy girl—ten fingers, ten toes. Congratulations Mrs. Martin. Congratulations. Your daughter is beautiful. Congratulations."

Jane Martin was exhausted. She was sweating all over and she hurt. She vowed never to have another baby.

She never would, but she wasn't alone. Very few women in the United States would ever give birth again. Giving birth in the United States would become a rarity for at least an entire generation, and for that matter, fertility around the world, and even warfare would never be the same.

1

CHAPTER 2

Professor Kirby Wadsworth entered the lecture hall about two minutes before his lecture was to begin. He was punctual as usual, and the two minutes gave him just enough time to walk across the room, arrange his notes, and begin his lecture exactly on time. Beginning his lecture exactly on time was part of his obsession with numbers and mathematics. He began precisely at 8:30 AM.

"Ladies and gentlemen, good morning," Kirby began. "Today I am going to talk about the most important problem facing the United States. It is the most important problem facing the world ---OVERPOPULATION. Overpopulation is destroying our environment. Overpopulation is destroying the world. Acres and acres of forest land have been converted to blacktop, cement and concrete. And look what is predicted for the future. The United States population will double in the next one hundred years, and other parts of the world will be worse.

"All you students probably think that AIDS is a great medical disaster, a social disaster. Wrong! All wrong! AIDS is a blessing in disguise that is helping to control the world's population. The black plague in the fourteenth century helped control the population. Pol Pot helped control the population. Joe Stalin, Mao Zedong, Hitler. They all did.

These dictators were considered some of the most evil people of our century, but they all helped control the population. Every now and then it is necessary for one of these "evil" people to arise, and do his part in controlling the population, and thus contribute to saving the world....

"Limit immigration to the United States. That is a position advocated by some, but what does that accomplish? Immigration is only a shifting of the population. Right now there are too many Chinese in China, too many Italians in Italy, too many Indians in India, and there are too many of all these ethnics in the United States. There are too many people in the cemeteries. On the other hand, there are not enough people in the cemeteries. There are too many people alive....

"The prognosis; it is going to get worse...

"Too many doctors are trying to prolong life, and medical research is actually failing mankind, not aiding it. Medical researchers need to develop something that causes people to die at a certain age. And it has to be administered in infancy, and it has to be irreversible....

"Another problem. Our longevity is increasing. People expect to live into their eighties, and by the end of the next century people may expect to live into their nineties. All these people are using up the world's natural resources....

"Perhaps we should close the medical schools, and close the hospitals for a couple years. Let's stop the drug companies from making antibiotics. Let's stop them from making anti cancer drugs. Let's stop the children's immunization programs. The medical community has to stop extending the life span."

Intuitively Kirby knew his lecture was just about over, and he looked down at his watch for verification. He was right. That was how his mind worked. He was one of those people who knew the exact time without looking at a clock.

"Alright," Kirby continued. "We are out of time for today, but I have an assignment for you. For your next class I want you to answer a few questions. Part one. What is the best way to control the population of the United States, and what is the best way to control the population of the world? And while preparing your answer, don't limit yourself to methods that are legal or moral or ethical, and don't pay any attention to any societal or religious restrictions. And for part two, a one word answer, would you be willing to implement such a plan?"

Socially Kirby Wadsworth was somewhat of a loner, although this was strictly by choice. He believed having close personal relationships diverted too much time from the pursuit of his other interests. Of course his main interest was his work, and his devotion to controlling the world's population. For enjoyment and mental stimulation he liked to solve mathematical problems, and for him, population control was the major mathematical problem. He carried all the population figures and population statistics in his head, working them over and over again, calculating and reflecting on their significance. He believed math was healthy for the brain, often doing mathematical problems before major intellectual challenges. He considered math the physical exercise of the mind.

CHAPTER 3

Ross Patterson sat alone at a desk in the faculty lounge. He was nibbling on some chips, sipping a coke and half heartedly watching television when Kirby Wadsworth entered. Ross was a full professor who was putting in his time until he retired in a few years. He had an average career, hadn't ruffled any feathers, and had progressed up the academic ladder as much on his social skills as on his research and teaching abilities. Ross didn't like Kirby. He was always afraid Kirby would jeopardize the Institute's major gift and grant programs because of his outspoken attitude.

"Well Kirby, glad to see you." Ross said. "I knew you lectured today, and I didn't even need to check the schedule. I could tell by the students' comments down in the lunch room. You know Kirby, it is always fun to be in the lunch room after you lecture. The comments are so entertaining." Ross Paterson smiled to himself, and sarcastically repeated some of the comments he had heard. "I wonder if the FBI knows about that man. If he were in high school, I bet he would be chosen as the student most likely to be a mass murderer. He should be under surveillance. I hope he doesn't live in my neighborhood. How can they let him teach here? He's insane."

Ross smiled again, but then became more serious, and directed his comments directly to Kirby. "Kirby, tomorrow Professor Spratt is going to waste precious minutes of his class time explaining how you graduated cum laude from some Ivy League school, and how, since that time, you have published some excellent research. Phil will explain how you have tenure, how you have a right to your opinion, and how, of course, a diversity of opinion is always important in all outstanding institutions. Kirby, if you ever need a substitute for your class, let me know. I'll call Joe Stalin. He'd fit right in." Ross laughed at his own sarcasm.

Kirby listened, but was unfazed by Ross's comments. He was more interested in getting his cup of coffee than in what Ross Patterson was saying.

This upset Ross even more and he continued speaking. "One good thing I can say about your lecture is that the students listen. They listen, but they are not quite sure what to make of what you say, or what to make of your assignment--- find the best method, legal or illegal, to control the population, and would you assist in its implementation. That's rough on the students, asking them to plan something illegal. It's like asking them to plan a robbery, or a murder or something. You are like Leopold and Loeb, trying to come up with the perfect crime. I don't think that's right. Suppose a student decides to act on a concept he formulated while taking one of your classes. Is that going to bother your conscience, or are you going to rationalize it by saying you were just trying to get the students to think? Maybe we should start a new class, "How to Succeed in the Criminal World" or "How to Commit the Perfect Crime."

Kirby was completely unaffected either emotionally or rationally by Ross' attack, and he responded very sarcastically. "Ross, let's look at what usually happens at this 'so called prestigious Institute for Population Demographics.' Most faculty members give a few lectures about some stupid platitudes, and as far as I can see, they really don't accomplish much. Let's see now. What did you do today, Ross? Oh, I know. You picked up your paycheck. Congratulations. That's an accomplishment. But then again, you spent part of your time worrying about me, a completely unnecessary exercise that you won't have to do next year. I'm taking a sabbatical in The People's Republic of China, and I'm going to advise the Chinese on population control.

"And do you know what the Chinese government liked about me? Do you know why they chose me? They liked the question I give my students at the end of my first lecture. You know the one, legal or illegal, moral or immoral, ethical or unethical, the best method for controlling the population, no restrictions. They believe I have more potential than the other candidates. They pointed out that what is illegal in one country may be legal in another country, and they also pointed out that the government of China is much different than the government of the United States. Another thing, remember what is illegal one day may be legal the next. All it takes is five Supreme Court Justices and the world is changed. Look at abortion. One day it was illegal, and the next day it was a woman's right.

"Our country is filled with such examples. It wasn't too long ago that American surgeons were sterilizing mentally handicapped young women right here in the United States, and American prisoners were the lab rats for scientific experiments. You never know what is going to be in vogue from one year to the next. It's like the fashion industry. Sometimes the skirts are short; sometimes the skirts are long. One day Dred Scott was property; soon after, the Fourteenth Amendment made him a real man."

Ross Patterson jumped to his feet, and pounded his fist on the table. "Kirby, that's scary. Using the phrases "in vogue" and "fashionable" is not appropriate when you're talking about peoples lives. I'm not sure what you're going to do in China, but I predict that some day I will be reading about it in the newspaper, and it won't be happy feel-good journalism. The students are right; you're sick. I'll be glad when you're gone, and I believe the Chinese will regret having ever invited you to their country."

Kirby remained very calm. "Gee Ross, I'm sorry you feel that way, but I am truly pleased to see you exhibit some emotion. I only wish that you and some of our other colleagues would show that passion when dealing with our work here at the Institute."

Ross responded angrily, "Kirby, You're not one of my colleagues. You and your cronies down at that end of the hall are not representative of this Institute. I think you're all mentally unsound, putting forth the ideas that you do, and for your information, every time I walk by your office, I walk by as quickly as possible, so people don't think I associate with you in any way whatsoever."

"That's very interesting Ross," Kirby replied, "and I really would like to continue this discussion, but, I have to meet with one of my mentally unsound cronies right now. I'll tell him you were asking for him."

Kirby's associate Adam Foster was waiting for Kirby when Kirby arrived at Adam's office. "Sorry I'm late," Kirby said, "but I was just talking to your old friend Ross Paterson. He said to say hi. He also said he liked your work, and wanted to know if he could join you for coffee some time."

"I'll bet he did," Adam said, chuckling to himself.

Kirby then became more serious and spoke, "I'm sure

you saw the article in this morning's paper about our county commissioners allowing townhomes to be built on one hundred and twenty five acres near the airport. How's that for keeping promises?"

Adam shook his head disgustedly, "I guess that means we have to work harder. I'll write some more letters, and tomorrow, when Jane Olsen and I meet with Congessman Welch, we'll be more forceful, and we'll see if we can prod him along a little bit. Congressman Welch promised he would help. He's just as concerned about the environment as we are."

Kirby responded sarcastically, "Congressman Welch, yes, he's concerned about the environment. And all the other politicians are too, especially during election years, and they all say they'll support us, but when it actually comes down to doing something, they always vote for the rich developers."

Adam spoke again, "I'll set up pickets down at the courthouse. Some of the students have agreed to help. They said they would protest in front of the commissioner's offices, and also the state capitol building. Some even agreed to go to Washington."

"Adam," Kirby answered. "How many letters have you written, and how many times have you picketed in front of the courthouse, and how many times have you met with those politicians? Face it, those methods don't work. They don't even get the attention of the media any more, and they certainly don't get anybody to vote with us. Those methods are not effective."

"Kirby, don't give up. We just need more letters and more meetings with those guys. I'm sure I can get more students to help, and perhaps the increased pressure will make the politicians act."

"Adam, I'm not giving up. I just believe it's time for us to stand up and say we were wrong. We have to admit that those benign old methods just don't work. We have to do something different."

"Okay Kirby, I hear you. Let's talk about it."

"Let's talk about it! That's all we do around here is talk about it. We have private conversations; we have classroom discussions; we have faculty discussions, and then we have committee meetings. I've talked about it so long, I'm ready to explode. The population is continuing to grow, and its time for us to make a decision.

"Kirby, control yourself. I've put a lot of time and effort into planning those meetings, and arranging for people to walk those picket lines. Do you think I considered that fun?"

"No Adam, I don't think you considered that fun, but I also think you are becoming an observer of the cause, and not a participant. Does your heart ever pound when you discuss population control, or do you ever have to get up from your chair and walk around the room because you're so excited about how much you're going to accomplish? You've changed Adam. You're becoming like the other professors around here. No passion. You don't take it personally, and you have to take it personally. It has to be a part of you."

"Kirby, I've worked hard for this cause, and I've worked hard for a long time. I believe I've worked as hard as you have, and I'm going to continue to work hard. I'm not going to quit."

"Yes, you have worked hard, but what has been accomplished? Not much, and I believe it's because of our benign methodology. Let's look at Football U. in the southern part of the state. When the students want to get rid of a football coach, what happens? First, there will be some letters to the editor. Nothing happens. Then they might hang the coach in effigy, and when they're really upset, they tip over cars, and they set them afire. They burn couches in the streets; they break windows, and they do all kinds of nasty things. That's when the gears begin turning, and officials start to react."

"Kirby, what are you suggesting?"

"Adam, you know what I'm suggesting; I'm suggesting civil disobedience... demonstrations. We have to do something that gets everybody's attention, maybe even use a little violence. We've tried all the peaceful methods, and none of them has worked. We have to try a new strategy. The new housing development is just a symptom of over population, and overpopulation is destroying the world. It's that simple. Do you remember the Berrigan brothers? When they were protesting the Viet Nam War, they broke into government offices and poured blood and napalm onto government files. The Berrigans and their associates were prepared to go to jail for their actions. They were committed. We're not committed, not even close. We've discussed this subject for years, and we still haven't done anything. All we ever do is talk."

Adam responded, "Suppose civil disobedience doesn't work. Then we still won't have accomplished anything. We'll have a criminal record, and may even end up spending some time in jail."

Kirby stopped and spoke very emphatically, "I'm going to repeat myself here. It's all a matter of commitment, and that's something we don't have. Look at those suicide bombers in the Middle East. They're committed. They attempt to solve their problems."

"Kirby, what are you saying, that we should use bombs, or recruit suicide bombers?"

"No, that's not what I'm saying, but what I am saying is that nobody is going to help us. If we want to solve the population problem, we have to do it ourselves. Besides, something like a few suicide bombers won't help. When the world is overpopulated by millions, what does a bombing that kills ten people accomplish?"

Adam answered, "Kirby, I'm getting a little confused here. Just what are you talking about? Are you proposing using massive explosives?"

"What would that accomplish?" Kirby replied. Even killing ten thousand people won't solve anything."

Adam began to feel uneasy, but continued the conversation, "Kirby, I assume you're just fantasizing, but there are some chemical bombs, which if activated and placed properly, may be able to kill up to sixty thousand people. But that's not reality. Now what are we talking about here?"

Kirby responded very directly and very seriously, "Adam, you know as well as I do, even sixty thousand people are not enough. Millions of people have to be eliminated. That's what I want to do, get rid of millions."

Adam was stunned. He sat speechless and stared directly at Kirby. Finally Kirby broke the silence, "You heard me right. We have to eliminate millions of people. Millions."

Kirby recognized disbelief and possibly even horror on Adam's face, and quickly reacted. "I guess that's something to dream about, isn't it?"

Kirby then quickly shifted gears. "But let's talk about it. How can we eliminate millions of people from the population? This is an academic institution, and at academic institutions all ideas are fair game for discussion. You agree with that, don't you?"

"Yes, I agree with that. I also believe discussion is as far as this topic should go. Suppose you were in seminar with your students. What would you say? Would you propose that same old ethical question about the end justifying the means? Would you say the world's overpopulation problem is so severe that any method of controlling it is acceptable?"

"Adam, forget about ethics and morality for a moment. Let's just start the discussion. Let's begin by looking at the past. Stalin slaughtered twenty million people in a relatively short time period, and Hitler slaughtered fifteen million. They're both substantial numbers, but like I tell my students, those numbers weren't substantial enough. The world is still overpopulated. In addition, the methods those gentlemen used are not available to us, but let's talk about the methods that *are* available to us. The resources of this Institute are essentially limitless. We have chemistry labs, microbiology labs, and every other kind of lab you can name. We have all kinds of research facilities.

"Producing a natural disaster is not beyond our capability, and the good thing about a natural disaster, quite obviously, is that you can blame nature. I'm talking about famines and disease epidemics. The Irish Famine of the mid eighteen hundreds was pretty good, and there were several other successful famines and epidemics, but the real winner and still champion for reducing the world population is E. Pasturella. Now that was effective."

Adam asked, "E. Pasturella, what's that?"

Kirby enthusiastically responded. "E. Pasturella is the bacteria that caused the Bubonic Plague, the Black Death. In the fourteenth century the Black Death killed one third of the population of Europe. Europe's population declined from about seventy five million people to fifty million people, and it was all accomplished by rats and fleas. Can you imagine that? Rats and fleas are better than an atomic or nuclear bomb. I believe we need something like that today.

14

Let's extrapolate those Black Death figures to the United States today. If one third of the United States population was eliminated, the population would decline from about two hundred fifty million to one hundred sixty million. That would solve the United States population problem, and it would solve it not for just a few years, but for centuries. If the epidemic happened to spread worldwide, all the better."

Adam's face turned white. "Kirby, are we still brainstorming here, or do you have something specific in mind?"

Kirby replied, "We're still brainstorming, but at some point the brainstorming has to be transferred into action, or nothing will ever be accomplished, and I believe it is our moral obligation to prevent overpopulation from destroying this world of ours."

"Kirby, I don't like the tone of this conversation, and I hope you don't do anything rash. I don't want to see you described in the newspaper as some crazed university professor trying to fulfill his messianic prophecy, and I certainly don't want to read about half the population of the United States being killed."

How the newspapers would write about his past and future work, Kirby was not sure. He hoped they would write that his work was successful. He hoped they would write that he had helped control the population not only of China, but of the entire world. He also hoped the newspapers would state that Kirby Wadsworth had performed his work for the love of humanity. But truthfully, it really didn't matter to Kirby how his work was described, or how his intentions were described, as long as his work was successful.

CHAPTER 4

For a number of years Kirby Wadsworth had been acting as a consultant to the Chinese government. For the most part it was long distance communication, but on occasion he would fly to China, spend a week or two, and then return to the United States.

Kirby was helping the Chinese develop a program to control the population of mainland China. He had helped them implement a few preliminary strategies, and even though these produced some short term achievements, Kirby realized that as a nationwide program, more was needed. Kirby believed there had to be a different approach in order for the Chinese population to be successfully controlled, and Kirby believed he had it.

Now he had to convince Yu Chen, the Chinese Assistant Minister of Health. For a number of years the two of them had been working together on China's population control program, and Kirby felt reasonably certain that Yu Chen would at least listen to his unorthodox proposal.

Finally the day came. Kirby left his Holiday Inn and walked the short distance to the new Chinese Ministry of Health Building. This part of the city had a very modern international look. There were modern skyscrapers, upscale shopping areas, and wide busy streets. It was like any other large international commercial city. The people, pictures and decorations identified it as China. Kirby could see the more traditional Chinese buildings and architecture in the background as he passed the smaller side street intersections. Traditional Chinese boats filled the interconnecting inland waterways.

As usual Yu Chen received Kirby very warmly, "Good morning Kirby, what can I do for you?"

Kirby hesitated for a moment, took a deep breath and then responded, "Yu Chen, our population control program isn't working. We need to change it."

"Okay Kirby," Yu Chen replied. "What do you want to do about it? I assume you already have something in mind."

Kirby answered, "As a matter of fact I do. In fact I've got a completely new plan. It's more radical, but it will definitely be more effective. If we develop this plan properly, we can solve the world population problem for years. We can take care of China, the United States and even the entire world. I believe it is our moral responsibility. The increasing population is destroying the earth, and we cannot allow that to happen."

Yu Chen chuckled. "Your plan sounds quite ambitious. Tell me about it."

Kirby began, "The existing population control programs are based on very short time spans. There is too much of a bureaucracy, and too many people are involved. My plan will eliminate population growth for at least two or three generations. It takes the responsibility completely out of the hands of the bureaucrats."

Yu Chen listened intently as Kirby described his plan in detail. He stared at Kirby in disbelief, and quickly looked at the door to make sure it was closed. He said, "I can't take that plan to my superiors. They'll think I lost my mind, and I wouldn't be surprised if they fired me. I can't risk it. Why don't you develop that plan back in your country, and if it is successful in the United States, then bring it over here to China."

Kirby replied, "That sounds reasonable, but there is a major problem with your suggestion. The development phase is too risky for the United States. There are too many restrictions and too many regulations in the United States, and the risk of discovery is too great. The development phase requires some human experimentation, and I think that can be handled much more discreetly in China, particularly since the experimentation is to be done without obtaining informed consent from the participants."

Yu Chen grimaced and said nothing, but repeatedly shook his head in a negative and incredulous manner.

Kirby pleaded, "If you don't want to, then let me present the plan to your superiors. That way you have nothing to lose, and if the plan succeeds, you will be known as a great man. At least hear me out."

Yu Chen listened to the entire proposal, and then finally spoke. "Kirby, I'm very skeptical of this plan, and even fearful, but because of our personal relationship over these years, I will at least present it. I will present it to Chou Chang, the Minister of Health. I have supported him for years, and we have a very good relationship."

The week passed, and Kirby heard nothing. Then suddenly, two days before Kirby was to return to the United States, Chou Chang, the Minister of Health, summoned Kirby to his office. In addition to Yu Chen and Kirby there were five other people in the office, four of them were high ranking government officials. There was Chou Chang, the Minister of Health, Lu Huang, the Minister of Trade, Mei Lee, the Minister of Finance, and Chin Dong, the chief medical researcher for the country. Sun Lee, M.D. was also there. Sun Lee was one of Chou Chang's most able assistants and his confidant. Neither Chou Chang nor Yu Chen were physicians and, when necessary, Sun Lee provided the true medical advice to these two ministers.

Chou Chang spoke directly to Kirby, "I understand you have a proposal. Explain."

Without any hesitation, Kirby began to speak. He was ready. He had been ready for his entire adult lifetime.

"Gentlemen, we can help each other. But we need to work together. Your goal is to control the population of China, and my goal is to control the population of the world, and in particular, the population of the United States. I can help you accomplish your goal, and you can help me accomplish my goal. Over the past few years your efforts to control the population of China have been a failure. It's time for a new method."

Several members of the Chinese delegation winced, and moved uncomfortably in their seats. They were surprised at Kirby's blunt and direct language, but Chou Chang remained motionless. Of course, Kirby didn't see anything wrong with his approach. It was just Kirby's mathematical and scientific background showing through. When you have a problem, you admit you have a problem, and then you solve the problem.

Sun Lee, M.D., a trained physician and Chou Chang's right hand man, interrupted, "Okay Professor Wadsworth, what is this plan and how is it going to work?"

Professor Wadsworth responded, "Sun Lee, the plan is actually quite simple. We're going to destroy the ovaries of a large number of Chinese women, so they will be permanently unable to bear children."

Sun Lee spoke again, "How's that Professor? You're going to permanently destroy the ovaries of a large number of Chinese women. How are you going to do that? Short of surgery and radiation, I'm not familiar with any medical process that can purposely destroy a woman's ovaries."

Kirby replied, "I'm not familiar with any such process either, but I believe such a procedure can be developed rather easily. The science is basically already out there, and it just needs to be channeled toward the ovary. For a long time now doctors have been able to selectively target the thyroid gland for treatment, and they can even destroy the entire thyroid gland if they wish. All the patient has to do is take a pill. American drug companies are already marketing diet pills which directly attack a person's fat cells, so why can't a pill be developed which directly attacks a woman's ovary? I believe it can, and I believe it's just a matter of time before it is developed. It would really just be an extension of our present day birth control drugs. Right now the ovary and ovulation are affected by birth control methods that are becoming easier to administer, and that are lasting for a much longer duration. Your laboratory should be able to combine these concepts, and in some way develop a permanent birth control agent, a product that destroys a woman's ovaries. In the near future I believe all women will be able to be chemically sterilized by ingesting a pill that affects only the ovary."

Sun Lee questioned further, "Suppose we develop such an agent, how are we going to get the women to take it?"

Kirby responded, "They won't know they're taking it. We're going to administer the drug to them without their knowledge."

"They won't know!" Sun Lee exclaimed. "We're supposed to distribute this ovary killing agent to millions of women without them knowing it. How are we going to do that?"

"Sun Lee," Kirby answered, "I don't know how we're going to do it, but you have one billion people in this country, and it seems to me that out of that number you should be able to find one person who can solve that problem."

Sun Lee spoke, "Do you have any ideas? You must have thought about it."

Kirby answered, "Yes, I've thought about it, but I would prefer not to create any biases in your research scientists."

Sun Lee persisted. "This project doesn't seem very well thought out. It doesn't seem feasible or even possible."

Kirby was direct. "It doesn't seem possible to you because you haven't thought about it. Let me give you two examples. Years ago our United States president, John Fitzgerald Kennedy, gave a directive to put a man on the moon, and before long it was done. In World War Two the United States created the Manhattan Project. The best scientists were assembled with the sole purpose of building a bomb that would end the war. It worked. Now what you need to do is assemble your best scientists and best biologists, and begin what we can call the Mao Project, the aim of which is to control the population of China, and as far as I'm concerned, to control the population of the world."

There was still some skepticism, but generally everyone saw the possibilities. Eventually they all gave their stamp of approval. Kirby thought to himself; *My presentation was just a formality. Those officials had already discussed and approved my plan before they even set foot in this room.*

Kirby was invited to work on the project full time. Under Chou Chang, the Minister of Health, Kirby and Sun Lee would work together to develop and coordinate the entire project. Kirby was to move to China at the end of the next academic year.

Kirby sat comfortably in his seat and watched the clouds lazily pass by as he flew back to the United States. He was in a completely satisfied state of mind, and he felt like he had really accomplished something. He was in a good mood, his conscience was clear, and his goal of world population control was now a possibility.

CHAPTER 5

The news spread rapidly throughout the Institute of Population Demographics that Kirby Wadsworth was going to work in China next year. Kirby was probably one of the best known professors in the Institute, mainly because of the extraordinary challenges he gave to his students. Some considered him a clear thinker and very provocative, although certainly very close to going off the deep end. Others considered him to be warped and dangerous.

Near the end of the semester, most fellow workers dropped by Kirby's office to offer their best regards for his coming year abroad. Kirby always greeted these well-wishers warmly, but there always seemed to be an anxious interface during these happy or sorrowful good-byes. Kirby was aware, of course, of his reputation at the Institute and smugly chuckled to himself as he gathered his papers and slides for his last lecture of the year. *It's nice to have tenure,* he thought to himself.

As usual Kirby began his lecture right on time. "Good afternoon ladies and gentlemen. You probably are all wondering where the semester went, are you not? This is my last lecture of the year, and I would like to discuss two topics with you today. First I would like to list, and then discuss your recommendations to control the world population.

Most of the submitted recommendations were mundane and impractical. Some students would use biological, chemical, or radiological weapons. Others would eliminate the people in the nursing homes, or in the prisons, or people over the age of eighty, or those who require intensive medical assistance. It is interesting to me that every student chose to eliminate people who are sick, or who are socially undesirable, or who are a burden on society. Nobody chose to eliminate any portion of the population that did not fit into those categories, or even to eliminate people randomly. What's wrong with eliminating healthy people and productive people, and why not eliminate people based on the quantity of natural resources they consume? Universally your answers indicated to me that your concepts are being limited by society's restrictions. There wasn't much originality to the answers, and thus, guess what." Kirby hesitated momentarily, and then coyly continued. "There were no A's for that assignment."

There was a general moan throughout the lecture hall until a bristling student raised his hand. "You're the teacher. Why don't you expound on the subject for a few minutes?"

Kirby responded, "Thank you, I will, and that actually introduces the second topic of discussion for the day, a concept used in animal population control, a concept called "Harvesting". Although I have several formal lectures devoted to "Harvesting," it is truly a simple concept. One of the purposes of deer hunting season is to control the deer population. When the deer population becomes too large for a particular geographic area, excess deer need to be eliminated. They need to be harvested. This strengthens the remaining deer population, and it improves the entire ecosystem.

"The human population is now excessive, and it is increasing. In the United States at this time the birth rate

24

is very high and it exceeds the death rate. This means the population will continue to grow, and the increased population will put even more stress on our natural resources.

"Did you people know that the insurance companies have extended the mortality tables out to the age of one hundred and twenty? Can you imagine that? One hundred and twenty years old. Pretty soon people are going to be saying that Methuselah died at a young age.

"What is the United States going to do with all those old people? Do you think having all those old people around is healthy for our country, or for the world? We are using up our natural resources, and we are using them up at a faster and faster rate. Plus fifty percent of the people over the age of eighty five don't even know where they are. Think about that. People are living longer, but they don't know they're living longer. How ironic is that?"

Kirby paused briefly and there was no verbal response from the students. There was a quiet muffled laughter, but it was also a very nervous and uneasy laughter. Kirby continued, "What do you people think? Do you think harvesting is a legitimate method for controlling the human population?"

A student immediately raised his hand, "You can't just harvest people. That's morally wrong."

Kirby responded, "Why is it morally wrong? Maybe it's just a custom of society. Suppose I said there is no such thing as morally right and morally wrong; everything is either legal or illegal. If an action disrupts society it is wrong and illegal; if an action does not disrupt society, it is right and also legal. Of course, the rights and wrongs constantly change depending on the whims of the particular society. The rights and wrongs also depend completely on an individual culture, and what is right in one culture can be wrong in another culture. Look how marriage is treated. In some cultures a man is allowed to have more than one wife. But not in the United States. In the United States having more than one wife is wrong, but maybe wrong isn't the correct word. Maybe illegal and not socially acceptable are the terms that should be used."

A second student said, "Harvesting a life is completely different. You can't do that."

"Yes, it's different," Kirby replied. "But why can't you do it? I am sure everyone is aware there used to be human sacrifice in religious ceremonies."

The second student replied. "That was years ago in very primitive cultures. Our culture is more advanced."

Kirby shot back, "I agree that our culture has advanced since earlier civilizations, and our culture is still advancing, and perhaps it is advancing to the stage where human harvesting will be legitimate. For instance, right now, here in the United States, infanticide for handicapped individuals up to three months of age is being discussed in our prestigious universities."

The first student asked, "Are you advocating harvesting for humans?"

Kirby answered, "I'm not advocating anything. I don't believe I stated my position on the subject, but I am trying to get you to think about all the possibilities, and I'm sure there's someone someplace that believes human harvesting should be considered. Because there is no absolute right or wrong, all he has to do is get the law changed."

Another student joined in, "The United States would never sanction human harvesting."

Professor Wadsworth replied, "I agree that the United States at this time would not sanction human harvesting, but not because of cultural reasons which can always be changed, but mainly because the image of deer harvesting consists of guns, and blood, and death. If a less violent method of harvesting human beings became available, I believe the country might not only tolerate it, but eventually would approve of it. It would fall into a contemporary borderline category like euthanasia and assisted suicide. A non-violent, bloodless, and painless method of harvesting humans might be accepted."

A student in the back said, "No President of the United States would ever accept it in any form whatsoever."

"Why?"

"Because it's wrong."

"It's illegal, and not wrong."

"I think there are absolute rights and absolute wrongs."

"Thank goodness you're thinking, because one of the reasons I'm at this Institute is to get you thinking—although I'm mainly here to help solve the problem of the world's excess population. I'm definitely not here to decide what is right and what is wrong, and I'm also not here to solve a traffic control problem. I'm here to solve a problem which is destroying the world, and I take that problem extremely seriously."

Kirby smiled, "I believe that was the topic of my first lecture months ago. We're right back at the beginning. Let's end the year on that note. Thank you all for your attention. I have enjoyed teaching and learning with you. Have a good summer, and I will see you when I return from my sabbatical in China."

CHAPTER 6

Lu Bin opened the laboratory door slowly and immediately gasped for air. The stench was suffocating. "God, what's that smell?" Lu Bin cried out to no one in particular, and really not expecting a response. Normally Lu Bin was the first one into the laboratory each morning, and he expected to be absolutely alone.

However, he was not alone, and a vocal response from Sam Lee startled him. "Good morning Lu Bin," Sam Lee said. "Welcome."

"Welcome. You've got to be kidding," Lu Bin said. "I could smell a little bit of an odor when I was walking down the corridor, but in here it's unbearable. How are we supposed to work in here today? I certainly won't be able to. If I have to stay in this room, I'll choke to death."

Sam Lee laughed as Lu Bin looked around the room, and finally continued speaking, "What's going on in here? There's a dead monkey at every single work station in the entire laboratory. No wonder it stinks in here. And look at them all. Their abdomens are all cut open, and they're widely exposed. What's going on? Sam Lee, did you know about this? Is this why you're in the laboratory so early this morning?"

Sam Lee replied, "Yes, I knew about this, and in a few minutes, that smell that you now consider to be so nauseating, is going to be the sweetest smell you ever experienced."

Lu Bin responded, "Sam Lee, tell me what is happening here. If you want to work on a monkey, that's fine, but all the other monkeys should be in their respective coolers. I'll help you put them back, and you can explain to me later."

Sam Lee yelled to his colleague at the other end of the laboratory table, "Lu Bin, wait. Don't touch anything. I want you to go get Chin Dong and then come right back here. I've got a presentation to make to the two of you. We've got it."

"Got what," Lu Bin replied.

"What we've been working on all these past months. What you and I have devoted our whole life to this past year or so. Go get Chin Dong. I don't want to take the chance of anything being disturbed, and I want these results verified by two independent observers right away."

Lu Bin quickly left the lab and practically ran down the corridor to Chin Dong's office. He entered without knocking. "Chin Dong! Sam Lee says he's got it. He wants you to come to the dissection tables right away. He said he doesn't want to take the chance of anything being disturbed before you verify his results."

Chin Dong understood immediately, and was out of his chair, past Lu Bin, and out the door before Lu Bin could even finish delivering the message.

He ran toward the laboratory, flung open the door, and nearly assaulted Sam Lee. "Is it true? Show me. Prove it to me!"

"Easy Chin Dong. I have everything arranged in the proper sequence, and we need to go through all the steps calmly, logically, and scientifically."

Sam Lee then stopped, looked directly at Lu Bin and

Chin Dong, and began. "First of all I want to assure both of you that all the standard procedures and protocols were followed exactly for the entire experiment, and now to be scientifically proper, are there any questions pertaining to the methodology used?"

Lu Bin and Chin Dong answered almost simultaneously, "No, no questions."

"Okay then. To briefly review, Stage One of this experiment consisted of administering the chemical which we decided to call, Ovamort, to 1000 mice. This phase of the experiment was considered reasonably successful with 887 mice demonstrating shrunken and non functioning ovaries. After chemical and dose modification of the Ovamort, this phase of the experiment was repeated with almost 100% of the mice demonstrating shrunken and non functioning ovaries. No untoward side effects were noted.

"Stage Two consisted of administering Ovamort to 200 female dogs of varying sizes and breeds. This phase was immediately successful with almost 100% of the dogs demonstrating shrunken and non functioning ovaries.

"We just finished Stage Three and I want you both to examine the ovaries of each and every one of these 100 female monkeys. I will demonstrate the first two, and then I want you to evaluate the remaining 98 independently.

"In specimen number one look very closely and you will note that both ovaries are shrunken and non functioning. Do you both agree?"

"Yes, I agree," they both said.

"Here is monkey number two. Ovaries are the same. Do you agree?"

"I agree," they both said

Sam Lee gave a sigh of relief and then spoke, "I think you'll find the remaining ninety-eight monkeys to be exactly the same, but I want you to verify the results yourself. Lu Bin and Chin Dong, you are on your own."

It took longer than Sam Lee thought because Lu Bin and Chin Dong were more meticulous than Sam Lee anticipated, but finally they were finished.

"What do you think?' Sam Lee asked.

"We both agree,' Chin Dong replied. "We were just comparing notes and the ovaries in every single monkey are the same---shrunken and non-functioning."

"Fantastic!" Sun Lee said, "We've got it."

"I agree," Chin Dong said, "but I have one question. These are animals. How do you know the effect will be the same in humans?"

Sam Lee replied, "I don't know for sure, but because the results were the same in the mice, in the dogs and in the monkeys, I believe they will be the same in humans."

Chin Dong spoke, "I agree with you. Ovamort's effect will be exactly the same in humans, as it was in the lab animals. Professor Wadsworth was right. All we had to do was put our minds and our money together, and success would follow. Thank you again Professor Wadsworth for your idea. Destroying a woman's ovaries is possible, and I might add, based on our experiments, it is very easily done. I can't wait until our next general meeting when we can present our conclusions to our other colleagues. Let's call the meeting for tomorrow."

Chin Dong hesitated and then very abashedly spoke to Sam Lee and Lu Bin, "You know, I probably shouldn't say this, but I can't wait to try this Ovamort on some humans."

CHAPTER 7

Kirby reflected on the first meeting of sixteen months ago. At that time Kirby was trying to convince the Chinese ministers that he had a good idea. He was trying to convince them that it would work. Sixteen months ago there were only six people in the room. Now there were a few more. Chin Dong, China's chief medical researcher, had brought several members of his medical research team with him.

Kirby remembered that first meeting very clearly. He remembered Yu Chen introducing him, and he remembered uttering his first words of the presentation.

"Gentlemen, we can help each other. But we need to work together. Your goal is to control the population of China, and my goal is to control the population of the world, and in particular the population of the United States. I can help you accomplish your goal, and you can help me accomplish my goal….."

Now it was sixteen months later and the mood in the room was completely different. Back then there was almost no emotion in the room. Everything was matter of fact. Today the mood in the room was gleeful. Kirby looked around the room to evaluate the expression on everybody's face—to see if everybody was happy, to see if the project was ready to proceed. There wasn't one frown of pessimism. We're ready to go, Kirby thought.

Gazing around the room, Kirby thought to himself. I don't know what they call a nerd in Chinese, but that hyperactive guy bouncing from conversation to conversation surely seems like one. Kirby later found out his name was Sam Lee. Sam Lee worked directly under Chin Dong, and he was the main laboratory research investigator for the project. He looked like a nerd and probably was one, but right now he had so much energy, he would be used with fourth and one at the goal line. Sam Lee was ecstatic, and now so was Kirby. It was obvious Sam Lee had developed what Kirby needed. He had developed what the world needed. He had discovered Ovamort, the ovary destroying agent that would be the solution to the world's problem of overwhelming population growth. The "development" half of Project Mao was a success. Now the distribution phase was to begin.

First there would be a three to six month field trial in several scattered locales of mainland China. If successful, then the real project could begin.

The Department of Health, under the direction of Chou Chang, Yu Chen and Kirby, set up the experimental field stations and worked on the logistics. All women of childbearing age living in a few small rural towns scattered throughout the country were to report to the field station clinics for a free history and physical. The stated purpose was to inform women of childbearing age about the most advanced methods of birth control. To ensure the women showed up, a free meal was promised to all the participating women and the accompanying men. Naturally most residents showed up. It seems to be part of human nature to try to get something for free. Kirby reminisced on his one time guest lecturer visit to the exclusive Greenbrier Hotel in West Virginia. Even the rich stood in line at tea time to get free cookies.

In the Chinese field trials each woman attended a lecture, and was then given a choice of three standard methods of birth control. She could choose birth control pills, she could wear a birth control patch, or she could take an injection. After each woman made her choice and had started on a particular method, she was entitled to the free food.

Kirby watched the entire procedure. He observed the laborers assemble the series of tents which functioned as the entire improvised medical compound. He saw the smiling, trusting, and even grateful young women go through the complete process. They were thankful what the government was doing for them. He saw them leave the lecture tent, and head towards the nurses station. He saw them make their birth control decision, and then happily join their male companion for their promised reward. As advertised the free food was delicious, and in general the men and women consumed their meals eagerly.

The women were instructed to return in four months for medical follow up, but whether they returned or not was irrelevant. The damage was already done. These innocent and ignorant women had surreptitiously been given Ovamort, the drug developed in Project Mao, and the drug which permanently destroyed women's ovaries. Hopefully it was already working, and hopefully none of these women would ever give birth again.

At the end of the trial period Kirby couldn't wait to get to the field station. He couldn't wait to talk to the unsuspecting guinea pig women, the women who had been so horribly deceived.

As the women began to trickle into the field station clinic, there was a tremendous amount of confusion, and a lot of screaming and shoving. A triage clerk was obviously separating the women into two groups.

Kirby was puzzled and immediately asked the triage clerk, "What are you doing?"

The response jarred him. "I'm putting the pregnant women in one room, and the non-pregnant women in the other room."

"What are you talking about?" Kirby yelled. "There shouldn't be any pregnant women."

"Well, there are," she responded. "There aren't many, but there are some. I've put the pregnant women in the room at the end of the hall. The non-pregnant women are right over there in the side room." The side room was filled with a group of young women who knew they weren't pregnant, and they were weeping, angry, and yelling.

Their mothers had told them what had happened. The mothers of this group were furious, and they were screaming and threatening the clinic staff. The mothers knew the symptoms, and although they hoped it wasn't true, they knew. The mothers knew why the women were not having their periods. They knew that none of the women were pregnant. They knew the meaning of the hot flashes, the irritability, the sweating, and the heart palpitations. Why were these young women going through menopause at such a young age? What had the clinic done to their young daughters?

Kirby wasn't concerned. What had happened to these women was for the long range benefit of mankind, and, in actuality, no one was really hurt. *Yes,* Kirby thought to himself. *A small number of women would be unable to conceive, but the number was relatively miniscule, and while the women had been permanently sterilized, their bodies were otherwise completely intact. There really hadn't been any harm done, and what a service those women had performed for humanity, even though they did it unknowingly and unwillingly. If some women's reproductive organs had to be sacrificed in order to help achieve population control, so be it. Thank goodness for those women.*

Kirby walked swiftly to the room at the end of the hall, the one containing the pregnant women. His usual calm, methodical demeanor was gone. He was frantic, his experiment, his life's work was in jeopardy. What was wrong with these stupid Chinese medical researchers? He opened the door, and stared at the small number of women sitting in their seats. He shouted at Dr. Bin Lai, an attending clinic physician. "No woman in this room should be pregnant. No woman. What did you do wrong?"

Bin Lai quickly responded, "We didn't do anything wrong. I don't think any of these women are pregnant. Some of the pregnancy tests are back already, and so far they're all negative. These women didn't have their periods, and therefore they just assumed they were pregnant. They're all relatively young, and for them there was no other explanation—if you miss your period, you're pregnant. The triage clerk made the same mistake. None of these women are pregnant."

Suddenly Kirby realized what had happened. His experiment had worked! None of the women had conceived over the four month period. They weren't having their periods, because their ovaries had been destroyed. Kirby was ecstatic. "SUCCESS," he yelled, as he bent over completely backward, and flashed a smile like nobody had ever seen before. He extended his fist clenched arms into the air, and continued his joyful yelling, "Success, success. We've done it. We've done it. We're on our way. We're on our way!"

He raced back to Bin Lai, first grabbing his hand, and then throwing his arms around his neck. "Bin Lai, you're a genius. I knew you were a genius all the time. And all your researchers, they're geniuses too. I never doubted for one moment that the success of the program was anything but inevitable. We've got to get in touch with Yu Chen, and Sun Lee, and Chou Chang, and all the rest of them. They've got to know. Success, success, I knew it."

Suddenly he pulled back from Bin Lai. *God, what am I doing?* Kirby thought to himself. *These people are going to think I'm crazy, but, then again, who cares? Having a product that can permanently sterilize a woman without her knowing it is a major achievement. It can change the world, and Ovamort will be more influential than the polio vaccine or penicillin or many other so called wonder drugs. Ovamort is better than waiting for those politicians down in Washington, D.C. to overcome their inertia. Talking to them is just a waste of time. To succeed, you have to be different. You have to do it yourself.*

Kirby's dream of controlling population growth was changing from a dream to a reality. The trial period was successful, and he was now on to his next challenge, the world wide distribution of Ovamort, and the actual destruction of millions of women's ovaries. Kirby Wadsworth was ecstatic.

The results were the same in the other field trials scattered throughout China. The same scenes occurred. The same emotions were present. The women still had some hope, but mainly there were feelings of anger, depression and despair. Feelings of betrayal were present too.

But what did that matter. The experiment was a success.

37

CHAPTER 8

Sun Lee was there when the doors opened, and he waited impatiently for the other Chinese ministers to arrive. He was bursting with enthusiasm, waiting to begin his presentation, a presentation the ministers were completely unprepared for.

After the ministers had arrived and were comfortably seated, Sun Lee began. "Ladies and gentlemen, the Ovamort experiment was a complete success. We now have an agent that can destroy the ovaries of any female in the entire world." He paused briefly while a soft murmur of joy rippled around the room. This was followed by a short, self-congratulatory round of applause.

Sun Lee once again began to speak, but was interrupted by Yu Chen. "I have spoken to Professor Wadsworth and he is extremely anxious to begin his new program as soon as possible. We owe him a great debt of gratitude, and it's too bad he is not here to share this moment with us."

Mei Lee, the only female in the group, then spoke, "I don't think we should be congratulating ourselves. We sterilized many innocent Chinese women without their knowledge, and now we're planning to sterilize many, many more. I don't think that's something to be proud of."

Sun Lee responded, "Mei Lee, that doesn't make

any sense. Look at our population control program now. Women are often physically abducted, and taken to the local operating rooms where they are forced to undergo late term abortions and forced surgical sterilizations. You know as well as I do that these women are literally kidnapped from their homes and taken to the surgical suites for these procedures. Do you think that's better than using Ovamort? Do you think forcefully aborting a woman one day from her delivery date is better than administering Ovamort to her?"

"No I don't," replied Mei Lee. "Those procedures are heinous, but I also believe that using Ovamort on these women is unacceptable."

Sun Lee responded, "Mei Lee, you have to keep in mind the words of Professor Wadsworth. Remember how he always said that we really weren't injuring anyone. We were just stopping the women from reproducing. That's the way you have to think about it."

Mei Lee angrily raised her voice, "What do you mean we really didn't injure anyone? We sterilized those women, and if Professor Wadsworth actually believes we really didn't injure anyone, then he is a sick and warped individual."

Sun Lee responded, "Professor Wadsworth is not warped. He is dedicated to his cause, a trait that I find admirable. We all should have such dedication. Yes, we sterilized those women, but other than having been sterilized, those women are exactly the same as they were before the sterilization. They're still healthy, and they can walk and talk just like they did before. They can still participate in all the events of the community, and their mental capacity has not been affected one iota."

"Sterilization is a major change for a woman," Mei Lee responded.

"Mei Lee, there has been no change," Sun Lee sharply shot back.

Mei Lee flushed, "I strongly disagree with that opinion, and I have strong reservations about this entire Ovamort program. I'm not sure we should be giving an ovary destroying agent to a large segment of our female population without their knowledge and consent. It isn't right. Some of these women will be my friends, and the wives and daughters of my friends. How can I possibly continue to associate with these women after deceiving them so horribly? Besides, I don't want my daughter sterilized. She's beautiful, and she's smart. She wants to have a child, and I want her to be capable of having a child. I don't want her sterilized."

Sun Lee replied, "I realize my suggestion to sterilize the children of our personal friends, and to sterilize even our own children was too strong and too idealistic. I anticipated people would balk at such a suggestion, and I knew they would attempt to thwart its implementation. Therefore, I have developed a plan whereby we would not be affected personally."

Sun Lee smiled, "Remember everyone, we are proposing a "birth control" plan for our country, not a "birth elimination" plan. We are going to control the number of births; we are not going to eliminate births entirely. Therefore I am proposing a "selective birth control" plan. We will designate the areas where the Ovamort is to be distributed. We will ensure that certain locales of China will be spared, and that other locales will be targeted. For instance, we can target the areas where the people are poorly educated, and we can target the prisons and the mental institutions, and perhaps some outlying areas where some of those fringe dialects are spoken. It won't be a random distribution."

Mei Lee spoke, "That is cruel and cold."

Sun Lee responded, "Mei Lee, it is not cruel and cold. It is a difference in philosophy, and I believe it is a philosophy that is going to make China flourish. We have to use Ovamort, and we have to use it without telling anyone. Otherwise, many women will refuse the medication. Ovamort is the best method we have for controlling China's population, and we must use it. This program is for China, our homeland. We must do it for China."

There was no further response and Sun Lee quietly looked around the room, trying to gauge the mindset of everyone that was present. The hesitation was longer than the usual pause used to collect one's thoughts, and it provoked a considerable amount of uneasiness, but finally he spoke. "But let's not concentrate exclusively on controlling the population of our own country. Let's focus on other countries as well. Look at Taiwan. Why don't we control the population of Taiwan?"

Yu Chen spoke, "What are you talking about? You sound like Kirby Wadsworth with his grandiose concept of controlling the entire world's population. Stick with the problem at hand."

Sun Lee responded sternly, and also enthusiastically. "It all depends on what you consider the problem at hand. I personally think that Ovamort has a bigger role for our country than just controlling our country's birth rate."

The other ministers stopped their idle chatter, and looked directly at Sun Lee. Yu Chen finally spoke, "Sun Lee, what are you talking about?"

Sun Lee hesitated until he had the full focused attention of every minister in the room. He then answered, "I have been thinking about a more important use for our discovery. Suppose we administered Ovamort to the population of

Taiwan. Ovamort is better than any weapon currently in the hands of any terrorist anywhere in the world. Ovamort is a weapon, and I think we should use it as a weapon."

No one spoke and Sun Lee continued, "Let's review some history here. Our country, The Peoples Republic of China, was proclaimed in 1949. Taiwan was a separate entity at that time, and it is still a separate entity. Over the past fifty seven years, our efforts to annex Taiwan have been a failure. It's time for a new strategy."

There was stunned silence until Sun Lee finally continued, "The old philosophy and the old methods of usurping control of a country are unpopular, and they cause people to protest. There is a natural reaction of disgust when terrorists bomb buildings, or torture people, or kill people. People object when roads and bridges are destroyed. They complain when they can't get back and forth to work, and people all over the world react to war. The United States and the United Nations would rush to defend Taiwan. Opposition appears, and people take sides. Righteous groups picket. Pictures of dead children are particularly anathema.

"What I'm proposing is more acceptable, and people of the world won't care if we take over Taiwan peacefully. Most people outside of China don't even know where Taiwan is, and they will not protest a coup in which nobody gets hurt. Moreover, Taiwan is rightfully one of our provinces anyway, and this is a chance to unify our country."

Sun Lee was becoming more enthusiastic as he continued, "What does the plan consist of? It's just like Kirby Wadsworth said, except I'm going to substitute the words Taiwan and Taiwanese. The plan consists of an attack on the ovaries of the Taiwanese women so that they are unable to bear children. Once the attack is successful, the Taiwanese women will be incapable of reproducing. Now let's extend that farther. Imagine what will happen to Taiwan if there are no Taiwanese children. There will be an economic collapse. And who will care if there are no children in Taiwan? Who will care if there is an economic collapse in Taiwan? No one. No one at all."

Yu Chen was afraid. "A plan like that will take years. It will take forever."

Sun Lee replied, "It will take years, but it will not take forever, and remember, we have been trying to put Taiwan out of business for fifty seven years already. This project will take half that time. Twenty years is nothing. We have tried various other methods for many many years, and nothing has worked. Many of you received your education in the United States, and many of you took business courses. You know that a good CEO of a corporation has to plan five to ten years into the future. You have to invest for the long term. This project has a time frame of approximately twenty years, and it will result in the actual take over of Taiwan."

Yu Chen was still dubious and spoke again, "What about the United States? Won't they intervene?"

"No," Sun Lee replied emphatically, "The United States will not intervene. The United States will realize there will be no reason to intervene. The deed will already have been done, and the Taiwanese women will already have been sterilized. Their ovaries will already have been destroyed."

The group remained silent until Sun Lee asked, "Are there any questions?"

No one spoke, and in the silence Sun Lee thought he could see everyone dreaming of Taiwan being annexed to mainland China. He could see their body language expressing their eagerness and enthusiasm for the plan.

Still no one responded and Sun Lee added, "Let's go back to Yu Chen's question then. 'What about the United States?'" He paused briefly, and then continued, "Let's discuss that topic. Why not destroy the ovaries of the American women, and make them incapable of bearing children? Perhaps we shouldn't bother going after Taiwan; perhaps we should go directly after the United States. If the United States falls, Taiwan will fall anyway. Remember back years ago when Nikita Khrushchev, the former and late Russian Premier, pounded his shoe on the table at the United Nations and proclaimed he would bury the United States. Instead of proclaiming he would bury the United States, he should have decided to prevent the people of the United States from being born. It would have been more effective."

Sun Lee continued, "Are there any questions?"

Yu Chen spoke in a very fearful voice, "We will be killed. We can't just implement a program of such magnitude without the approval of a long list of our superiors."

"You're right," Sun Lee said, "and, in fact, this attack on the United States has already been approved by our superiors. Chou Chang and I have met with Vice Premier Zhao and Premier Chu numerous times over this past year, and everything has been approved. We're ready to go. Vice Premier Zhao and Premier Chu and the other ranking cabinet members sanctioned the entire program from the beginning. They sanctioned Ovamort's development, and they sanctioned its use not only in China, but also in the United States. They realized the economic devastation that would occur following our successful Ovamort program in the United States, and they are eager for its implementation."

Yu Chen spoke again, "Do Premier Chu and Vice Premier Zhao really expect to take over the United States?"

Sun Lee, smugly smiled and answered, "No, they don't, but they expect the American economic devastation to weaken the United States sufficiently so that its role as the world's only superpower will be undermined."

Yu Chen then asked, "How are we going to proceed with this attack, and how are we going to distribute the Ovamort so widely?"

Sun Lee responded, "That was completely worked out during the research phase of the program. The distribution won't be a problem, and again the effect will be devastating. The American news commentators and financial experts talk about an oil shortage and high interest rates causing economic problems in the United States, but they are nothing compared to a shortage of people. An increasing population base is the key to the American economy, and without an increasing population base, there will be a recession, and then a depression, and then economic collapse."

Sun Lee continued, "If any of us is ever implicated in this plot, the Chinese government will deny they knew anything about the existence of Ovamort, or the existence of us, and we will be on our own. We will be treated just like our foreign spies are treated when they are discovered during their espionage activities."

Everyone sat speechless until Sun Lee spoke once again. "Now we have only one more topic to discuss."

"What's that?" Yu Chen asked.

"It's Professor Kirby Wadsworth," Sun Lee replied.

"What about him?" several of the other ministers replied almost in unison.

"What about him?" Sun Lee asked rhetorically. "What about him? Professor Wadsworth is too much of a liability, and he must be executed."

Yu Chen gasped, "Executed! What are you talking about? Kirby was our inspiration. He brought us the idea, and because of him, Ovamort has been developed, and our birth control program will be a world model. Every year we can determine the number of females who will be allowed to reproduce, and the number of females that need to be sterilized. I do not believe he should be harmed in any way. He is our hero."

Sun Lee responded, "Yes, Professor Wadsworth helped us develop a fantastic birth control device, and I am extremely grateful, but now its development is complete, and we don't need him any more. Ovamort is also not just a birth control device. It is a weapon. We have the power to exploit its potential and further our country's objectives. We can essentially attack other countries with it, and destroy their populations. It is better than any terroristic weapon we have. With the United States as a target, I believe Kirby's conscience might prod him to rebel. Visualizing the old homestead being attacked by a foreign power might be too much, even for a man on a mission. I believe he is a threat that needs to be eliminated."

Yu Chen replied, "I don't think Kirby will care what we do. Professor Wadsworth has already advocated experimenting on innocent human beings, so I don't think we have to worry. His fanatical goal is world population control, and nothing else matters to him. As long as his goal is achieved, he will not be concerned. Leave him alone."

Sun Lee again responded, "We can not risk it."

Chou Chang finally spoke, "We have plenty of time to decide, and I can understand both viewpoints. Vice Premier Zhao left that decision and all other decisions up to me. Personally, I happen to like the American aphorism 'Dead men tell no tales,' but on the other hand it might be more efficient to keep Kirby alive in case a problem arises in our program. After all, he is our expert. But enough of this already, let's celebrate our accomplishment. This meeting is adjourned. Go and enjoy yourselves and I will see you all at the celebration dinner next week."

The celebration dinner held the following week was terrific. It was more lavish than the usual government party, a fact obvious to everyone. No expense was spared, and everyone was happy. The food was excellent and the drinks flowed readily. Everyone clapped, feasted, and drank in a common exultation. Kirby was treated royally. Everyone was treated royally. The different speakers praised the success of the program, and in particular, the people most responsible for its success. Very few knew that it was not just the well organized distribution of the usual mundane birth control devices that caused the success, and only the inner circle knew it was the ovary killer, Ovamort, that was the active agent that caused the plan's success.

Actually the party served several purposes. One was to acknowledge the initial success of the program. That was the advertised purpose, but the real reasons were to officially inaugurate the bloodless and covert assault on the population of China, and also to begin the bloodless and covert assault on the population of the United States.

Kirby reveled in the program's success, and the anticipation of future successes. He was now in the manic phase of his personality. He was bursting with energy and ready to explode. He couldn't wait to begin the next phase of the program.

At last the party seemed to be winding down. The band stopped and the dinner plates were being removed. The bar was still open, but some guests were beginning to leave.

Chou Chang and his ministers, however, did not show any signs of leaving and they were actually having a rather heated discussion in the corner of the banquet room. Kirby couldn't hear the content of the discussion, and he disgustedly thought to himself, *They should be rejoicing. Here we've had a monumental scientific breakthrough and they're arguing. Compared to our success I'm sure it's a trivial matter, but obviously they feel differently, and since it doesn't pertain to me, I'm going to enjoy myself.*

Actually Sun Lee was still presenting his very strong opinion to the other ministers. "We cannot let Kirby Wadsworth live. He is too much of a liability and must be killed."

Finally the Departmental ministers finished their discussion and were getting ready to leave. All the Chinese Departmental Ministers had their usual chauffeur driven cars, as did Chin Dong, the chief medical researcher. This was a treat and a real honor for him. He was not accustomed to such excesses.

Kirby was afforded the same luxury, and had his own chauffeur. He was an honored guest. He was completely relaxed as his chauffer driven car moved slowly through the quiet narrow streets to the front of his residence. There was very little traffic, and the ride was quite pleasant, but at the same time he was happy to be home. He exited the car slowly, and walked to his residence even slower. Kirby was slightly inebriated from the three Manhattans he had consumed, plus he was tired from all the excitement. Thank goodness his driver Lin Chen was there to help him.

Kirby unlocked the lock, opened the door, and stepped inside. He turned to say thank you just as Lin Chen was reaching into his pocket. "Here," Lin Chen said, "It is a letter from Chou Chang. He said to give it to you."

Kirby opened it slowly and began reading,

Dear Professor Wadsworth,

Thank you very much for your assistance over these past months. Ovamort has been developed because of your initiative and your boldness, and now we are entering the next phase of the program, the distribution of the Ovamort. Dr. Sun Lee will assume the leadership responsibility for this phase of our operation, but I am hopeful you will continue to play a major role in the completion of the project.

Thank you again,
Chou Chang

Sun Lee, M.D. was now the designated representative to lead the project in the United States. He was a physician, and could follow the progress of the Ovamort itself. He was American trained, spoke English fluently, and was familiar with American customs and traditions. He was the choice to implement the plot in the United States. His new address would be the Chinese Embassy in Washington, DC.

China's administration of the Mao Project had actually begun immediately after Kirby Wadsworth's original meeting with the Chinese ministers. China just assumed that the medical research would be successful. Why wouldn't it be? With the best minds in China working on the project and, with the added incentive that China's population problem would be solved for generations, no one even considered failure.

With such confidence China instituted an open business climate. It opened its doors. It welcomed American businesses, and American businesses came. China asked for assistance and American businesses willingly gave.

Simultaneously China was welcomed into the United States, and began setting up some of its own factories, acquiring some American companies, and participating in various company mergers. These were plain vanilla businesses—food producers, furniture companies, clothing manufacturers, pharmaceutical companies, etc. There weren't any exotic businesses and none pertained to national security.

The most important business however was International Pharmaceutical, a large pharmaceutical company based mainly in the United States, but with an international exposure as well. International Pharmaceutical would surreptitiously produce all of the Ovamort necessary to chemically sterilize the child bearing aged women in the United States. Of course, that wasn't all International Pharmaceutical produced. International Pharmaceutical was a large firm with multiple, legitimate, pharmaceutical products— all of which provided the perfect cover for its main enterprise, Ovamort production.

CHAPTER 9

Jack drove slowly into his driveway, and was greeted immediately by his wife Nancy who was puttering in one of her many flower gardens. Actually Nancy was more than just a putterer. She had beautiful flowers blossoming throughout her entire three acre estate. The house itself was equally as attractive. The front was completely brick with two large white columns framing the ornate main doorway. An oval driveway extended from the property line, past the main entrance, and back down through a stand of trees to a rural secondary road. Inside there were three large bedrooms, a living room, dining room, family room, den and library. In addition, there was an enormous, elaborately decorated master suite with a large picture window that gave a sweeping view of almost the entire grounds. Gazing out that window was one of Nancy's favorite pastimes.

"How did it go today?" Nancy said.

"Miserable," Jack abruptly replied.

"I take it from that response you didn't win," Nancy answered.

"No I didn't win, but I should have, and that's what's annoying. I had them all beat, and I let them slip away."

"Jack, I don't understand why you play that game. You ride in that cart all day, don't get any exercise, and nine out of ten times you come home unhappy. And your friends are just the same. Why don't you take up something where you have fun, something that makes you happy?"

"Forget it. I'm not having any fun here either. I'm going in and shower. We've got the football game tonight."

"What do you mean "we've" got the football game tonight? "You've" got the football game tonight. I'll be stuck in the kitchen listening to Joan, and all she talks about is her children, and how perfect they are. Everything they do is always better than what everyone else does. Her son John seems like a nice boy, but that Carol is a brat. I hope she has a headache or something, so she has to stay in her room. And you can help me get out of that kitchen by insisting that Joan and I come out and watch the ball game."

"Okay, Okay. I will. Now I'm going inside to get ready, and you better get your rear end moving too."

Joan Rosenbloom was what the other hospital employees would call the typical DW (doctor's wife). She was snobby, and slightly arrogant. She was friendly to those whom she considered to be in her peer group, but tended to ignore those in a less fortunate financial situation, unless of course she needed their assistance. She thought of herself as being in high society, but actually there was no high society in the city of Merriom. There was just a group of people who were playing pretend, although they didn't realize it.

Joan Rosenbloom's house fulfilled all the prerequisites for being accepted into Merriom's pseudo elite society. It was a million dollar house in the proper neighborhood with five bedrooms, five bathrooms and a three car garage. The living room and dining room were both rather spacious, and together with the separate family room, were obviously designed for entertaining. The obligatory interior decorator had supplied the proper furnishings and color schemes. Oriental rugs were ubiquitous.

The marble foyer was equally splendid, and the lights shone perfectly upon the arriving guests. As usual, Mr. and Mrs. Holder were impressed.

When the food was ready to be served, it seemed like Joan and Steve's two children appeared out of nowhere.

"Hi John," Jack Holder said in a loud voice. "You're not going to have any wild parties when your parents are over in Europe, are you? I don't want to be reading about you and your friends in the newspaper, but if you need me, just call. I know somebody who can post bail for you."

Joan quickly intervened. "Jack Holder, you leave John alone. I'm completely confident everything will be fine the entire time Steve and I are away. John's very responsible, very mature. He's already a junior at Clancy Prep, and pretty soon he'll be a senior, and then before we know it, he'll be off to college.

Clancy Prep was the prestigious coeducational prep school considered to be a pipeline to the Ivy League. It was expensive, but considered well worth the price. Clancy Prep had a strong academic curriculum and a good extra-curricular program. If John graduated near the top of his class at Clancy, he could expect to be admitted to the college of his choice, presumably one of the Ivies. That was what Joan Rosenbloom hoped for. It was still over a year away, but an Ivy League school was the only place for Joan Rosenbloom's son.

Jack then directed his attention to Carol. "Carol, what grade are you in? Well, no matter what grade you're in, I'm sure you're one of the best and the brightest."

Carol responded, "I finished number three in my class

last semester, but that was because of some bad luck. I expect to be number one this semester."

Jack chuckled and furtively glanced at his wife Nancy, who appeared as if she were ready to vomit.

Carol was two years younger than John, and was also a student at Clancy Prep. Mrs. Rosenbloom had always emphasized how important it was for Carol to go to Clancy, not only for the academics, but also because she would be meeting the right people.

The children had been appropriately recognized, and Joan, almost without thinking, passed onto her next thought. "Jack, Nancy, where are you going on your next trip? Oh, that reminds me. I saw the diamond pendant Ben Wilson bought for Holly. I guess Ben must be having a good year, because Holly told me the pendant came from Tiffanys. Isn't it nice to receive presents that come in those little blue boxes?"

It wasn't too long ago that Joan didn't even know what Tiffanys was. Her mother and father certainly never bought anything from there, nor did any of her relatives. But Joan Rosenbloom wanted a new tradition. Her family was to have the best. Joan liked the new clothes, the fancy jewelry, and all the toys her husband had. She never wanted to be poor again, and if possible, she didn't want anybody to know her background. As far as every new acquaintance was concerned, Joan Rosenbloom had always been well off.

Indeed, Ben Wilson was having a good year, as he had for the past several years. Real estate was moving in the town, plus Ben had acquired some rental apartments, and also some commercial real estate. He had accumulated quite a real estate portfolio over the years, and the more it appreciated, the more he could borrow to purchase even more real estate. Ben even owned the mall, probably the single most valuable commercial piece of real estate in the city.

The conversation waxed and waned depending upon the status of the football game. At times the men were quite demonstrative, and even obnoxious and crude as they shouted at the television, and watched nervously as the game see sawed back and forth. But Nancy didn't care. At least she was out of the kitchen and watching the game. Finally Wellsburg pulled away in the fourth quarter, and garnered its first victory of the season.

"Well, that was easy," Jack Holder said. "There was never any doubt. Now what time do the fireworks start? I don't want to miss them."

"Don't worry Jack, you won't miss them," Steve replied. "They generally begin about fifteen minutes after the game, so we have plenty of time. Remember, they're in a different time zone than we are, so it's probably not quite dark enough out there. Have another drink, or some more to eat. There's plenty left."

The conversation was abruptly interrupted by Joan's yelling, "The fireworks are starting. Grab another beer, and get in near the television." She then went to the base of the stairs and yelled, "John. Carol. Come on back down. The fireworks are starting."

Nancy was the first to speak after the fireworks ended. "Gosh, that was awesome. I didn't realize they would last so long and those color displays were amazing."

After a few more oohs and aahs from everybody, Jack Holder addressed the children, "John, your mother keeps telling everyone how well you're doing over at Clancy, and I'm sure you're just tearing that place up, but you have to plan for the future. If you're going to go to one of those Ivy League schools, you're going to need a car. If I were you, I'd get a convertible. Start working on your mother right now. I'm sure she'll give in, and get you what you want."

"And Carol," Jack continued, "I thought you were going out tonight, the way you're all dressed up. Look at you. You're so grown up. You're quite the young lady"

Carol responded, "Mom said I should always try to look my best."

Jack replied, "Well, you look great. I'm sure all the boys will soon be after you."

"Some of them are after me already," Carol replied.

From across the room Joan spoke, "Jack, doesn't she remind you a little bit of Jackie Kennedy?"

Jack was enjoying the entire scene, and doubly so because he knew how much it irritated his wife. He pushed further. "Pretty soon you'll be off to college too. It's amazing how fast time goes by. That'll be exciting for you."

"Yes. I'm looking forward to it. It should be more of a challenge for me. I can't wait."

Nancy Holder had as much of that conversation as she could stand, and finally spoke, "Come on Jack, it's late. It's time to go."

Jack then talked directly to Steve. "Steve, next week is a home game, so let's all get together for a tailgate. Nancy and I will have it."

Joan Rosenbloom responded. "Good idea. And while we are planning our social calendars, everybody is planning to go the General Hospital's Fall Dance, aren't they? . Remember what a good time we had last year. It's also one of the few times during the year when we get a chance to dress up. I'll call the Wilsons, and the Fielders."

"Great," Nancy answered, "That'll be fun. Joan, maybe we can have lunch together this week. I'll call you."

CHAPTER 10

Going to the office every day was one of the most enjoyable parts of Dr. Rosenbloom's medical practice. Unlike the hospital, the atmosphere was pleasant. There was a camraderie among the staff, and there was a feeling of trust. Dr. Rosenbloom liked the friendly banter in the office, and he liked the directness the staff exhibited when they disagreed with him. Of course, there were occasional outbursts of anger, but they were rare, and they were quickly forgotten.

"Good morning Dr. Rosenbloom," said Joan Stevens, his office manager. "Mrs. Eyler wants to talk to you about her bill, and we know what that means. She doesn't want to pay. Oh, excuse me, she can't pay. Do you want to speak to her, or do you want me to say you're busy?"

Dr. Rosenbloom answered, "Joan, you're too cynical, too negative, and you know that's bad for your health. I've told you before that people who have a positive attitude, and who are optimistic, and who perform acts of kindness are happier and healthier. Let me tell you the benefits of..."

"Doctor, I've heard all that stuff before. Now, we've got a busy day. What do you want to do? Do you want to see this lady, or do you want me to send her away?"

"No, no, no, I'll see her. Send her in."

"Okay doctor, but don't you be giving away our Christmas bonus. You're a softie for those 'poor boy' stories that these little old ladies tell you, and half those stories aren't true anyway. I don't understand how you can be so gullible."

Mrs. Eyler entered the room very slowly, slightly afraid, and tremendously embarrassed. "Good morning Mrs. Eyler. Sit down, and make yourself comfortable," Dr. Rosenbloom said. He knew how difficult it was for people to talk about their bill, particularly when they couldn't afford to pay.

"Thank you, Dr. Rosenbloom," Mrs. Eyler replied. "I know you're busy, and I don't want to take up too much of your time, but I would like to speak to you about my bill. Is there any way you can reduce it, or at least give me extra time to pay? I'm having some hard times right now, and I don't think I can swing it."

Dr. Rosenbloom felt just as uncomfortable as Mrs. Eyler, but he wanted to know why she was unable to pay. If there was a legitimate reason, the bill would be forgiven immediately, but Dr. Rosenbloom knew several instances where people who had more money than he did, had refused to pay their bill. "What's the problem Mrs. Eyler?"

"Doctor Rosenbloom, I can't afford it. My husband left me, and I'm having it pretty rough. My son Tony needs seventy nine dollars for school, and my daughter Gail needs eighty dollars, and with Christmas coming up, I don't have the money. I can't disappoint my children. It's the best part of their lives."

Without any hesitation Dr. Rosenbloom spoke. "Just a minute, Mrs. Eyler, I'll be right back. Let me get your bill."

Mrs. Eyler sat alone in Dr. Rosenbloom's office, completely mortified, and now wishing she had never come.

The wait seemed endless, but finally Dr. Rosenbloom

reentered the room, and immediately handed her an envelope. "Mrs. Eyler, don't worry about your bill. It's all taken care of. I have written "Paid in full" across the top, and I have spoken to our billing clerk. If by accident you get another bill, just call the office, and ask whoever answers the phone to please check the records once again."

A tear formed in Ms. Eyler's eye as she pulled the bill from the envelope. She read the "Paid in full," which was neatly written across the top of the page. It was signed Dr. Rosenbloom. Suddenly her heart jumped. "There's money in here," she exclaimed.

"Yes, I know," Dr. Rosenbloom said. "You need seventy nine dollars for your son, and eighty dollars for your daughter. I agree with you. It is the best part of their lives, and I don't want them to be disappointed either. You don't need to tell anyone about the money. No one here will ever know."

Mrs. Eyler's single tear changed to crying as she hastily counted the money. "Doctor, there's two hundred and fifty-nine dollars here. You made a mistake. There's one hundred dollars too much."

"I didn't make a mistake Mrs Eyler. The extra hundred dollars is for your Christmas dinner."

Mrs. Eyler jumped from her chair, and hurriedly left the office, abruptly brushing against Joan Stevens as she exited.

Joan Stevens quickly headed toward Dr. Rosenbloom's office. "What happened? What did you say to make her bolt like that? Did you finally say no to someone?"

Dr. Rosenbloom replied, "I guess she did leave rather quickly, but you know how it is Joan. People have to be accountable. Now, what am I supposed to do next? I don't want to get too far behind."

"Actually Doctor, you're getting a break today. You have an open slot at 2:15, so you better enjoy it while you can. I can't remember a day when the schedule wasn't completely bursting, but then again, you can see our very own Kelly at that time, or haven't you noticed? She's absolutely beaming. She's so excited about being pregnant, she's ready to explode—it's her first."

"Good for Kelly," Dr. Rosenbloom replied. "Get a pregnancy test on her, and I'll talk to her later."

"Thanks Dr. Rosenbloom, she'll appreciate it."

"Kelly, sit down and relax," Dr. Rosenbloom said later that afternoon. "I want to discuss your pregnancy test with you. The test came back negative, which, of course, means you're not pregnant. I'm sorry."

Kelly was dumbfounded, "That can't be. I missed my period, and I'm always completely regular, like clockwork. The test must be wrong; it has to be."

Dr. Rosenbloom replied. "Let's discuss this for a minute. Sometimes the test can be falsely negative when the woman is less than four weeks pregnant. That's a possibility, and of course, there are many other possibilities for a young woman to miss her period. It could be emotional. It could be a change in physical activity; for instance, a lot of female athletes go a long time without having a period. It could be hormonal or medicinal, or it could be a host of other reasons. Some girls even stop having periods because of their desire to become pregnant, but don't worry, no matter what it is, we'll find the reason. Let's schedule a complete history and physical for you, and in the meantime we'll get some lab work, and then when that's all done, we can sit down and discuss the results."

CHAPTER 11

The following Friday Dr. Rosenbloom had a patient scheduled for 2:15 PM but he didn't have any for 1:30, 2:00 or 3:45 PM. That was odd. There should have been a full book. His receptionist, Mary Farrell, probably had made some scheduling mistakes. Dr. Rosenbloom was not happy, because he knew he would be called to the emergency room to deal with what should have been a routine office visit.

He grumbled to Joan Stevens, his office manager, "Joan, grab the scheduling book from the front desk and come back to my office for a minute. I want to ask you a few questions."

"Yes Doctor, I'll be right there."

Dr. Rosenbloom was not his usual friendly self when Joan entered his office. He was agitated and tapping a pencil on the desk.

"Let me see that scheduling book," he quickly barked. "Why aren't there any patients in these time slots? Nothing's crossed out so it's not because of cancellations. It's because nobody was ever scheduled. What is going on here?"

Joan replied, "Doctor, there just weren't any patients."

"What are you talking about? I don't understand."

"Doctor, check the future schedules."

Doctor Rosenbloom quickly flipped through the pages. The following Friday was even worse. There were even more openings on the schedule. He checked the remainder of the month and the following month. There were vacancies not only on the Fridays, but also on some of the Thursdays.

"Joan, what happened to our backlog of patients? We used to have an eight week waiting period. What happened?"

"Doctor, there is no waiting period. I don't know what happened, but the waiting period is gone."

"What do you mean, it's gone? An eight-week waiting period just doesn't disappear. Why didn't somebody say something to me?"

"Doctor, it took a while for all this to develop. There was the eight week backlog, and then another four weeks when there were still a considerable number of women still trying to schedule an appointment. That filled up the schedule for another four weeks. That's a total of twelve weeks. It's only been recently that the phone has stopped ringing. Nobody noticed it. I didn't notice it, and obviously you didn't notice it."

"You're right. I didn't notice it, but I didn't notice it because I was too busy seeing patients. I had a lot of sick patients to take care of, and I couldn't be checking the scheduling book every minute. That's why you're here."

"Doctor Rosenbloom, I had no reason to suspect anything. We've had a full schedule for years, and I figured people would always be making babies, so it really didn't attract my attention.

Doctor Rosenbloom was quiet for a moment and then spoke, "Have you heard any rumors? I haven't had any malpractice cases against me, nor any bad publicity as far as I know."

"No, I haven't heard anything, but I really haven't talked to anybody."

"Have any of the office staff mentioned anything?"

"No, they haven't. Not one word."

"I don't get it. Why's my practice different? I go to the doctors' lounge at the hospital every day and not one single doctor has mentioned his practice was slow. All my colleagues are still complaining about how hard they're working, and how many hours they're putting in. Maybe this is just a fluke of nature, and the practice will be back to normal before we know it." He then stopped and thought for a moment, "But I truly doubt it. One month, yes, possibly two, but not three or four months. Something's wrong."

He thought a little more, "Joan, you speak to the office managers from the other physician's offices every now and then, don't you?"

"Yes I do."

"What are they saying? Have they mentioned anything about their practices being slow?"

"No, they haven't. In fact their chief complaint seems to be their inability to hire enough staff to keep up with the workload."

Dr. Rosenbloom rose from his desk and paced nervously from side to side, "What's going on then? This is affecting my practice only. There's got to be an answer."

Joan Stevens spoke, "There isn't a new obstetrician in town so the patients can't be going elsewhere, at least not in this town, and expectant mothers don't like to travel out of town. They like their obstetrician and hospital close by."

Dr. Rosenbloom looked straight at Joan Stevens and spoke, "Joan, I want you to answer this question truthfully, and I realize it's embarrassing, but is it me? Am I too gruff with the patients, or is it my personal hygiene, or perhaps there's something else about me that is chasing the patients away. What do you think? I need to know."

"No Doctor, it's not you. Occasionally you're a little gruff, but the patients know your personality by now, and you've been that way for years. No, it's not you."

"How about the office staff, or something about the office itself?"

"No, it's nothing in the office."

"How about our fee schedule, or our method of accepting insurance company payments?"

"No, it's not that. We're the same as all the other physician's offices."

Dr. Rosenbloom grabbed the scheduling book again. "The pattern is obvious. The number of vacancies is still increasing. You know Joan, the more I think about this, over the past two or three weeks, we've had more than the usual number of young women in here who missed their periods, yet they weren't pregnant. Look at our own Kelly. All this has to be related."

He tried to think back. Was there something unusual that happened about six to nine months ago that would cause a decrease in the number of pregnancies? He thought about the blackout of years past, but that caused a temporary increase in the number of pregnancies, not a decrease. What happened that could have caused a decrease? Nothing, a blank.

"Joan, maybe I should contact the State Health Department and have them evaluate the situation. Maybe something is occurring that the Health Department needs to know about, or maybe they know something already. But I hate calling them, because it's generally a nightmare getting through to somebody who knows something, and it is even more difficult trying to get them to answer a question without all kinds of reservations and disclaimers, but before I do anything, do you have any ideas, any ideas at all?"

"No, doctor, I don't. Sorry."

Dr. Rosenbloom finally said, "I'm not going to call the Health Department just yet. Frank Rush is a former classmate of mine, and he's only about twenty miles from here. He's a straightforward guy, and if he knows anything, he'll tell me. I'll see if he is having a similar problem."

Doctor Rosenbloom didn't waste any time. "Hi Frank, Steve Rosenbloom here, I'd like to ask you a few questions if you have the time."

""I have plenty of time Steve, and I never thought I'd say this, but having plenty of time isn't as pleasant as I thought. How about you? I guess you're feeling some pressure about now, right?"

Steve Rosenbloom replied, "It sounds like you already know why I'm calling. What's happened Frank? What is going on?"

"Steve, I don't know what happened, but it is still happening, and I believe it is going to get worse."

"Frank, don't tell me that. My practice is heading downhill already. How about you?"

"I'm doing okay but my practice has changed. I haven't had many new OB patients for some time now, but you already knew that, didn't you? That's why you're calling. Telling a young man and a young woman they would soon be the parents of a nice healthy baby was one of the fun parts of my practice. It was a delight. I was happy. The parents were happy. The staff was happy. Everybody was happy. Now nobody's happy. Nobody's getting pregnant, and my practice is starting to fall apart too. My income is down. The patients are unhappy. The staff is unhappy. I'm unhappy, and I don't see an end to it. Have I cheered you up enough Steve?"

"That's not what I wanted to hear Frank. I was hoping you would say it was a virus or something, something that was self limited, and that had already disappeared. What's the State Health Department saying? Have you been in contact with anybody down there?"

"Yes, I called them and I got through right away. Instead of being put on hold, or shuffled from secretary to secretary, I was immediately put through to the Director, Dr. John Murphy. He said I was the first OB man from this area to report a decrease in early pregnancies, but that other OB doctors around the state had already reported a similar decrease. Dr. Murphy didn't know the cause, but said that other states were reporting comparable experiences, and that it appeared to be a national problem. He said he would call me back. So far he hasn't."

Dr. Rosenbloom spoke, "You mean he didn't give you a hint as to what is going on."

Frank Rush replied, "Dr. Murphy doesn't know anything. He gave me all this Irish blarney about how back in the eighteen hundreds in some God forsaken place, there was a precipitous drop in the number of pregnancies, and then all of a sudden the pregnancies spontaneously rebounded, and no one ever knew the cause for the drop or the cause for the rebound. He talked about hormone deficiencies and vitamin deficiencies and epidemics and famines and viruses, but, in truth, he doesn't have a clue."

"God, Frank, I don't know what to do, but be sure to keep me posted, and if any good news comes in, give me a call."

"I will Steve, and keep your head up, but don't expect a phone call."

Dr. Rosenbloom put the phone down, took a deep breath, and quietly murmured. "I hope he's wrong."

Dr. Rosenbloom left his office and walked towards his car. He was half in a trance. How long would his practice survive without new patients?

He was suddenly interrupted by a loud call from John Vogel. "Hey Doc, I need to speak to you. You're prescribing too many birth control pills. You need to ease up on that pencil of yours."

John Vogel, the owner of the local maternity shop, and Curt McKeon, the owner of a children's shop approached him. John Vogel jokingly spoke, "Doc, I'm not moving my obstetrical inventory. We're going to have to take your prescription pad away." The forced laughter of the two businessmen quickly dissipated, and John Vogel continued speaking. "Seriously now Steve, something's wrong. What is it? You've got to be in the same boat I am. Pregnant women determine our fate, and I'm sure you've noticed that pregnant women are kind of scarce around here. My business isn't going to survive much longer, and yours isn't either. Now what's happening?"

Dr. Rosenbloom awkwardly responded, "Gentleman, I'm sorry. I'd love to hang around and talk, but I don't have the time right now. I have an important meeting to go to, and I'm late already."

Dr. Rosenbloom nervously laughed, rudely brushed by them, and continued towards his car. He thought to himself. *They don't know what's coming.*

CHAPTER 12

Dr. Rosenbloom's obstetrical practice continued to deteriorate, and only a further decline could be foreseen. Over the course of this time period he had had several discussions with his wife about their finances. These decided nothing. Now something had to be done. His income was continuing to drop, and his end of the month payments were still coming due. Like most doctors, other than a retirement plan, he really hadn't saved much money. Money was for buying toys, and buying jewelry, and taking trips and enjoying life. It was not for saving. Now lifestyle cutbacks were necessary.

Steve Rosenbloom knew this was not going to be a pleasant evening, and therefore had waited for a weekend night, after dinner was over, and the children were out with their friends.

Steve was drinking his after dinner coffee, and nervously watching Joan clear the table. He was waiting for the proper moment to tell her the bad news, but with bad news there never is a proper moment.

Joan stopped for a moment and glanced at her husband. "Steve, what's the matter with you? You've been quiet all evening. Don't you feel well, or are you just tired?"

Steve blurted back awkwardly and quickly. "Joan, we

have to make some changes in our lifestyle. We have to decrease our spending."

Joan quickly replied, "Steve, don't start with that financial stuff again. We've already been through all that, and besides, this isn't a good year to cut back. John will be a senior at Clancy, and Carol will be a sophomore, and they're both going to need new wardrobes. In fact John has to start shopping now, so he will look nice and spiffy when he goes on his college interviews. He's planning to visit about six colleges, although at this point I would say he's leaning towards Yale. At least that's the way he's talking, and I'm sure that if he got early admission, he would grab it. And can you believe that Carol will be a sophomore already?

Don't you dare tell our children that they have to cut back. I want this year to be perfect for the both of them. If you really think that it's necessary, I suppose I could cut back a little bit myself. That should help."

Steve looked directly at his wife, took a deep breath, and spoke once again. "Joan, I'm sorry, but we cannot afford to send John away to college. He has to enroll at Holmesdale Community College, and if our finances improve, and he does well at Holmesdale, maybe he can transfer at the end of two years."

There was no response and Steve decided to push on. "And Carol can't go to Clancy next year. We can not afford the tuition anymore. She has to go to the public high school."

Both Joan and Steve were waiting for the other to speak. Joan was hoping she had misunderstood what Steve had just said, or that Steve would now say it was all a joke. Steve was hoping Joan would say she understood, and that everything would work out fine.

Finally Joan spoke. "What are you talking about? You

can't possibly be serious. Carol needs to go to Clancy, and John needs to go to one of the Ivies. I can't imagine you would even consider any other options for our children. That's the end of it. I don't want to discuss this any further."

Steve became more emphatic, "Look Joan, we have to discuss our finances, and we have to discuss them right now. I have tried to explain all this before, but you don't seem to understand what is happening. My practice is failing, and my income is falling, and it's falling precipitously. We are in debt, and we can not afford any more frivolities. You NEED to think and act like you did when you were growing up back in Crossville. You NEED to think and act like your mother and father did, and you need to start shopping like your mother and father did."

Joan replied just as emphatically, "Never. Never again. I acted like my parents for twenty-four years, but I never thought like them. I always wanted better, and I fought to make myself better. I married a doctor so I wouldn't have to scrimp and save, and my children didn't have to live the way I did. Now you're saying that our life has to change. Why don't you go get a job moonlighting, or work part time in the emergency room? You used to do that. You want me to go back in time, what about you, and what about all your toys, and all your frivolities? What are you going to do?"

Joan stopped screaming for a moment. Her mind and body were both moving frantically. She was rapidly pacing around the kitchen when she suddenly resumed her verbal attack.

"I never knew a doctor who had financial problems. There's one doctor in the whole wide world with financial problems and I'm married to him." Suddenly Joan's expression changed dramatically as all kinds of ugly images flashed through her head. "Wait a minute. The only doctors with financial problems are doctors with other problems as well. Are you an alcoholic? A druggie? A gambler? What is it? Is there another woman?"

"Let me see your arms." Joan demanded as she rushed towards Steve.

He quickly extended both arms. No needle tracks.

"Get me your checkbook!"

"You won't find anything there either," Steve said as he thought about the double entendre of his response. Considering the circumstances, he correctly decided to ignore it. "Joan, there is no other problem. The money just isn't coming in like it used to. We have to cut back."

"Steve, I can't cut back. I struggled too much and too long when I was younger. What will everybody think? What will they say?"

"Who cares what they think, and who cares what they say? Besides, they are in the same situation we are, or they will be shortly. I'm an obstetrician so it hit me first, but soon it will be the pediatricians, and then it will be the surgeons or the emergency room doctors, and pretty soon the entire medical community will be affected. The lawyers, the bankers, the businessmen and even the priests and ministers will also be affected. We won't be alone Joan; everyone is going to feel the pain.

"Now let's continue this discussion tomorrow morning before one of us says something we will regret. We can break it to our children gradually, but we can't wait too long. You know how rumors spread, and I don't want the children to hear the bad news from anybody else."

Steve didn't sleep much that night. He continuously turned from side to side, constantly thinking about his discussion with Joan. He anticipated other dreadful discussions, not only with Joan but also with his children, John and Carol. Joan slept even less. For the most part she wandered around the house, alternately reading, watching television, or eating. Occasionally she would lie down, but her active mind prevented her from sleeping.

She was sitting at the kitchen table when Steve came down the stairs. It was early in the morning, and they were both exhausted. Joan had finished eating an entire package of cookies, had several empty soda cans in front of her, and she was actively munching on peanuts from a nearly empty peanut can.

Joan was much more docile than the previous night. "Steve, I am sorry about last night. I shouldn't have spoken like I did. We've had a good life, and no matter what happens, we will continue to have a good life. We will fight this as a family. Good times come and go. Bad times come and go, and I am sure this is just one of those temporary bad times. I also think we both should be there when we explain it to John and Carol. There might be some temporary anger and disappointment, but I believe they'll understand."

"Joan, I'm glad you think they will understand, because I'm not so sure. John and Carol are used to a pretty affluent life style, and now all of a sudden that's going to disappear. I'm not sure John is mature enough to cope with such a radical change, and Carol's still a baby, but I hope you're right."

"Of course I'm right. They'll be just fine, but I'm concerned about your office staff. How are they going to handle it?"

Steve replied, "I'm not even sure what I'm going to say to them. I have to think about it."

"Steve, you don't have anything to think about; you don't have a choice. You have to terminate some of your employees. You told me you don't have the money coming in like you used to, so you have to cut the expenses accordingly."

"Joan, my office staff has been with me for years. They're more than just an office staff, they're my friends, and I'm sure they consider me their friend as well. I can't terminate them."

"Steve, last night you were telling me that I had to face reality. Well now, you've got to face reality. You have to terminate some of your staff. Decide who you can eliminate, and eliminate them. Personally, I'd get rid of the ones making the highest salaries."

CHAPTER 13

"Hey Mom," John said enthusiastically as he strode into the living room. "We have to start planning our trip this summer. School will be out in a few weeks, and summer will be over before we know it, so we need to get moving. I have about four colleges to visit, and I want all my applications in by September. Optimally I would like to have everything wrapped up by Christmas."

Joan Rosenbloom could see the enthusiasm and pride in her son's eyes. He was in one of those moods where he just bubbled with excitement, a seventeen-year-old man eager to set off to college, eager for his next challenge.

Mrs. Rosenbloom felt a sudden numbness come over her entire body. She ached for her son. Although Joan and Steve had planned to tell John together, they never found the appropriate moment. This time, however, Joan knew she had to say something. Even though Steve was not there, she could not procrastinate any longer. She sadly began to speak, "John, your father and I have been meaning to talk to you about college. Your father has not been bringing in as much money as he used to, and we've been trying to figure out ways to reduce our expenses. As it stands now, we don't believe we can take on any new obligations."

She tried to soften the shock, but there was no way she

could do it. John was a perceptive boy and he knew what was coming, but he waited, and hoped that the final words were not those that he now was anticipating.

Joan continued, "John, we can not afford to send you away to college. We don't have any choice. I know you're disappointed but there is nothing your father and I can do."

John stood perfectly still. Then fighting back the tears, he responded with a cracking voice. "Mom, you told me that if I did well at Clancy, I could go to the college of my choice. You and dad told me I could go anywhere. You told me it would be good for me to get away, that it would be the best thing for me--- socially, financially, and intellectually."

Mrs. Rosenbloom softly answered, "Yes I did John, and I'm sorry, but times were different then. Our financial condition has deteriorated considerably, and we have to cut our expenses."

"And my college education is the expense that is being cut," John replied.

Mrs. Rosenbloom snapped at her son. "John, your father and I have discussed it, and we think you will do just as well at Holmesdale"

John barked back, "Holmesdale. Holmesdale is a community college. For my entire lifetime all I ever heard was how Holmesdale was for underachievers, or for those students who didn't quite have the necessary brain power to go elsewhere, and now you want me to go there. I'm not going to Holmesdale. I'll borrow the money."

"John, you can't borrow the money. You don't have any income, nor do you have any collateral, and your father and I certainly can't cosign a note for you. I'm sorry."

Steve Rosenbloom sat quietly at the kitchen table listening to his wife as she described her discussion with John.

Actually Steve was only half listening. Since the family's financial misfortune, Steve was unable to concentrate as well as he used to. He was physically present, but mentally he was only partly there. Joan continued talking, "Steve, don't just sit there. Before John gets home, the two of us have to go upstairs and tell Carol what is going on. I think she will understand. Steve, Steve, are you there?"

"Yes, I'm here, and Carol won't understand. For years we've been glorifying Clancy Prep, and telling her how important it was for her to graduate from there. At this point I think it would be irrational for her to understand."

"Steve, you're underestimating your daughter. Now, come on. We've got to do it. Let's go."

Joan knocked on Carol's door, and then both she and Steve entered.

"Carol, your dad and I want to talk to you about school next year."

Carol lifted her head from her book and excitedly answered. "Sure, what is it?" She expected she would be told of a proposed shopping trip for next fall's new clothes, but there were no smiles on her parents' faces. There was no happiness in their eyes. Something was wrong. "Mom, Dad, what is it? What's the matter?"

Mrs. Rosenbloom spoke. "Carol, we need to make you aware of what is happening. Your father is not making as much money as he used to, and we have to cut our expenses. We have already spoken to John, and he is aware of our financial situation. John understands that we can not afford to send him to an Ivy League school, and he is going to go to Holmesdale Community College next year."

"Holmesdale Community College," Carol snapped. "That's not fair. John has been counting on an Ivy League school for as long as I can remember. An Ivy League school was all he talked about when he was filling out his applications. I never heard him mention Holmesdale, and I never heard you or dad mention it either. Where's John now? I want to hear what John has to say about this."

Mrs. Rosenbloom replied. "John will be home in a little while. And Carol, we all have to pitch in; we all have to sacrifice. We can not afford to send you to Clancy next year." Mrs. Rosenbloom paused. "But your dad and I both think you will like the public high school just as well. We also think you will get just as much out of it."

Carol snapped at them again, only louder and in a more angry tone. "You've got to be kidding. What will our friends think? What will their parents think? I have to go to Clancy, and John has to go to an Ivy League school. The two of you have told us that all our lives. John can't go to Holmesdale. That's where the dummies go."

Mrs. Rosenbloom responded, "Carol, a lot of intelligent people go to Holmesdale. I'm acquainted with several of the teachers there, and they are excellent. John will get a good solid education there, and you will get a good solid education at the public high school"

Carol replied, "Is this my mother talking? Why did John and I study so hard all these years, if John is going to end up going to Holmesdale, and I'm going to end up graduating from the public high school. We could have fooled around a lot more, and gone out carousing on Friday and Saturday nights instead of hitting the books like we did. And what about you and your fancy trips, and your fancy clothes, and your fancy jewelry?"

Mrs. Rosenbloom yelled, "Carol, shut up. We're all together in this as a family. Every one of us has to cut back. That includes me. It includes your father. It includes John, and it includes you. Now simmer down, and control yourself."

"Control myself? And what else did you and dad decide that John and I have to cut back on?"

Mrs. Rosenbloom answered, "We're still in the process of arranging the family's priorities."

"Family priorities—what does that mean? Is John going to get the new car you promised him?"

'No, he's not. We can't afford it, and John understands that."

"I'm glad John understands all this, because I don't. Am I going to get the new clothes you promised me?"

Mrs. Rosenbloom replied, "We'll probably have to make some adjustments."

"Make some adjustments...That means I won't be getting them."

"Carol, our spending habits have to change, and there is nothing we can do about it. Now your father and I are going to leave you alone for a while, and when you're calmer and able to discuss this matter appropriately, then come down to dinner. We can discuss this further when you are more rational."

CHAPTER 14

D r. Rosenbloom spent an extra long time at the hospital that morning. He didn't want to go to the office, because he knew the whole day would be miserable. He had to terminate a nurse and a secretary, and he had to warn the remainder of the staff of possible further layoffs. He felt like a traitor.

The day dragged. The office was tense, tempers were short, and the staff was jumpy. They knew what was coming, they just didn't know to whom.

Although the day itself seemed to last forever, and despite his attempt to extend his last office visit as long as possible, Dr. Rosenbloom's last appointment went by much too quickly. When Dr. Rosenbloom finished seeing his last patient and exited the examining room, his stomach was churning and his pulse was racing. He never had to terminate an employee before. His practice had consistently grown, and employees were always added, never eliminated.

As Dr. Rosenbloom was about to enter his office, Joan Stevens, his office manager approached him. "Dr. Rosenbloom, I would like to speak to you for a moment if you have the time."

"Fine" he replied. Anything for a brief reprieve, although he didn't really like the tone in her voice. It was so matter of fact, stern, even slightly cold.

They both entered his office, and Dr. Rosenbloom closed the door.

Mrs. Stevens was very nervous, which was unusual. Normally she was calm and relaxed. "Dr. Rosenbloom, I know the office is not doing well, and the entire staff can see what is happening. We don't know why it has happened, but it is obvious our patient load is dropping precipitously, and according to the rumor mills, nobody else seems to know why it has happened either. But anyway, the staff had a meeting at lunch time today, and we talked about the problem. We all need our jobs and we all need the benefits, and because we figured you were going to cut the office staff this afternoon, we came up with a proposal. Do not fire anyone. Instead, we will all take a fifteen percent reduction in salary, and then we'll just hope these troubled times run their course. The entire staff agrees."

Dr. Rosenbloom gave a sigh of relief, "Joan Stevens, you just made my day. I've been fretting all weekend about this office, and I've deliberated for hours over every possible scenario that I thought would keep this office afloat. I thought about each individual, and how each and every decision would affect each individual and her family. Thank you. Tell the office staff I accept their proposal, and tell them it was a very pleasant surprise, and Joan, you know as well as I do, that all recent surprises have been absolutely horrible events."

"I know that, Dr. Rosenbloom, but maybe there's another pleasant surprise waiting for you. There's a gentleman here to see you. He's some kind of office manager who specializes in Ob-Gyn practices, and he says he has all kinds of ideas to make your office profitable. Because of our situation, I figured you might agree to see him. I know you don't like to meet with sales reps, but why don't you see him? You never know."

Ms. Stevens opened the door to the waiting room and invited Mr. Joseph Moran back to Dr. Rosenbloom's office. Mr. Moran spoke first. "Dr. Rosenbloom, I know it's late, and I don't want to take up too much of your time, but I think you could benefit from my services. I specialize in making OB-Gyn practices profitable, and I believe I can improve your bottom line.

Dr. Rosenbloom quickly interrupted. "What makes you so sure?"

Mr. Moran replied, "Because that's my business, and I'm good at my business."

"Mr. Moran, this sounds too good to be true. Who do you represent?"

"Doctor, I like to say I represent the people, and what I do is either buy or manage Ob-Gyn practices around the country. I'll come in, evaluate the practice, make the appropriate recommendations, and then, depending on how much the physician wants to participate in the management of the practice, I either implement all the changes myself or the responsibilities are shared. It would be all up to you. Either way you will be able to earn a comfortable salary, and depending on what you desire, you will be free from all the paperwork."

"I don't get it," Dr. Rosenbloom said. "What are you going to do that is so different that it will suddenly change my practice into a profitable concern?"

"Doctor, there are a lot of ways a medical office can make money besides the old traditional method of treating patients. You know better than I do, but there aren't many women getting pregnant these days, and therein lies the opportunity. There are still some babies being born to women around this country, and some of these women will probably want to put their babies up for adoption. With your help I will arrange for these valuable babies to be properly placed, and I can assure you they will all be placed in a good home. Of course you and I will split the placement fees, and, again, I can assure you, those placement fees will be substantial. I am essentially providing an adoption service."

"Mr. Moran, you aren't providing an adoption service. You're selling babies, and you want me to help provide the babies. I don't want any part of that, and I think you should leave."

"Just a few more minutes of your time doctor. I can understand your reaction, and I can empathize with your feelings completely. That particular arrangement would be such a radical departure from your present OB practice, but I thought I should at least make you aware that such an endeavor exists."

"Mr. Moran, you're making me rather uneasy the way you so casually discuss such an idea."

"Doctor, I'm not being casual. It's just straight forward business."

Mr. Moran, I'd be more comfortable if you left."

"Doctor, wait. If you don't like the prior idea, there are other ways to make your office profitable. For example, all the young girls in this area have not been affected by this infertility blight, and those that have not been affected are a prime commodity."

Dr. Rosenbloom angrily interrupted, "Mr. Moran, I don't appreciate you describing those young girls as a prime commodity. It's very offensive, and it's denigrating to all women."

"Dr. Rosenbloom, just listen for a minute. Years ago a girl's menstrual cycle was described as the curse. No more. People ask me all the time for lists of girls who are still capable of having children, girls who are still having their periods. All you have to do is provide me with such a list. I will pay you per person, and I will pay you very handsomely. Now that's harmless enough, isn't it? That's just a matter of some innocent paperwork."

"Mr. Moran, that is also a violation of the law. Get out of here. I want no part of you, or any of your schemes. I have always run my practice in an honest ethical manner, and I'm not going to change now. I would go bankrupt before I would participate in any of those activities."

"Dr. Rosenbloom, it's interesting you would bring up bankruptcy, because I happen to know your financial situation isn't very good."

"How do you know that?"

"Because that's also part of my business, and actually that information is so easy to obtain that it's essentially part of the public record. But let's get back to your personal finances. You've worked hard for a long time to accumulate what you have, and now you're in danger of losing it. My proposal can not only save you, it can also increase your wealth substantially, and I can foresee that after a few years you might elect to sever our relationship. I would be agreeable to that. Easy in, easy out."

"Mr. Moran, like I said. I would prefer to go bankrupt rather than be associated with you or any of your schemes."

"Dr. Rosenbloom, you would only have to be associated with me very peripherally. I would hire a local person to handle all the details. In fact, I believe you have several people on your staff right now who are very capable individuals, and who could supervise the whole operation."

"You investigated my staff?"

"Of course I did. They're already trained as OB personnel. They know the terminology, they know the routines, and the transition would be very easy. Besides, they've been loyal to you for years, and professionally they rely on your judgment. If you spoke enthusiastically about this enterprise, I'm sure they would sign on the dotted line immediately, and they would continue to be loyal employees. Most of them aren't in the best financial situation either. You would not only be saving them financially, you would be saving yourself as well."

"Mr. Moran, is that supposed to be a guilt trip, because I'm sure none of my employees would have any desire to be involved in your so called enterprise. They wouldn't sacrifice their principles."

"Dr. Rosenbloom, it's amazing how principles become…not sacrificed…but interpreted in a different light when people are faced with certain decisions, particularly when those decisions affect children. How about your children, Dr. Rosenbloom? I understand John is an excellent student, Ivy League material from what I hear. It's too bad he'll never have the opportunity to get an Ivy League education, but you could change that. Holmesdale Community College is adequate, but it's not Harvard or Yale. Perhaps you would like to reconsider your decision. Carol would benefit as well."

"Mr. Moran, you're becoming more disgusting every minute of this conversation. For the last time, get out before I call the police."

"Whatever you wish Dr. Rosenbloom, but please think it over. Actually I thought you were becoming more positive about the program when I mentioned the benefits your children would receive. You hesitated a little bit, and I thought you were on the verge of saying yes. Maybe you were, and I'll keep in touch in case you change your mind. Have a good day, and give my best regards to your wife, and especially to your children John and Carol. One more thing, I'm sure you realize that if you don't do it, some other obstetrician will."

CHAPTER 15

The room had more than the usual cast of characters for the President's daily briefing and strategy session. It was also much earlier in the day than usual. In addition to President Freeman and the other usual attendees—such as the Vice President, the Secretary of Defense, the Secretary of Homeland Security, the Secretary of HEW, the White House Chief of Staff, and the other Cabinet members—many other security and health care personnel were there. The Directors of both the FBI and CIA were there—the NIH Infectious Disease Chairman Dr. Joan Amato, Surgeon General Dr. Stan Hession, and the chief obstetrical consultant to the U.S. Government, Dr. Phillip Waters. Many others were there as well.

President Freeman and Don Hudson, the White House Chief of Staff, were the last to enter the presidential conference room. It was a big room with a large oval table that could accommodate approximately thirty people. Everyone was sitting when the President and Don Hudson arrived, but they rose immediately upon seeing the President enter the room.

Fresh fruit and fresh flowers were place strategically around the conference room every single day. That was the whim of Mrs. Freeman.

Otherwise the conference room was rather ordinary. There were the usual pictures of past presidents and other distinguished statesmen, but nothing particularly striking. The only eye-catching aspect of the whole room was the highly sophisticated technological and communication equipment along the far wall.

President Freeman began the meeting. "Alright somebody, tell me what's wrong. Why aren't our women getting pregnant?"

The room was uncomfortably silent, and although everyone was acutely aware that in another situation, a joke would be forthcoming, no one said anything.

"Okay," the President said, "Let's start at the beginning. Dr. Waters, you're the chief obstetrician for this country, tell me everything you know about why our young women aren't getting pregnant. What's going on?"

Dr. Waters replied, "I'm sorry Mr. President, but I'm afraid my knowledge of the subject is very incomplete. We're working on it, but there are still a lot of unanswered questions. I do know that the women aren't getting pregnant because their ovaries have been rendered non-functional, and therefore our women are physically incapable of becoming pregnant. However, we don't know why their ovaries have become non functional. We just know the result. We also don't know whether it's permanent or temporary."

President Freeman replied, "That's not a very enlightening report, Dr. Waters. It's also not very optimistic. Does anyone have any ideas?"

No one answered, and President Freeman spoke again, "Dr. Amato, you're the infectious disease scholar in this country. Is it an infectious disease, a virus, a bacteria, a mutant strain of something? What is it?"

Dr. Amato answered, "I don't know sir. We're still in

the early stages of our testing, but so far the results are very disappointing. Nothing specific has shown up, and there is no evidence of any particular causative agent."

"Another very informative answer," the President said sarcastically.

"Dr. Hession, how about you? What do you think? You're the Surgeon General"

Dr. Hession replied, "Mr. President. From all the information I have, and I must admit that my information is somewhat limited, the women are not getting pregnant because their ovaries have been destroyed. Their ovaries are not temporarily non functional, they have been permanently destroyed, and they are not going to recover. We know what happened; we just don't know *how* it happened, or *why* it happened. "

"This is just great," the President responded. "Everybody knows what happened, but nobody knows how or why. I want to know how and why, and I want to know right away. I also want to know what's being done to find out, and when we're going to know something."

Dr. Hession replied, "Mr. President, we're investigating everything. Our laboratory, plus every other sophisticated research laboratory in the country is working on this. So far no results, but we're hopeful."

The President snapped at him, "You're hopeful. What are you so hopeful about? As far as I can determine, no one in this room knows anymore than any other common ordinary Joe out on the street. I don't see any reason to be hopeful."

The President then hesitated momentarily and apprehensively looked down at the table in front of him, "I was hoping I wouldn't have to ask this question, but because I didn't get the answers from the medical community that I was hoping for, I have to ask."

President Freeman then turned to John Watkins, the Secretary of Homeland Security. "John, what do you think has happened? Is this the work of terrorists? If it is, it's the mother of all terrorism."

Secretary Watkins answered, "We don't know sir, and, believe me, we have been desperately trying to find out, but there are no rumors or suspicions anywhere. We have called in all our chits, and nothing. We have contacted all our national and international sources everywhere, and nothing has turned up. Nothing. Nobody has taken credit for it, and everyone is claiming both innocence and ignorance."

"Come on John, how about your gut feeling? You're the national expert on such matters, and it's all supposed to be second nature to you. What do you think? Is it terrorism or isn't it?"

"Mr. President, I don't know what to say. We don't have any evidence of terrorism, and until we have more information, I don't think it would be right to speculate. After all, viruses have to start some place, and this could be a virus that started right here in the United States."

Dr. Amato, the Infectious Disease expert, spoke very quickly, "As I said before, we don't have any evidence that the cause is a virus or any other infectious agent, and I believe it would be reckless conjecture to say that it was."

The room was quiet for a short time and then President Freeman spoke, "Well, what am I going to tell the American people? I can't go up to the podium and tell them I don't know anything. I'm also receiving grief from some of our district Congressmen, as well as senators and state representatives. They're screaming about plant closings and production slowdowns in their districts, and they're extremely concerned about their constituents losing their jobs, and let's face it, this could be just the beginning. I'm sure you all realize that if we don't reverse this process soon, the United States is going to be in for one big financial disaster."

Don Hudson, the White House Chief of Staff spoke, "Don't tell the people anything. Procrastinate for a while, and in the meantime maybe somebody will find some answers. Until then avoid all public appearances, and keep completely out of the public's sight. If the people discover that you don't have a satisfactory answer, your image is going to take a nosedive. Perhaps you can leak something, or have Dr, Hession, the Surgeon General speak. He can address the nation, and he can give a very bland response. He can tell everybody there is a problem, and that President Freeman and the Surgeon General's office have devoted a tremendous amount of time, effort, and money to find the cause and the cure. Dr. Hession can say that President Freeman is deeply concerned, and that the President and his staff are working around the clock trying to find the solution. Of course, terrorism can't be mentioned, and without telling a lie, Dr. Hession can lean a little bit toward an infectious disease etiology. It won't sound quite as bad, and people will tend to accept it a little better."

President Freeman was grasping for anything, "That sounds reasonable to me, and at least it will suffice for the short term. Let's do it, and for God's sake, everybody get to work, and find out what's happening. Tomorrow this is going to be all over the media. It's going to be on the front page of every newspaper in the country, and the people are going to expect some kind of response, and I want to be able to give it to them. Now is there anything else before we adjourn?"

Dr. Hession, the Surgeon General spoke, "In case it comes up in a question and answer session, there is one more problem that everyone needs to be aware of."

Don Hudson immediately spoke, "We just went over that. The President will not be participating in any question and answer sessions until we have more information about this problem. Even if we have to claim a minor illness, the President has to remain isolated from the press."

President Freeman responded, "Thank you for your concern Don, and Dr. Hession, what's the problem?"

Dr. Hession answered, "A large number of the women who are unable to bear children are having mental problems. Many of them are suffering real and deep cases of depression. In the worst cases they're suicidal. They are putting a real strain on the psychiatric services of this country, and until we find a solution to our infertility problem, their psychiatric problems are not going to go away. Everyone needs to be aware of this psychiatric problem, and we probably should be making plans to offer some assistance."

President Freeman responded, "Thank you Dr. Hession."

Dr. Hession spoke again, "That's not all. The men are not faring any better. The American Psychiatric Association is reporting relatively large numbers of men being concerned about their virility and their ego, because of their inability to impregnate women. There are increased numbers of severe male depression, and just like the women, in some cases they are committing suicide. Other men are becoming paranoid, and the increased number of homicides has been directly attributed to their mental health problems. There is also a severe strain on the social services, family services, ambulance services and even the law enforcement agencies. All these services have to respond to all these psychiatric emergencies, and they're being overwhelmed."

President Freeman responded, "Can't we just tell the men that it's not their fault, and that it's actually because of the females that the pregnancies aren't occurring?"

Don Hudson immediately spoke, "No, we can't blame the females. That would alienate some of our female voters, and we need every last one of them."

Dr. Hession responded, "Mr. Hudson, can't you ever think in a mode other than improving images and garnering votes? The real reason we can't say it's because of the females is because that statement would deepen the depression of the females even further."

Don Hudson shot back, "Dr. Hession, it's my job to think in terms of images and votes, and frankly, I'm doing my job, and I must say that neither you nor your two illustrious physician cohorts seem to be doing yours. All you can say is 'I don't know.'"

Dr. Hession barked back, "What would you have us do, give an unverified report, or even worse, an untrue report, just so you can issue a favorable public relations statement?"

President Freeman intervened, "Hold it everyone. I understand how frustrating it is not to have a satisfactory solution to our problem, and it makes everyone's job very difficult, but we're all on the same team here. Let's remember that, and now let's adjourn."

President Freeman was right; the story was all over the newspapers the next day, although, depending upon the background and viewpoint of the authors, the content of the articles varied widely. In the Denver financial paper the mood was upbeat. Several articles were devoted to the economic consequences of the infertility blight, and they all arrived at the same conclusion—there really was nothing to worry about. The financial experts cited the decrease in the index of leading economic indicators to categorically declare that there would be an economic downturn, but believed that it would be minor. The downturn would not pass into a recession, and there would probably be an economic expansion at the end of the next quarter. The cause of the economic downturn was an unexplained temporary decrease in the number of pregnant women across the country, and as soon as the number of pregnancies increased, and the pregnancy rate reversed itself, everything would be fine.

On the other hand most newspapers had a more pessimistic, or rather a more realistic viewpoint.

Recesssion Is Predicted was the front page headline of the Chicago newspaper. The Chicago financial pundits described the probable recession as a serious national problem. The lack of births was an amazing phenomenon that was starting to destroy the United States economy. There would not be an economic ripple effect, they predicted; there would be an economic tsunami effect. Maternity shops would close, as would children's clothing stores and infant and toddler furniture departments. Floral shops and photography studios would be affected. Both large and small hospitals would be closing wings, and shutting down obstetrical and pediatric units. Numerous nurses, secretaries, clerks, pharmacists, and technologists would be laid off.

National chain stores were already starting to feel the pain, as were baby food producers, gift shops, and candy stores. The unemployment rate was rising, and other economic indicators had all turned negative. The purchasing manager's index, the index of leading economic indicators and the GDP were all bad and getting worse.

Some authors mentioned the strong possibility of a depression, while others stated that a depression was inevitable. The economy was starting to spiral uncontrollably downward, and there did not appear to be anyway to reverse its descent. It was just a matter of time, and no amount of federal easing was going to help.

CHAPTER 16

Pete Vangard, the senior FBI agent, and his associate Emily Chandler were already in the room when CIA Agents Tom Lewis and Glen Hardy arrived. Tom Lewis was in charge of this particular phase of the operation.

Agent Lewis began the meeting with the usual polite introductions and preliminaries, but then went directly to the problem at hand. "Ladies and gentlemen, the United States is having a very serious problem. Over the past several months there has been a tremendous decrease in the number of pregnancies. The experts don't know how or why. All they know is that a large percentage of our American women are unable to become pregnant because their ovaries have been destroyed. It started about four months ago, and since it affected so many women, and it affected them so suddenly, we are speculating that it was a single agent that disseminated throughout the United States about six to nine months ago. We need to learn what happened. Our mission is top priority, and we have been instructed to discover what happened as soon as possible."

FBI agent Pete Vangard sarcastically responded, "We need to solve this problem as soon as possible, a problem that occurred six to nine months ago. Now that sounds like top priority to me. I thought some terrorist, or some renegade country was going to launch a nuclear missile or something. It was my impression something was imminent. I must be at the wrong meeting."

Tom Lewis ignored Pete Vangard's comment and continued to discuss the case. "This is not just an ordinary assignment. The president, all his advisors, and his entire cabinet are all very worried. They've been meeting about this problem constantly, because it may pertain to national security. The President has allocated all kinds of manpower, equipment, and money to the case, and we are fortunate to have been chosen to participate. I've had some unusual assignments in my career, but nothing like this has ever happened before. Off hand, I can think of several possible causes, but obviously everyone is concerned about terrorism.

"To begin our investigation we need to contact the Center for Disease Control in Atlanta, better known as the CDC, and also the Institute for Population Demographics.

"Pete and Emily, I want you to use all the available resources over at the Federal Bureau, and find out what you can from the Institute for Population Demographics. Listen to what they're saying, and ask them if they have any theories. All governmental departments and governmental services are at your disposal: the Internal Revenue Service, the Immigration and Naturalization Service, the Department of Education, every department you want. Every government computer expert and every government computer are available to you. Glen and I will do the same at the CIA, and we'll take the Center for Disease Control. We'll all get together in forty eight hours and compare notes. In the meantime, if anything urgent arises, I'll contact you. Now are there any questions."

Emily Chandler quickly replied, "Yes, I have a question. What are we waiting forty eight hours for? Can't we get this thing moving quicker than that?"

Tom Lewis was surprised by the brashness of the junior FBI agent's response. He thought to himself, *What kind of people am I going to be working with? I don't need two FBI agents who have a chip on their shoulder.* However he pleasantly replied, "I just thought forty-eight hours was a reasonable time period. It guarantees that we will have a meeting rather soon, and of course, if something comes up, we can always meet before then. Now are there any other questions?"

No one responded.

"Fine," Tom said. "Two days then." He then quickly added, "And sooner if necessary."

Emily Chandler nervously stood by her chair as she deliberately fidgeted with her briefcase while CIA agents Tom Lewis and Glen Hardy efficiently and methodically gathered their papers and left the room. At the same time Pete Vanguard was slowly assembling his papers, and waiting for the door to close behind the departing CIA agents.

The door had barely closed when Pete turned to Emily and spoke. "Now, what did you think of that? Top priority—not this case, not at this date. This case should have been top priority a year ago, when something could have been done about it. Now it's over. It's done. I don't consider the investigation of an event that occurred six to nine months ago top priority. Come on, let's go home."

Emily's lips quivered as she glared directly at Agent Vangard.

Realizing something was wrong, Agent Vangard spoke, "What's the matter Emily? You sick or something? You don't look quite right."

Emily snapped at him, "No, I'm not sick, but I'm not

feeling quite right either. Look at me. Look at my left hand. See my wedding ring. It means I'm married, and do you know what usually happens when two people get married? They have children. Well, I don't have any children, and I'm now physically incapable of having children. Not being able to have children haunts me every day, and I'm sure it will continue to haunt me. You may not be interested in pursuing this case, but I am. I'm going to solve this case, and I don't care whether you participate or not."

Pete was completely taken aback by Emily's outburst. He was obviously very embarrassed, and he meekly responded, "I'm sorry Emily. I wasn't completely aware of your personal situation. I always thought you were a career woman, and that you were childless by choice."

Emily answered, "That was true years ago, when I first married, and that is what makes it so much worse. My husband and I could have had children years ago, but we both decided to postpone having children until it was more convenient, and then when we were ready, it was too late. My husband and I both went through all the tests, but by that time there was nothing we could do. I'm just like all the other women in this country. My ovaries have been destroyed. I don't know how it happened, but I'm determined to find out, and if it was some terrorist, or some group of terrorists that deliberately destroyed my ovaries, I want revenge.

"God Emily, I'm sorry. I didn't know what you were going through, but you can't let your emotions interfere with your work. We're FBI agents, and we're not supposed to seek revenge. We're supposed to seek justice, so maybe you should recuse yourself from this case. If you want, I can get George Anderson to take your place."

"George Anderson? Don't you dare even think about getting George Anderson to take my place. You're my superior, but this is my case. If you don't want it, fine, but I do. Give me the freedom and the authority, and I'll solve it myself."

"Emily, you're too emotionally involved. Besides we don't know what is happening here. We don't even know whether there has been a crime committed, and, as of yet, there certainly isn't any evidence of terrorism. You could be wrong about your personal problem being related to the national problem, and even if it is related, we don't know what caused the national problem. You heard Tom Lewis. Nobody knows what's going on. It may be a virulent strain of some virus which has crossed the country."

"Come on Pete. If it was simply a virus, the President or one of his subordinates would be all over the television telling us that it was simply a virus, but he's not doing that. The President has Tom Lewis, the Assistant Director of the CIA, down here asking us to help them find out what happened, and you know as well as I do that Tom Lewis, Glen Hardy, the President of the United States, and every informed government cabinet official thinks it was a deliberate act. You heard Tom Lewis mention terrorism. I'm sure that's what he suspects. I also think Tom Lewis has already been down to the CDC, and he has come up empty. He now wants to spread the blame around, and he has invited us to join the party."

"Emily, there are a lot of assumptions in that logic of yours, and you may be right, but if you're going to behave like a religious zealot, you'll be exposing a lot of people to unnecessary danger. That includes me. It includes you, and it includes everyone else who is involved in this case. Remember, revenge destroys the hunted, and it destroys the hunter."

Emily replied, "I guess revenge was the wrong word to

use, not because it's a bad motive, but because of those silly little aphorisms people quote. Like you just did. What are the good motives: duty, hope, love, hate? Is hate any different than revenge, or do we just use hate to obtain revenge? Hate works; it worked for you."

"What are you talking about?"

"I'm talking about Justin Farland, your academy buddy who was wasted by some terrorist a few years ago. Hate consumed you, but it also pushed you until what's his name was captured and convicted. I remember you saying how hate allowed you to work without sleep and without food. Some of your actions back then scared me, and I could have reported you to the chain of command, but I didn't, and now I'm demanding you leave me on this case."

"Emily, that was different. Justin Farland was the victim of an assassination, a murder."

Agent Chandler responded, "Yes, it was different alright. That terrorist destroyed one insignificant man, but that man was your friend, and I tolerated you for that entire year while you were pursuing the assassin. You're going to do the same for me, because whoever did this has destroyed the lives of millions of American women, and, in particular, because I'm one of those women whose life has been destroyed. Even if it kills me I'm going to find who did this."

"Emily, slow down. First of all, I don't believe your life has been destroyed, and secondly you don't know what's going on here. This could be the work of some nut like the Unabomber."

"Pete, you've got to be kidding. This is a nationwide catastrophe. This isn't the work of some local sicko. The whole country is affected, which means this had to be done by somebody not only with a considerable amount of money, but also with considerable other resources as well. I'm sure some organization will likely take credit for it pretty soon, and because it was so successful, I expect they will use the same technique again, and I expect they will use it soon. We have to catch these guys, and we have to catch them now, because I'm sure they're plotting their next attack. Whether you think so or not, it *is* an attack."

Pete spoke, "Emily, you're absolutely wrong when you say I'm not interested in this case, and in fact, nothing could be further from the truth. As far as the content of the case itself, I don't think it's as emergent as Tom Lewis says, because the actual event occurred six to nine months ago. However, any time the President and his Cabinet are directly involved in a case, that's a good case in which to be a participant, but only if you handle it properly. This case is a possible career maker, and that's why I want it. If we don't make any substantial mistakes, and if we get our names in the bright lights and headlines every now and then, it's an automatic promotion and perhaps a chance to skip a few rungs while climbing up the ladder. This case is good for the career."

"Good for the career. *That's* why you want to solve this case, because it's good for your career? There are millions of women out there unable to become pregnant, and you want to solve this case so you can get a promotion. That's unbelievable."

"Emily, as long as the case is solved, what difference does it make what my motive is? You talked about motives just a little while ago, and you talked about several emotional abstract motives such as love, hope and hate. How about some concrete motives like money, or a promotion or a fatter retirement? They're just as valid, and probably more so, because I believe the emotional motives interfere with a person's judgment."

Emily replied, "And the concrete motives like money and a promotion don't interfere with your judgment? I don't believe it."

"Emily, we're not accomplishing anything here, and you're actually reinforcing my opinion that you're too emotionally involved to be assigned to this case. Now let me think for a minute."

"Go ahead and think, "Emily said, "but you better be on the right wave length."

Pete hesitated for a moment before continuing, "Emily, I know better, but I'm about to make a bad decision here. You shouldn't be involved in this case, but realistically, I know that one way or another, you will be involved. Therefore, I believe it's better if it's official, and I know it's better if you're working with me rather than somebody else. At least I can watch you, and maybe even get you to exercise some restraint every now and then. We can work out the details later, but you have to remember that on the eighth day God made me the boss. Welcome aboard. Now let's go home and get some rest.

Emily was tremendously relieved that she would be remaining on the case, and at the same time she was disgustingly astounded at Pete's lack of insight.

Emily spoke, "Pete, did you ever study philosophy when you were in college?"

"Yes I did."

"How about Descartes and his 'Cogito, ergo sum?' or maybe you're more familiar with the English translation, 'I think, therefore I am'"

"Yes, I remember that. Why do you ask?"

"Because if the converse of that were true, you wouldn't be here," Emily quipped.

"I don't get it," said Pete.

"That doesn't surprise me," replied Emily.

Pete didn't comment and the uncomfortable silence persisted until Emily finally spoke, "Pete, something's wrong, isn't it? I've worked with you long enough to know something's not right. Your remarks to Tom Lewis weren't typical, and your non- response to my stupid little joke was completely not you. What is it?"

Pete hesitated for a moment and then responded, "Emily, I've been having some severe stomach pains recently, and I had an attack a few moments ago when I was in the room. I consider myself to have a pretty high pain tolerance, but I think I need to see a doctor."

Emily replied, "I knew it. I knew it. I knew there was something wrong, and, although, I'm sure it will turn out to be nothing, I feel for you. Sometimes those unexplained pain episodes can be incapacitating. Let me know what the doctor says."

CHAPTER 17

Yu Chen and the other ministers assembled for their routine meeting to assess the progress of the Ovamort program in the United States. Yu Chen was nervous. He was worried about the progress the program was making, and he hoped that the ministers would have some advice. Addressing Chou Chang and the other ministers, Yu Chen spoke, "We have discussed this problem before, but it is starting to worsen. There are more pregnancies occurring in the United States. They were at first very sporadic, occurring in unwed thirteen and fourteen year olds, but now as the children are getting older, the pregnancies are occurring more frequently, and I'm concerned. We need to make some decisions here, but first I'd like you all to hear what Chin Dong has to say."

Chin Dong began, "According to our medical research, Ovamort did not affect any prepubertal females. The ovaries had to be active and mature for the Ovamort to be effective. Therefore the female children who were less than approximately twelve years of age when we administered the Ovamort are all capable of having children. More and more of these children are entering the child bearing age, and soon the number of pregnancies will increase exponentially, and that's our problem."

Yu Chen immediately spoke, "According to Professor Wadsworth, what Chin Dong just described is a major problem, and it is, in fact, a threat to the success of the whole population control program. Professor Wadsworth believes the first Ovamort dose was reasonably effective, but according to his mathematical model, its effect was not great enough, because of the young women who are now becoming pregnant. In order for the program to succeed, the number of fertile females has to be brought below the critical mass level, and according to Professor Wadsworth we are not quite there yet. Reaching this critical mass level is crucial, and if we do not reach it, the program will fail, and everything we have accomplished so far will be for naught. Professor Wadsworth believes more females have to be targeted."

Yu Chen paused for just a moment. "What I have just stated is the professional opinion of Professor Wadsworth. I am not advocating that position, but everyone needs to be aware of it, and we need to discuss it immediately."

Sun Lee spoke, "Kirby Wadsworth and Chin Dong are extremely talented individuals, and based on their work and their opinions, I don't believe we have any choice. We have to administer another dose of Ovamort. In the year immediately preceding the introduction of Ovamort, the population of the United States grew by three million one hundred thousand people, and there were approximately four million births. The Ovamort introduction will prevent those four million births, and instead of growth, the population will decrease. Preventing births is the same as killing people, and we will have essentially killed four million Americans. If we extend that out, say for five years, we will have prevented the births of twenty million Americans, which means we essentially will have killed twenty million

Americans. And we will have done it peacefully, without using any of the old fashioned methods of biochemical or radiological terrorism. I think what we have accomplished so far is extremely impressive, but according to Chin Dong and Professor Wadsworth, it has not been impressive enough, and we have to do more. Let's stop and reflect for a moment. Think what the decrease in the population will do to the American economy. Because the economic growth of a considerable number of industries in the United States is dependent on population growth, the decreased population will eventually cause a depression, and then an economic collapse, and we will succeed. However, if there is a resurgence in the number of pregnancies, as Chin Dong predicts, we will fail. Therefore I believe another dose of Ovamort is necessary."

"I disagree" said Lu Huang, the Minister of Trade. "The United States is reeling right now, and with all due respect to Professor Wadsworth, I truly believe he depends too much on those numbers of his. Everything is so mathematical. The American economy is already starting to weaken, and I say let it go. I think we should pursue other opportunities. We already have the Ovamort, and I think we should contact the IRA in Ireland, and help them distribute the Ovamort in Northern Ireland. I also think we should contact the Palestinians and help them distribute the Ovamort in Israel. We can even use Kirby Wadsworth's speech." Lu Huang spoke in a voice mimicking Kirby Wadsworth. "Northern Ireland has been out there since 1917. Israel has been out there since 1948. Your policies have been failures. You need to change your philosophies." He then reverted to his normal voice. "We might also consider using Ovamort right next door in India."

"No" exclaimed Sun Lee. "We can not let other people

know what we are doing. We have to do it all ourselves. Besides in those other locations we would have to determine whether we can put the proper distribution channels in place."

Chin Dong spoke, "I am a medical researcher, and I am not sure I should be involved in making such decisions or even discussing such matters. I suppose that should be left to my political counterparts, but I have some strong opinions. Ireland is insignificant. It is a small country with a small number of people, and it is a weak country. Israel is small and strong, but not a major enemy. In the Middle East and also in the remainder of the world, Islam is a major enemy. Perhaps we could use Israel as a ruse when dealing with Islam, and actually attack Islamic females with the Ovamort. I agree that some consideration should be given to India and Pakistan. They have too much potential. They are enemies to be dealt with."

Sun Lee spoke again. "I want to once again strongly emphasize the work of Chin Dong and Professor Wadsworth. Unless we continue our attack on the United States, we will fail. It would be very easy to reactivate production and distribution in the United States, because the mechanism is essentially still in place, and the volume of Ovamort we would need for a second distribution would be very small. Although still very critical to our success, it is essentially a mop up operation that can be handled very easily. By the time we administer it, the second distribution of Ovamort would hit those females who will have entered into puberty over the last year or two. That should do it. That will leave only a small number of young women who can conceive when they get older. If necessary we can give one more dose in a few more years, but I expect the United States will already be stumbling by that time."

Yu Chen spoke, "I believe that administering another dose of Ovamort in the United States is too dangerous. When the first dose of Ovamort was administered, it was completely unsuspected, but the situation is now completely different, and there is too great a chance of discovery. I'm sure the United States officials are monitoring every newborn, every pregnancy, and even every young girl who is starting her menarche. They're in a panic situation right now, and would be very suspicious of any action that is even remotely out of the ordinary. The chance of being discovered is too high."

Sun Lee replied, "We've got to do it, or we're going to fail. I agree the United States will soon realize the importance of its young girls being able to become pregnant, and I know the country will rush to protect them, and even encourage them to become pregnant. As of yet the United States officials do not know how we caused their national disaster, or even that we did it, but they are feverishly working on a solution. Therefore I believe there is some urgency in sterilizing these young women before the United States institutes preventative precautions. We must act while we are still capable."

Mei Lee shuttered, "What are we doing? We're permanently sterilizing young girls who are just entering puberty. These aren't women we're talking about. They're children, essentially babies. Doesn't anyone care? We're assaulting babies. What are we going to do next?"

Sun Lee replied quickly. "Mei Lee, you have to think about this logically. It's not just a brave young man with a gun who is your enemy. Women and children are also your enemy. The entire culture is your enemy, and the entire culture must be destroyed. The Americans did that to the American Indians, and in order to soothe their consciences, the Americans first demonized the Indians. Demonizing a culture makes it mentally easier to annihilate that culture. The early Americans called the Indians heathens and savages, and justified the annihilation. The Arabs are justifying their hatred of the Americans today by calling them infidels. Maybe if we did something like that, you would be more enthusiastic about our program."

Mei Lee responded, "You want me to be enthusiastic about sterilizing millions of young girls?"

Sun Lee snapped at her, "Mei Lee, you can't let sentiment interfere with your decisions. We're talking about the welfare of China, and you can't let your personal feelings hinder your judgment. You must admit Ovamort is a very sound program, and you must be willing to sacrifice so that our country can prosper."

"Sacrifice! You're sacrificing other people, and you're doing it without their knowledge, I don't like it."

"You don't like it. What would you prefer, our benign Ovamort methodology or people being killed and mutilated by bombs and bullets? Our method is infinitely superior to an invading army that is raping and torturing women, and making them real casualties of war. Genghis Kahn would slaughter every man, woman and child. He would even kill all the dogs, and he would literally level the towns. We're not doing that. You haven't seen any death or destruction, and not one singe individual has been injured.

Mei Lee responded, "What are you talking about, not one single individual has been injured? Don't you think that the millions of women we sterilized have been injured? They have been severely injured."

"Mei Lee, what we are doing could be considered a new revolutionary form of warfare. We're using a bloodless battlefield, and I actually consider us to be the heroes in this whole operation. You mentioned earlier that we're assaulting babies; we're not assaulting babies. In a real war, that's where babies are assaulted, and they're killed and they're mutilated. In a real war hundreds of thousands and sometimes millions of soldiers and civilians are killed and mutilated. Hospitals overflow with innumerable people devastated by all kinds of disfiguring and life threatening injuries. Water supplies and food supplies are destroyed, and infectious diseases permeate entire populations. Cities are leveled, homes cease to exist, and entire families disappear. Overcrowded and diseased refugee camps become the new metropolitan living quarters, unless of course, you happen to be housed in an overcrowded prison camp. You don't see any of that suffering in our program, and I believe we have launched a new benign type of warfare. It might become a prototype for all future wars—or do you want to revert back to the days of Nagasaki and Hiroshima? Thousands of Japanese civilians literally melted. Then there were the post bombing complications. There were radiation injuries, severe burns, blood disorders and other health problems. These were followed by the long term complications of more radiation injuries, genetic defects and a high rate of cancer development. Mei Lee, we're on the right track."

Lu Huang was impatient. "All this philosophy is interesting, but it really doesn't help us, and I would like to get back to our main goal. If we have to do something, why do we have to do the same thing? Why can't we do something different, like combine the Ovamort attack with some minor military action. That might hasten our cause, and maybe some real terrorist attacks would help. To begin with, perhaps a disruption in Hawaii, away from the Continental United States. We could cause a disruption in that state without any difficulty. I don't believe that Hawaii should be an American state anyway. I think it could just as easily be a Chinese province."

Sun Lee was dumbfounded. He had not expected such a harsh opinion, or such a ridiculous opinion. He wondered whether it was excessive pride or perhaps mental illness that was influencing the opinion. "If you start using force, the American people will become aroused. It will pique their interest, and incite their patriotism. In general the American people don't care about government. They care about their presidency, and they care about their young soldiers being killed in battle, but basically nothing else. We discussed this topic previously, and we all agreed. Let's stick with the plan, only Ovamort and no violence."

Lu Huang persisted, "Well then, maybe not military action but perhaps something else. You always tell us how well and how widespread Ovamort is delivered. Why not use the Ovamort delivery system to deliver toxic chemicals or toxic bacteria. I believe a nice dose of bacteria spread around the United States would be interesting. And as for the plan, why can't it be adjusted? Why so rigid? If not the method, why not the schedule? Why do we have to stick with the schedule? Let's speed it up. Some of my ideas would help in that regard."

Yu Chen sternly replied, "Lu Huang, you mentioned those ideas before, and do you remember how strongly Professor Wadsworth reacted. I remember him stating that our moral obligation was population control, and that we were achieving that goal by Ovamort distribution. He strongly opposed your methods. He didn't want anyone to be hurt."

Sun Lee then emphatically offered his own opinion once again, "Our main problem now is the increasing number of pregnancies in the United States, and we can not divert our attention to any other country until we are absolutely sure we are finished with the United States. I live in the United States, and there has been a tremendous change in the beliefs of the American people. No longer are pregnancies out of wedlock considered to be wrong. There is no longer a stigma attached to unwed mothers, because any pregnancy is a good pregnancy. Children are being urged to marry younger and younger. Motherhood is being glorified more and more, and a pregnant female is a celebrity. You would think these pregnant females were athletes or rock stars. They're being invited to mayor's offices and even governor's offices so that politicians can have their pictures taken with a pregnant female. The other day the Governor of Pennsylvania was trying to get Mary Brier, an anonymous former welfare recipient, to support his reelection.

"Health care is always a popular topic in America, but it has changed. The pregnant women are being seen by the department chairmen in the best health care facilities, and are being supplied with the best equipment and the best food, while it is the others who are seeing the interns in the crowded clinic buildings.

"The citizens are desperate for newborn babies, and they will get them unless we intervene. The population is on the verge of rebounding, and, one more time for emphasis, I believe another dose of Ovamort is necessary."

Everyone remained silent.

"One more thought," Sun Lee said. "I am still concerned about Kirby Wadsworth. You heard him object when Lu Huang shifted the discussion to methods other than Ovamort distribution. Professor Wadsworth objected strongly. His goal is strictly population control while our goals are more expansive. I'm afraid that if more drastic measures become necessary, he will waver, and therefore I think he should be eliminated."

Yu Chen once again spoke up for his long time associate. "I do not think Professor Wadsworth should be killed. He is the expert, and we need him. It was the professor's mathematical model that determined our program was inadequate. Suppose another problem arises, or worse, suppose a problem arises that our own people are incapable of discovering. We need him."

The dialogue persisted for some time before Chou Chang finally said, "Thank you all for your input, but it's starting to get late, and we need to terminate this discussion. I understand everyone's viewpoint, and my conclusion is that we need a second distribution of Ovamort in the United States in order to ensure our success. We will implement this distribution as soon as possible. I will further evaluate the situation for Northern Ireland, Israel and India. I will obtain more information and then decide what to do. Perhaps we will proceed against all of them, or perhaps none of them. We will see."

As everyone started to depart, Chou Chang beckoned to Sun Lee, "Sun Lee, I appreciate your concern about Kirby, and I agree that you can never predict the future, but murdering someone is a perilous activity. Just as it is impossible to predict what Kirby's future actions will be, it is also impossible to predict what will transpire during a murder. There is also a considerable amount of publicity and notoriety when someone gets killed."

Sun Lee replied, "I can't predict how Kirby will react to unplanned future events, but I can predict how he will react if he is dead. I also know how I would undertake Kirby's death, and I can assure you, there would be no mistakes."

Chou Chang responded, "Sun Lee, I really do understand your fear of Professor Wadsworth, but I believe that the risk of murdering him is greater than the risk of allowing him to remain alive. He is also a valuable asset to our program, so my decision at this time is that Professor Wadsworth is to remain alive."

CHAPTER 18

President Freeman began the meeting with the same old refrain, "Alright somebody, tell me what's happening. Why aren't our women getting pregnant?"

This time, Dr. Waters, the country's chief obstetrician, spoke right up, "Mr. President, we have some good news. It's amazing how circumstances can change so quickly, and it now appears that some of the younger females in our country are getting pregnant. They are the very young ones, the twelve and thirteen year olds, the ones who have just entered womanhood. There aren't many, but I believe there are enough to say there is a trend, and, of course, we're monitoring the situation very closely. Maybe it truly was a virus that has finally run its course."

Don Hudson exclaimed, "Thank goodness it's over. Now we have to get the economy rolling again, so we can get the President's approval rating back up."

The President spoke, "Thank you Don, we'll get to that later, and thank you Dr. Waters. That's the most optimistic report I've heard in a long, long time, and it's also the first scintilla of hope I've heard about this case,

Dr. Amato, the infectious disease expert spoke, "Even though the number of pregnancies is increasing, I still haven't seen indisputable scientific evidence that this disaster was caused by a virus, although I must admit that down in the Southeastern part of the country some of the blood studies are indicating a possible viral etiology. And like Dr. Waters said, if it was a virus, maybe it was a virus that has run its course."

President Freeman took a moderately deep breath and sighed comfortably as the tension appeared to ease slowly from his face. "What is this?" the President said. "two of our physicians giving optimistic and positive reports. I hope you're both right, and the cause is a virus, because it certainly makes a difference whether it was a virus or not, because if the cause was not a virus, or some other self limited event, and it truly was the work of terrorists, the terrorists will try again. The terrorists will realize, just as we did, that our women are becoming pregnant again, and they will act accordingly."

John Watkins, the Director of Homeland Security spoke, "If this heinous act were the work of terrorists, I'm sure they already have better statistics pertaining to the rebounding pregnancy rate than we do. I'm sure of that. However, I'm skeptical that terrorists were the perpetrators, because I don't know how they would have done it, and I also believe it could have been caused by a virus."

President Freeman spoke, "Well, if they did it once, they certainly can do it again, and we have to be vigilant, although I feel much better now that our chief obstetrician and our chief infectious disease specialist in this country say that it was possibly a virus. What do you say, Dr. Hession?"

Dr. Hession responded, "I agree with my two colleagues."

"Good," President Freeman said. "That makes it unanimous. All our physicians agree, plus we have the added bonus of our Homeland Security Director also being in agreement. I guess I have to go with my advisors. It was probably a virus."

Don Hudson then spoke, "Mr. President, now you can go before the American people, and tell them that although we don't have all the facts, the epidemic is over, and the country is headed in the right direction again. Let the people know what a good job this administration did."

President Freeman spoke, "Don, we can address our public relations status a little later, but first I would like to play devil's advocate for a moment. If the disaster was not caused by a virus, and it truly was caused by terrorists, what would the terrorists do now? What could we anticipate?"

John Watkins, the Director of Homeland Security answered, "If I were them, I would stick with success. I would use the same technique as before, and I would act immediately in order to squelch the rising number of pregnancies."

President Freeman spoke, "I agree, and if they're going to act immediately, that means we have to act immediately, so what should we do?"

John Watkins replied, "I'm not sure what we can do. We don't know what was done before, nor do we know by whom. All we can do is keep plugging away and hope we get some kind of a break."

President Freeman responded, "What happened to all the good news?"

Mr. Hudson spoke, "We have plenty of good news. Pregnancies in our young females are up, and according to our physician authorities, the cause of the prior infertility catastrophe was most likely a virus which has run its course. I would conclude there's no danger of it reoccurring. That's all good news, and we need to publicize those facts."

Mr. Hudson continued, "Right now our problem is the economy, and the cause of our problem is the lack of births, and that's what we have to change. Because our young women are now capable of becoming pregnant, we need to get them pregnant. We need to reward any woman who becomes pregnant, whether married, singe or divorced. We should consider having the government pay a bounty for each documented new pregnancy, and a greater bounty when delivery occurs. We need to open up the fertility clinics, and get those eggs out of the freezers and get them fertilized. We need to consider changing some of our immigration laws, and give preference to pregnant and fertile females. There are a lot of things we can do."

President Freeman spoke, "Those proposals are rather radical. We've always claimed to be the party of family values and family morality, and I suspect a significant part of the population would condemn those actions."

Don Hudson replied, "Mr. President, times have changed. Our economy is failing, and we no longer have the luxury of a high and mighty morality stance. We have to do what is necessary in order to stimulate the economy. We know what the problem is, and we need to fix it. We need to shed our righteous cloak and be practical about this matter, and I would recommend that you initiate some of these proposals right away. The effect would ease the minds of the populace, and it would also enhance your standing. The only thing that concerns me is your statement that a significant part of the population would condemn those actions. I suppose we would have to simultaneously institute a strong public relations campaign and a superior educational program in order to provide satisfactory damage control. We don't want to lose any of our supporters."

The room was completely silent and everyone's eyes were focused directly on the small area of the table immediately in front of them. There was no eye contact whatsoever. Finally President Freeman spoke, "Don, those ideas are certainly provocative, but I think we should postpone any action on them until a later date."

Don Hudson replied, "A later date may be too late. This is a possible bonanza for us, and we need to take advantage of the opportunity. Those activities which you are judging to be "too radical" are going to be very prevalent in American society very soon, and they will become full fledged American industries. We need to take advantage of the inevitable."

President Freeman replied, "What does that mean?"

"That means we take care of our friends, political contributors, and all our other benefactors. We support our loyal private enterprise community, and we dole out the pork appropriately. We want to guarantee their future allegiance, and of course, we obviously want to guarantee their future financial support."

President Freeman responded, "Thank you Don. I appreciate your viewpoint much better now, but I still think further discussion is necessary."

"Okay Mr. President, but I wouldn't delay too long."

The President spoke, "Thanks again. Now is there any other discussion?"

Dr. Hession answered, "We haven't touched on the severe mental illness that our men and women are experiencing. It is a major problem that is getting worse, and even with an enormous amount of counseling, I believe we're going to have a whole generation of Americans go through life in a severe depression. We don't have enough psychiatric facilities to care for all the men and women who are suffering from mental illnesses. Psychiatric budgets are strained beyond hope, and the proper medical care just isn't there. The best we can do is try to keep these people out of the mental institutions, and try to make sure they're functional."

Don Hudson spoke, "You mean to tell me that just because these men and women can't become doting parents, there's a possibility they will be non-functional in our society. I find that hard to believe. These people have to get over it, and get on with their lives."

Dr. Hession snapped back sharply, "Mr. Hudson, I don't know what your background is, but I suspect you were raised in a very cold family environment. You are insensitive to the anguish these people are suffering, and you don't sound capable of experiencing any empathy for these distraught individuals."

Mr. Hudson interrupted, "Dr. Hession, no one is interested in your evaluations unless they pertain strictly to medicine, and don't you ever…"

President Freeman quickly yelled, "Enough. I want to remind everyone that we're all working together here, and we need to cooperate. Personal attacks don't help, so let's all calm down, and get back to work."

CHAPTER 19

Pete Vangard and Emily Chandler were walking rather quickly up the steps of the administration building of the Institute for Population Demographics when Emily spoke, "Pete, you seem to be doing quite well today, the pain gone?"

"Yes," Pete replied. "I'm doing great. I'm completely pain free, and whatever I had apparently cleared up by itself. It must have been intestinal spasms or something, so I cancelled my doctor's appointment. There's no sense in paying some doctor's country club bill when I'm already better."

"Pete, you shouldn't have done that. Suppose your pain comes back, then you have to go through that same old rigamarole of trying to get another's doctor's appointment."

"I hear you Emily, but, right now, I've got a more pressing matter on my mind, namely our appointment with President Malone, the President of this Institute."

The administration building of The Institute for Population Demographics was the newest building on the entire campus—courtesy of the Murray Family Foundation. It was a building that caught your eye as soon as you set foot on campus. Its architecture was extremely modern. Some considered it avant-garde, while others considered it plain ugly. The first floor lobby was wide open, and decorated with large colorful imaginative paintings and modern metallic sculptures. The main focus of the room, however, seemed to be the policeman sitting behind the obtrusive security desk. To many it was a pure mortar and bricks building with absolutely no charm, but certainly had an expensive architect's signature.

"Good morning sir," Pete Vangard said. "We have an appointment to see President Malone."

"Your names?"

"Pete Vangard and Emily Chandler"

"Okay, you're listed here. Any bags?"

"No."

"Step over there where I can see you better.....Good..... Now turn completely around.....Okay, you pass. President Malone's office is down at the end of hall and then left. You can't miss it. Go ahead."

"Thank you," Pete replied.

From the security desk it was only a short walk to President Malone's office—an office with modern furniture, modern lighting fixtures, and again with no charm. President Malone's secretary promptly announced the two agents' arrival and escorted them into the inner sanctum.

"Good morning President Malone, I'm Agent Emily Chandler from the FBI and this is my partner, Agent Pete Vangard. You know why we're here, so let's get started. I hope you can help."

"Yes, yes, I know why you're here. Tragic, isn't it, all those women? I hope you can figure out what happened, but I don't think I'll be much help. I'm essentially a fund raiser. I attend banquets, give speeches, pat people on the back, and tell them what a great job they did, but I'm really not in the trenches like the other faculty members. However, I have opened the Institute to you. All faculty members, full and part time, have been instructed to cooperate with your investigation, so do what you need to do."

Agent Chandler spoke, "Thank you President Malone. We appreciate that, but I still would like to ask you a few questions, okay?"

"Sure, go ahead." President Malone replied.

"Thank you sir, and I hope you won't be offended by some of these questions, but I have to ask them. I'm sure you understand."

"Yes, I understand, and I won't be offended. Go ahead and ask."

Emily Chandler began with a barrage of questions. "First of all President Malone, do you think there is anyone in your Institute who might have done this deliberately, or perhaps his research project spun out of control, or maybe he had a nervous breakdown? What do you think? Any people on your staff like that?"

"No, there's no one here like that. You can put that idea out of your mind right now."

Agent Chandler questioned further, "President Malone, we have to start somewhere. Help us. You must have some ideas. Where should we begin?"

President Malone responded, "Well, this is an Institute where a lot of radical ideas are put forth, but they are just ideas. No one here has the resources to do anything. I've received letters complaining about different faculty members from time to time, but again I can't imagine any faculty member at this Institute being responsible for such a dastardly act."

Emily spoke, "Those radical ideas you mentioned. Just how radical are they?"

President Malone chuckled, "All institutions of higher learning have people putting forth radical ideas. That's the nature of the higher educational system, but I never thought there was anything to worry about."

Emily persisted, "Is there any one faculty member who immediately comes to mind, or who always seems to be in the middle of the fray?"

President Malone answered, "Professor Kirby Wadsworth's concepts cause a lot of turmoil around here, but I don't think he would actually act on them. I think he says those things just to make his class interesting, or to annoy the students and the other faculty members, but go talk to him. He's very knowledgeable about the subject matter, and he also seems to know the scuttlebutt around the Institute. He's a good place to start, and I'm sure he'll be happy to talk to you. He likes to talk to everybody, but I must warn you, be prepared to listen to his propaganda."

Kirby was sitting at his office desk with the door wide open when Pete and Emily appeared at his door. Emily knocked gently and Professor Wadsworth immediately looked up from his notes. Emily spoke, "Professor Kirby Wadsworth, I'm Assistant Special Agent Emily Chandler and this is my partner Pete Vangard. We're from the FBI, and we're investigating the tragedy that has struck the young women of this country, namely their inability to become pregnant. President Malone has given us clearance."

"Welcome, please come in, and please call me Kirby," Kirby Wadsworth answered. "Have a seat and make yourself comfortable. Tell me exactly what you want to know, and I'll see if I can help."

"Well professor," Emily responded, "we're investigating the infertility tragedy that has befallen the young women in this country. Do you know anything about it?"

"No. I'm afraid I don't," Kirby replied. "Only what I read in the newspaper, although I do know that it's *not* a tragedy. It seems more like a blessing to me. The only problem I can see is that this epidemic is not worldwide, but maybe over time it will spread. According to the newspapers, it's supposed to be a virus, isn't it?"

Emily and Pete were flabbergasted at Kirby's response, and were momentarily silent. Emily's anger level rose quickly, and she finally spoke, "Professor, there are a lot of depressed and angry women out there, and I'm one of them. And all because of your so called epidemic. These women can't bear children, and I'm determined to find out why."

Kirby replied in a very matter of fact fashion, "What did you say your name was? Emily Chandler, isn't it? Well Emily, you have to take a broader view of this. If you and all the other women of this country continued to have children, pretty soon our environment would be destroyed. The food supply would be exhausted, and it would be your progeny who would be suffering and starving. You wouldn't want that now, would you? I certainly wouldn't. Therefore, I don't feel too bad about this virus that has gripped our country."

Emily glared at Kirby Wadsworth. "Professor Wadsworth, you're an authority on this stuff, and I think you know it's not a virus, and I also think you know what happened, and, furthermore, I think you probably know why it happened and even possibly who did it."

"Emily, you're too upset," Kirby replied calmly. "Let's look at this situation rationally. No one's been hurt. No one's been killed. You haven't seen any bombs exploding, or people running around with guns or knives, have you? I can understand why you're angry, but after a while, you'll get over it. You'll also realize that the final result will be a better world. Once you get a chance to think it through, it will be as obvious as the rejuvenated environment you'll be seeing. I'm one hundred percent convinced of that. Now is there anything else you would like to discuss?"

Emily spoke quickly, "I don't want to discuss anything with you Professor, but I have to. It's my job, and what I'd really like to do is jump over that desk, and bash your head in. I think you're an evil person, and I think you're using evil means to accomplish your warped goals."

Kirby replied, "Ms. Chandler, I don't consider myself an evil person. On the contrary I consider myself a very compassionate person, and a very conscientious American patriot who is especially interested in preserving the future of the United States, and if it requires a generation of childless women to restore the United States to its proper environmental balance, so be it."

Emily angrily started walking toward Kirby, and Pete Vangard immediately thrust himself between the two. At the same time Pete Vangard spoke, "Thank you Professor. I think Agent Chandler and I accomplished something today, and I'm sure we'll be back. Have a good day."

As the two agents were leaving, Kirby offered one last thought, "Mr. Vangard, don't worry about Emily's anger. She's like all the other American women. They just have to learn to subjugate their selfish maternal instincts for the good of society."

Emily turned quickly and starting moving angrily toward Kirby. "Professor Wadsworth, if I weren't on duty, I would leap over that desk and bash your head in." Her pace toward Kirby unconsciously started to accelerate, and she seemed to be losing her self control. All of a sudden Pete Vangard jumped directly in front of her, once again thwarting her efforts to get to Professor Wadsworth. "Let's go

Emily," Pete reiterated. "I think we've accomplished quite a bit here today."

Pete hustled Emily out the door and out of the building. "Emily, what happened to you in there? You can't lose your cool like that. We don't want to have the Institute of Population Demographics officially protest that two FBI agents were threatening violence to one of the Institute's professors. We don't want to ruin our careers, we want to enhance them. Emily, whether he's guilty or not, you've got to learn to control yourself, or you'll be off this case. Now go home and get some rest."

Emily responded, "Pete, you heard that man. He said this infertility blight was a blessing. What kind of a response is that? Plus, did you see that smirk on his face. I think he's knows something, and I think he definitely knows it wasn't a virus."

Pete replied, "According to our last memo, the President's advisors are supposedly leaning toward a virus."

"I don't think so," Emily replied, "and I think Professor Wadsworth knows it."

CHAPTER 20

Emily Chandler's ride home was nerve wracking. She obsessed about her recent meeting with Kirby Wadsworth and his outrageous attitudes and opinions. These thoughts were occasionally interspersed with her reflections on Pete Vangard's unsympathetic and unbelieving attitude.

Thank goodness I'm home, she thought, as she pulled into the driveway of her well-kept suburban home. She gazed at her relatively spacious backyard, and sadly thought of its permanent emptiness, never to be filled with the laughter of children.

Opening the door she yelled to her husband. "Hello, I'm home. Where are you?"

Dave replied "I'm in the kitchen having a cup of coffee. How was your day?"

"My day was horrible. I never realized how big a jerk Pete Vangard is, and he's becoming a bigger jerk every day. Plus I interviewed a Professor Kirby Wadsworth today, and he is one of the most offensive people I have ever met."

Dave shook his head and sighed, "This sounds like it's going to be one fun night. Why don't we start with a nice glass of wine, and then you can tell me all about it. I believe this is going to be much more interesting than watching television."

"You don't sound very sympathetic. Where are the dogs? HAPPY! JENNY! There you are. Maybe I'll get some sympathy from you two."

"Alright Emily, why don't you start with your partner Pete?"

"Okay, but you won't believe it. Pete is still not sure this national infertility tragedy is the work of terrorists. He still thinks it could be an accident of nature."

Dave looked directly down at the floor before responding. "Emily, I don't want to sound too contrary here, because I know you've had a rough day, but why couldn't it be an act of nature? To me, it seems more reasonable to theorize that it was an accident of nature, rather than to theorize that somebody purposely spread a poisonous agent throughout the entire United States—and I want to emphasize, a poisonous agent that nobody has discovered anywhere. I'm sure your professional colleagues have discussed this to the nth degree, but I'm going to speculate anyway. How did the terrorists do it? Through the water system? Impossible. There isn't one water system in the United States; there are multiple water systems, and they all couldn't have been poisoned. Remember, almost the entire nation has been affected. In the food? I've heard of contaminated food causing problems from time to time, but in those cases the outbreaks have all been local, or, at most, regional. I've never heard of food poisoning on a national scale, and to accomplish that purposely would require that a tremendous quantity of food be affected. It also would require a nationwide distribution system. Through the air? That doesn't seem logical either. It would be an impossible project to affect so many women in so many parts of the country by an airborne contaminant. Look at the Chernobyl accident. That was airborne contamination, but the affected geographic range was only about one hundred miles, and the United States is three thousand miles wide. It just doesn't seem reasonable to postulate that it was an airborne contaminant. Spread by flies or rodents? That's possible, but it seems more reasonable to believe that it would have been a natural contagion rather than something artificially induced. Plus there is no evidence to support any of those hypotheses."

Emily responded, "I admit there is no hard evidence supporting a terrorism theory, but there's no evidence suggesting it was a natural phenomenon either, and I happen to believe it was the work of terrorists. I don't know how it was done, but terrorists did it somehow, and I'm going to find out how"

"Emily, accidents of nature like viruses and the flu spread across the entire country every single year. Why couldn't it be as simple as a virus? Remember the old polio epidemic. That was a virus that spread across the entire United States and directly hit nerve cells. Why couldn't this be a virus that has spread across the United States and directly hit women's ovaries?"

Emily replied, "Did you ever hear of a virus that spread across the country and hit only women's ovaries? Tell me, did you ever hear of one?"

"No, I never heard of one, but that doesn't mean it doesn't exist. What about the human papilloma virus? That's a virus that attacks a woman's cervix, so why can't there be a virus that attacks a woman's ovaries? I don't think you should abandon the viral etiology theory so soon."

Emily responded, "As far as I'm concerned, it's obvious we're dealing with something man made." Emily's expression then changed quickly, and she began to chuckle to herself. "Well, maybe you're right, because from what I can determine, there must have been a horrible virus that spread across this country and targeted only men's brains."

"Very funny," Dave replied, "Although I am glad to see you laughing again. It's good for you."

Dave hesitated for a moment and then spoke, "Okay, enough about that topic. Tell me about your Professor friend."

Emily replied, "His name is Professor Kirby Wadsworth. You should have heard him talking about how the epidemic was a blessing, and how it was good for our environment and for our country. I couldn't believe what I was hearing. I almost slugged him."

"You what? Emily, maybe your partner is right. Maybe you should get off this case. Your personal situation is driving you too hard."

"I'm not getting off this case. I'm going to solve it."

"Emily, just because this professor has a radical opinion, it doesn't mean he's evil, or even that he's wrong. I don't agree with him, but I can understand his viewpoint."

"You understand his viewpoint. You and I can't have children because of this disaster, and you stand there and try to justify his position. What's the matter with you? You're supposed to be supporting me, not giving me grief."

"Emily, I'm not giving you grief. I just want to help you face reality."

"Face reality? What do you want me to do, give up on this case, and say our national infertility problem is natures way of correcting the world's overpopulation?"

"No, that's not what I want," Dave replied. "I just don't want you to have a nervous breakdown. This case is consuming your life, an addiction as bad as alcohol or drugs.

Let go a little. From what I understand, the entire govern-ment is working on this case. Let someone else be the hero. I need you, and I need you to be home and functioning as a member of this family. I don't want to see you in a full blown clinical depression moping around some psychiatric ward. You're too valuable to me. Come on, relax. A lot of families don't have children, and because of this epidemic, it's actually now the norm. We'll have a good life, and who knows, maybe we'll even get lucky and our adoption will come through."

Emily spoke rather harshly, "Maybe our adoption will come through. What are you talking about? Haven't I just been having a conversation with you about how there aren't any babies being born. All those adoption papers we filled out, and all those physicals we went through, and all those background checks we had, were all a waste of time. There aren't any babies to adopt."

Dave replied, "I don't believe that. There are always babies to adopt. We just have to look harder. I'm not giving up."

Emily responded, "Now who's not facing reality? Jenny. Happy. Come with me. I've had enough of this discussion. Let's get another glass of wine and go watch TV. Maybe there's a reality show on."

CHAPTER 21

Two days later Pete and Emily were back in the same conference room waiting for Tom Lewis and Glen Hardy to arrive, when Emily noticed that Pete Vangard was sitting relatively motionless in his chair with sweat pouring down his forehead. "Pete, what's the matter with you? Are you having a heart attack or something? I'm calling 911."

"No Emily, don't," Pete quickly replied. "I'll be okay. It's just my stomach acting up, and the pain will go away soon. It always does, and please don't say I told you so, but you were right. Those stomach pain attacks didn't go away by themselves, and now I have to make another doctor's appointment."

"Maybe you should go to the emergency room," Emily said.

"I'm not going to the emergency room," Pete replied firmly. "If people know I'm not feeling well, they'll take me off this case, and I've waited for a case like this for a long time. I'll be okay. Just be quiet and don't say anything to Tom or Glen. I'll get through this meeting, and then I'll get a doctor's appointment right away."

Tom Lewis and Glen Hardy arrived shortly thereafter. Tom, with a worried and unhappy look on his face, began the meeting. "To briefly summarize, our trip to the CDC was worthless. We talked to everybody we could, and nobody knows what's going on. The affected women do not have any evidence of being infected by a virus. The investigators have checked the blood levels for every conceivable infectious agent, and they are all within the range of normal. There is no evidence of a single woman being infected by any virus that could have caused them to become sterile."

"Wait a minute," Pete Vangard said. "I thought it was *supposed* to be a virus. The last time we heard anything from our infallible hierarchy, they were leaking it out that it was a virus, and they were claiming they were gathering the last bits of necessary evidence before pronouncing that the culprit was a virus, and that the virus was finally under control."

Tom responded, "It didn't work out like it was supposed to. The official word now is that the cause is *not* a virus. Drs. Amato, Hession and Waters made the conclusion, and informed the President just recently. You are all familiar with those doctors, aren't you?"

Pete spoke, "Yes, I'm familiar with them, and what did they say?"

Tom replied, "They said that a virus doesn't behave that way. Viruses spread in a predictable fashion, and the number of people infected increases in a systematic progression over a period of time. That's not what happened in this situation. The whole country was affected simultaneously. Plus, a pattern of antibody production would have shown up in the blood stream by now. That didn't happen."

Pete spoke again, "I thought there were antibodies showing up in the blood stream down in the Southeastern part of the country, and it was just a matter of time before this would be confirmed nationwide. What happened?"

Tom replied, "It didn't pan out. Those particular anti-bodies remained confined to the Southeast, and apparently represented a local virus that is completely unrelated to the national problem. A virus is definitely not the cause.

"Now back to our CDC trip. After leaving the Infectious Disease section we went over to Toxicology. The same thing, nothing. Those investigators ran every single toxicity study possible, and no toxins were found in any of the blood samples. There was the normal percentage of drug addicts, but no abnormal increase. There was nothing to explain the infertility.

"Then we went to a subsection of the Toxicology Department. Same old thing, nothing. There was no increased incidence of food poisoning, or water poisoning, or exposure to any other noxious agents. I don't think we're going to get much information from the CDC. How about you two? What did you find?"

Agent Chandler spoke, "We didn't find anything definite, but I believe there are some possibilities. To begin with there is a professor named Kirby Wadsworth who is absolutely possessed about population control, and boy, does he ever have some weird ideas about what is acceptable and what is not acceptable. He basically told us that he thought this infertility problem affecting the American females was actually a blessing. That's sick, but that is what he believes."

Agent Chandler continued, "You know—and Pete can attest to this—I never did think it was a virus. I always thought foreign terrorists did it, but now I believe it was done by a man born right here on our own soil. I believe it was Professor Kirby Wadsworth."

Tom spoke rather sharply, "You believe it was Kirby Wadsworth? One man couldn't have done this. This epidemic is nationwide, and it affected the entire country simultaneously. How would one person have done it?"

Emily replied, "I didn't say he did it all by himself. I believe he acted in conjunction with some fanatical religious fundamentalist group, or perhaps some renegade cult. A lot of those off the wall religions and those strange secretive cults frequently have an awful lot of money, and they also often have a very broad and very well organized underground system. They could have done it, and they could have done it very easily, although I still don't know how it was accomplished."

Tom spoke, "How did you ever come up with the idea of it being a religious group or some type of cult?"

Emily answered, "I came up with it by the process of elimination. Foreign terrorists have never used such a technique before, and it is just so uncharacteristic of a terrorist group. In one way or another terrorists have always used explosives, and they have always targeted specific sites. Even when the Twin Towers were attacked, although using a completely different technique, explosives were used and a specific site was targeted"

Tom spoke again, "Part of your reasoning seems sound, but I never heard of any group espousing any theories or activities like the one we're investigating."

Emily replied, "You may not have heard of them, but they're out there. You can find groups that espouse anything. I realize this isn't Africa, but, for a short time, back in Africa in the early 1800's the Zulus killed all pregnant females. I admit it was for psychological reasons, but it was done. Maybe Kirby Wadsworth performed the pernicious act for psychological reasons, although I don't think so. If I had a choice between Professor Wadsworth being psychotic, and being a very sane determined individual who thought he was acting admirably, I'd choose the latter. Remember the Shakers, a former religious group in upstate New York. They believed sex was evil, and they became extinct because of their own beliefs. And remember Jim Jones in Guyana. How do you explain a person like him, and how do you explain his followers, followers who committed suicide on his command? Maybe Kirby's particular group achieves their goal by preventing procreation. The whole wicked scenario just seems to fall into the religion or cult category rather than the realm of terrorists"

Tom spoke, "That seems pretty farfetched to me."

Emily answered, "There is nothing farfetched when you're investigating a catastrophe like we're investigating. Remember when the Oklahoma City bombing occurred, no one knew who was responsible, and the media originally speculated that it was some unknown terrorist group, probably of Mid Eastern origin. And who did it? Timothy McVeigh and Terry Nichols, both Americans. I'm sure that most people thought it was inconceivable—Hey! How's that for an appropriate word choice, inconceivable—Anyway, I'm sure that most people thought it would be inconceivable that Americans would perform such an act as the Oklahoma City bombing. They would probably think it is more inconceivable that an American could be responsible for the infertility blight in the United States. But I do. I no longer believe it is some foreign terrorist group. I believe it is Kirby Wadsworth acting in union with some fundamentalist religion or secretive fanatical cult."

Tom asked, "Other than your intuition, what proof do you have?"

Emily answered, "I don't have any proof, but I've done a little checking on this Kirby Wadsworth gentleman and he belongs to the Hemlock Society, the Zero Population

Growth Committee, the Professors for Environmental Preservation, the Citizens for Population Control, and several other such societies. I also have his own words. Kirby said the entire catastrophe was a blessing, and he hoped it would spread worldwide. He described himself as a patriot who was interested in helping the United States, and he mentioned that if it took a generation of childless females to preserve the United States, so be it. I remember his words very clearly. He's our man. I'm going to get him, and I'm going to get his associates as well."

Tom spoke, "Emily, you haven't completely convinced me, but you've aroused my curiosity enough that I think you and Pete should pursue your theories. Go get something more substantial, and bring it back to me.

Pete and Emily headed straight to the Institute for Population Demographics to interview a few of Kirby's fellow professors.

President Malone, the President of the Institute, was the first stop. Pete Vangard started the conversation, "President Malone, this is all to be confidential, but we need to gather as much information as possible about Kirby Wadsworth, and we thought that talking to some of his colleagues might be a good place to begin. Do you think you can help us, or can you at least suggest some people who will be able to help?"

President Malone answered, "I won't be able to help you personally. I don't know anything about Professor Wadsworth except for his professional work, but what's going on here? What's the problem?"

Pete replied, "We don't know that there is a problem, but the more information we have, the better off we'll be. Now where should we begin? Who knows him best?

Who are his friends?"

President Malone answered, "You might talk with Ross Paterson. He wasn't Kirby's friend, and I would actually consider him Kirby's foe, but I think he knew Kirby as well as anybody. Ross was always suspicious of Kirby, and as much as he could, he tried to keep track of what Kirby was doing. Several times Ross came to my office complaining about Kirby, and about how he was bad for the Institute. He wanted me to put a muzzle on him."

"Where do we find this Ross Paterson?" Pete asked."

"His office is at the opposite end of the corridor from Kirby's. Go right up. Ross will talk to you, particularly if it's about Kirby, and even more so if it's negative. He wants Kirby off the faculty."

"Ross Paterson, I'm FBI agent Pete Vangard, and this is my associate Emily Chandler. We would like to ask you a few questions about Kirby Wadsworth. President Malone said you and him often were at odds over various topics here at the Institute."

Ross responded, "That's right, we were. I never really liked the guy, because I felt he was a radical trouble maker who continually disrupted the Institute's routine. I never felt he was a good representative of the Institute, and, in fact, I always thought he was a little bit dangerous."

Pete answered, "That's quite an evaluation, Professor Paterson. Can you give us something specific?"

"I sure can. For example, Kirby's signature question, which he gave to the students at the start of each semester was 'What is the best method to control the population of the United States, and what is the best way to control the population of the world. Don't pay any attention to what is legal, ethical or moral.' Now that's some question to pose to the students. I was always afraid he would entice some naïve student to do something illegal. I was also afraid he might cause the Institute to lose some grant money."

"Didn't anybody say anything to him?" Pete replied.

"Yes, people would admonish him from time to time, but he had tenure and that allows you to say whatever you want. One more thing. When he acted as a consultant to the Chinese Government over in China, he told me the rules and laws were different over there, and that maybe he could really accomplish something. I don't know what he meant, but it was a little bit disconcerting."

Pete spoke, "Anything else we should know?"

"I don't think so."

"Did you ever ask him what he thought the cause of the American women being sterile was?"

"Yes, I did."

"What'd he say?"

"He said he wasn't sure, but he thought the most plausible explanation was that it was caused by the wrath of God, and that it was actually another plague brought on by Moses. He then gave a condescending chuckle. I gave up talking to him; I can't stand him."

Emily chimed in, "Do you think he could, in any way, be responsible for the American women being unable to become pregnant?"

Without hesitating Ross responded, "I certainly do, and I'm sure if he did it, he's very proud of it. It would have made him feel like he accomplished something significant. He always exhibited a very irritating disdain for all his peers. He believed that all we do is teach, and that we really don't accomplish anything."

Pete spoke, "Is there anything else you can tell us?"

"No, I don't think so, but you should talk to Adam Foster,

one of Kirby's buddies. I think Adam recently worked on a project with Kirby. In fact, Adam was one of only a few people who could work with Kirby, although you must realize, Adam himself has some far out ideas as well. Good luck."

"Adam Foster, I'm FBI agent Pete Vangard and this is my associate Emily Chandler, and we would like to ask you a few questions about Kirby Wadsworth. Ross Paterson said you were working on a project with him. Is that correct?"

"Yes, that's correct."

"Tell us about the project, and perhaps a little bit about Kirby himself."

Adam answered, "Well, the project was primarily about environmental preservation and secondarily about population control, but we never finished it. We kind of dropped the project in midstream, and then we gradually drifted apart."

"Why is that?'

"To put it politely, I thought Kirby was getting a little too aggressive and a little too radical in his thinking, and frankly, I became frightened, so I purposely avoided him."

"Tell us a little bit more about that."

"At our last meeting Kirby said it was our responsibility to prevent overpopulation from destroying the world. He believed talking was becoming less and less of an option, and he mentioned that it was time to make a decision. He talked about bombs, and epidemics and famines, and he said it was necessary to eliminate millions of people. Like I said I became afraid and I avoided him."

Pete continued, "Did you ask him what he thought caused the infertility blight in the United States?"

"Yes I did, but he never gave me a serious answer. He

just murmured something about the great reparative process of nature."

Emily questioned him further, "Do you think Kirby could be the cause of the American women not being able to become pregnant?"

"It wouldn't surprise me one bit. I don't know how he would have done it, but I think he could have been involved in some way. He couldn't have done it alone, and in all probability he would have needed a lot of help, but yes, I think he could have been involved."

"Who would have helped him, any ideas?"

"No, sorry."

"How about his friends, or maybe his visitors? Could they have helped him?"

"Kirby didn't have any real friends. He was courteous to everyone, and very polite, but no real friends. As for visitors, I never saw any except for you two when you were in his office the other day. As far as I know, he didn't socialize with anyone. Occasionally he would go to a movie or a ball game or something, but almost always by himself. His whole life was his work."

"Any hobbies?"

"Not that I know of."

"Church?"

"No."

"Anything else we should know?"

"Probably a lot of things, but I can't think of anything right now."

"Mr. Foster, you helped us a great deal, and if you think of anything else, let us know. We'll be in touch."

Pate and Emily walked silently and quickly down the corridor of the faculty building, with Emily bubbling with excitement over the information the two of them had just received from Adam Foster and Ross Paterson. As soon as they cleared the doorway, and started down the stairs, Emily burst forth, "I can't wait to tell Tom about our findings."

Pete replied, "They're not findings. They're the opinions of two of Kirby's colleagues, and we have to be careful. We don't want to make a mistake."

Emily responded, "I think they're more than opinions. Ross and Adam were emphatic, and those answers weren't stated as opinions. They were stated as facts, and I believe that's significant. I'm going to follow up on this right away. I'm going to make a few phone calls, and do a little research myself, and I hope I have all the information I need by the time of the meeting tomorrow."

"Good idea Emily," Pete replied. "I'm going to make a few phone calls myself. Let's get together tomorrow morning before our meeting with Tom and Glen. That way we'll have a united front, and neither of us will be blindsided. It will also give us a chance to clarify any contradictory information we might receive, and it will ensure that our presentations are completely harmonious."

CHAPTER 22

"Okay Emily," Tom said. "How much progress have you and Pete made with your investigation of Professor Wadsworth?"

Emily quickly answered, "We've made considerable progress, although the case is not progressing in the direction I thought it would. Kirby belongs to all kinds of organizations, although he's not an active member in any of them. He pays his yearly dues, but never attends any meetings. Occasionally he'll write a scientific article for them, or write a letter to the editor in the popular press for them, but he's really not an active member. He also doesn't attend any services of any of the organized religions, mainstream or otherwise. He doesn't have a girlfriend, a boyfriend or even a best friend. He has teaching associates and faculty colleagues, but really no friends."

Tom interrupted, "I'm not sure what your point is here, Emily? What does all that mean, and what's happened with your fundamentalist religion or fanatical cult theory?"

"Let me finish," Emily replied. "I spoke to Bill Wolfe, the FBI's authority on such organizations and he assured me that Kirby Wadsworth is not a member of any fundamentalist religion or fanatical cult. Bill also said he didn't think it was a religious group or a cult that was responsible for the catastrophe. Bill knows all those groups, at least the fundamentalist religions, and he said that when a fundamentalist religion does something significant, it pronounces it publicly so that God and the whole world can see the great achievement. He also said that every now and then a small unknown cult will pop up, but it won't have the resources to cause a major catastrophe. They're usually small and very localized. This was not the work of a fundamentalist religion or a secret cult."

Tom spoke, "So this is another dead end. Kirby Wadsworth is not the culprit."

"No, I didn't say that. I still think he's the culprit, and we talked to some of his colleagues and they think Kirby could possibly be the culprit as well, and now I believe he aligned himself with foreign terrorists. He could be in partnership with anybody, but I already have my opinions."

Tom replied, "I'm sure you do, and I assume you've already done some preliminary work on those opinions of yours."

Emily answered, "Yes I have, and it's been very interesting."

Tom replied, "I don't want interesting; I want answers, and frankly your opinions haven't proven to be very fruitful. All your opinions have done is use up valuable time. We've been down the wrong road twice already, and we can't afford any more failures. When I use the phrase "we can't afford any more failures," I'm using it with two different meanings, the first as investigators trying to help the United States solve this puzzle, and the second as a group of individuals who are trying to maintain their jobs. Maybe you should give up on Kirby, and try a different tack for a while. We can't become fixated on one individual, or get stuck with tunnel vision. We've got to be flexible."

"No, Kirby is our man," Emily replied. "We just need more time to find out who his partners were."

"Emily, we may not have much more time. The higher-ups are continually on my back. They're emphasizing that the purpose of finding the perpetrators is not only to prosecute them, but also to prevent a repeat performance of the event. Right now we have no idea how or why this catastrophe occurred, and that means we have no way of preventing it from happening again. The hierarchy is fearful that the perpetrators will strike again. They can see that the number of pregnancies is starting to rebound again, and they realize that an enemy can see it as well. We have a lot of pressure on us."

Pete Vangard's political ears perked up, and he quickly responded, "You can tell your bosses that we've accumulated a lot of valuable information recently. Tell them we're still analyzing it, and also tell them that we feel we're going in the right direction."

Emily spoke "Because Bill Wolfe told us that Kirby didn't do it with the help of anybody here in the United States, it was obvious to us that we had to look overseas. It was also obvious that because his work is his whole life, we had to focus on his work associates. He has traveled to Cuba, several Middle Eastern Countries, China, Mexico, and South America. He associated with some evil characters in his travels, but there were no lasting relationships...except one. He did a sabbatical in China a few years ago, and he has maintained contact with several people over there. One of the people he still maintains a strong relationship with is a man named Yu Chen, the Assistant Secretary of Health for the whole country of China. Just for your information, and just in case it comes up in conversation, Yu Chen is a follower of Islam.

Tom quickly interrupted, "Good God Emily, I didn't know there were any Muslims in China."

Emily answered, "There are more than you would think. There are approximately twenty five million of them in China."

Tom spoke again, "You mean we're dealing with al-Qaida—a Chinese branch of the al-Qaida extremists. At our last meeting you told me we weren't dealing with religious extremists, and now you're telling me we are, except that they're foreign. It would've been easier if it was an American cult rather than al-Qaida. They've got the resources, and obviously they have the know how. If we're to prevent a repeat attack, we've got a lot of work to do. I also don't relish going back to the White House and informing everyone we're dealing with al-Qaida. Everyone is going to have a fit, and my head is going to be on a platter."

"Wait a minute," Emily said. "We did some further checking on Yu Chen. He's a follower of Islam, but he's not an extremist. He has never associated with any al-Qaida operatives, nor has he ever communicated with any of the mid eastern extremist organizations. He's a solid citizen of China, and his loyalty is strictly to China. In addition, every single one of our country's multiple spy agencies categorically denies there was any al-Qaida participation in this catastrophe. It's not al-Qaida that committed the heinous act. We can eliminate them, but we cannot eliminate Yu Chen.

"During my investigation I also discovered some other valuable information. Kirby Wadsworth spent some time in China about three years ago helping them with population control. I thought there might be a connection, so I checked with some of my sources. More about him later."

Agent Chandler had a list on the blackboard of all the United States companies that China had become involved in within the last five years. One of these companies was circled. She began her discussion. "These businesses were all acquired by the Chinese about three years ago. Prior to that there were almost no purchases, mergers, or commercial activities by the Chinese in the United States. There were some, but not too many. Then about three years ago there was a tremendous spike in the number of business ventures. This intense activity lasted about two or three years, and then it slowly decreased, but I must emphasize that it was only a relative decrease." She pointed to a graph on the blackboard, "Look at this graph. Here is when Kirby Wadsworth was in China, and this spike represents the sudden rise of Chinese business activity in this country. Here is when the number of pregnancies in the United States decreased markedly. I'd say there is a pretty strong time association pattern to all these activities."

Emily continued speaking, "Almost all the businesses the Chinese became involved in continued to operate just as they had with the previous owner. The Chinese would bring in three senior management people and two young trainees for each company. These people would observe and they would learn, but they did not really participate in the active management of these companies.

"International Pharmaceutical, the company that is circled, was completely different. The Chinese took over an entire wing—and I mean took over. They built a new transportation dock, and they put in a new security system. The entire wing was a separate and discrete entity, and none of the old employees were allowed in there. Instead of the usual five new Chinese employees, there were about sixteen new employees, all Chinese. This was a Chinese company, run by the Chinese, and with all Americans excluded. My partner Pete will fill you in on these employees."

Pete Vangard rose from his chair and walked slowly and also very stiffly to the front of the room.

Tom Lewis eventually spoke, "Pete, are you okay? You're walking kind of funny."

"Yeah, I'm okay," Pete replied. "I think I pulled a muscle in my back and I'm a little stiff, but I'm sure it'll work itself out in a day or two."

He then continued speaking, "Emily is being very kind when she said we worked on this together. She has done most of the work, and she certainly has been the one who has done all the pushing and shoving in order to achieve what has been accomplished so far. In fact Emily gave me the list of employees to check on. I have checked their credentials here in the United States and also their backgrounds over in China. My results are interesting. First of all there were no young trainees employed at International Pharmaceutical. Most of the new Chinese employees at International Pharmaceutical were MD's and PhD's which we would expect at a pharmaceutical research company. The other employees fit into a category that I would call management. Some of these management officials were trained and experienced management officials, but others were not. They were Chinese government officials before they came to the United States. While having management officials in a pharmaceutical firm makes sense, having government officials does not. In China these government officials worked directly under a man called Sun Lee, M. D. I will talk about him a little later.

Other than the employees just mentioned, no one else worked in that wing of the company. There were no janitors, no clerks, no stock boys, and nobody delivered food to that unit. All the employees working in that wing were highly qualified people. Every function in that unit was carried out by a Ph. D., an M.D., or some government or management official. That includes sweeping the floor, changing the light bulbs and cleaning the bathrooms. The Chinese wanted as few people as possible to know what was happening in that wing of the building, and they weren't going to take a chance that someone would find out."

CIA Agent Lewis spoke up, "What was the new security system like? How sophisticated was it?"

Pete was ready. "The security at International Pharmaceutical was extremely stringent, and the new Chinese security chief was not the typical security officer. Over in China he had a very high ranking security position. To be assigned to International Pharmaceutical, he either received a very substantial demotion, or he was assigned to a very important project. I believe the latter. The system itself was extremely sophisticated."

Tom interjected, "I assume we have an investigating team down there."

"Yes we do," Pete replied. We actually have two. One is investigating the facility, and the other is investigating the personnel. That's where I obtained my preliminary information, and we're supposed to get updated and more complete information as it is obtained."

"Good," Tom replied. "I hope they come through."

"Now back to Sun Lee and Kirby Wadsworth," Pete said. "I'm not sure how closely they worked together when Kirby Wadsworth was over in China, but we do know that they did have some contact. We know they participated in several meetings together, along with several other important officials, but we don't know what was said or by whom.

However, the fact they had any contact at all seems more than just a coincidence.

"Sun Lee, M. D. is a medical doctor assigned to the Chinese embassy in Washington, D. C. That doesn't make sense. I am also not sure what he really does in that embassy. As far as we can determine China has never had another medical doctor assigned there, and we know that a lot of these countries "hide" people in their embassies to conceal their true mission, and because it gives them diplomatic immunity if discovered.

This Sun Lee was also a busy man. He traveled all over the United States, but not to do medical work. He was into real estate. He purchased three pieces of property and leased one. These four properties are scattered around the United States and are practically out in the middle of nowhere. That also doesn't fit. Those properties need to be investigated right away. Emily and I will be investigating the property that Sun Lee leased, because it's the closest, and we can drive there right after this meeting. The other properties have already been assigned to other agents, and they're probably knocking on those doors right now. I'm sure they'll have some information for us tonight."

Emily immediately spoke up, "Actually, I'm kind of anxious to get going."

Pete Vangard, surprised, but then again, not really surprised, but a little bit concerned about Emily's impetuosity chimed in, "Emily and I will be leaving as soon as possible, and I hope we also have some answers by this evening."

Tom Lewis perceived the slight uneasiness in Pete Vangard's voice, but didn't say anything, filing it away for future reference, and immediately switched the conversation back to Kirby Wadsworth. "Pete, Emily, are you going back to question Professor Wadsworth?"

"Yes," Emily replied. "I can't wait to get that man in my sights."

Pete also replied, "Yes, we're going back, but I don't think it will do much good. Maybe we'll get some information by accident, or maybe he will divulge some information on purpose, but I doubt it. He's one cold determined gentleman, who believes what happened to all those American women is going to make the world a better place. We're going to pursue Sun Lee a little bit, and then we're going to revisit Kirby."

Tom hesitated only briefly and then spoke, "When you go back, I'd like you to consider bringing Ryan Stone with you. He's a very good interrogator."

"Who's he?" Pete inquired. "I've never heard of him."

Tom replied, "He's a good friend of mine, and he's helped me out several times in the past. I took the liberty of asking him over. Just a minute I'll get him."

Tom walked to the doorway and beckoned for Ryan Stone to enter. "Ryan, I'd like to introduce you to Pete Vangard and Emily Chandler, the FBI agents I told you about. Pete and Emily, this is Ryan Stone."

Pete Vangard spoke, "Mr. Stone, Tom says you're a very good interrogator, and I assume Tom briefed you about this case, so what do you think? Can you help us?"

Ryan Stone replied, "I have no doubt whatsoever that I can help you, but I think we need to change a few things. First of all, Professor Wadsworth has to be taken out of his own environment when he's questioned. Take him to a very cold or a very hot interrogation room, preferably in some isolated place, and do the questioning there. Make him feel uncomfortable. I also think we should use a few different techniques to encourage him to talk."

"What's that mean?" Pete asked sharply.

Without even changing his tone of voice, Ryan Stone answered. "Well, some pharmaceutical assistance combined with a little bit of physical pressure might help."

Pete exclaimed, "Pharmaceutical assistance? Physical pressure? If they aren't nice, euphemistic words for what I'm afraid you really mean. Tell me exactly what you are talking about."

"I'm talking about obtaining information. You need information, and I'll get it for you."

"I don't like the sound of this," Pete replied. "This is the United States, and Professor Wadsworth is a citizen of the United States. He hasn't been charged with anything, and so far, the Professor is just one weird human being with some weird ideas. Besides, we're still at the point where we don't even know if there has been a crime committed."

"You may be right Mr. Vangard, but after I'm finished with Professor Wadsworth, we'll know for sure whether he's been involved in a crime or not. In his case I would probably only need a minimal amount of pharmaceutical assistance. I can take him to the police station, give him a few drugs, and I bet I won't even have to lay a finger on him. He may not even remember receiving the drugs, and in a few hours I'll have the information you need. We can justify the interrogation on the basis of national security. What do you say?"

"What do I say?" Pete replied. "I say no. Emphatically no. This is the United States, and we don't use techniques like that here."

Ryan Stone spoke in a very matter of fact fashion, with no remorse or guilt whatsoever. "Yes, Mr. Vangard, we *do* use those techniques here; right here in the United States. Give me a chance, and I'll get the information for you. I'm very good at my work."

Ryan Stone then turned to Tom Lewis. "Tom, what do you say? You're in charge here, and you told me your superiors all the way up to the President are jumping all over your back. Give me a chance. It'll only take me a few minutes. I'll get you the information."

Tom Lewis responded, "Pete, there is some urgency here, and we need the information. The nation's pregnancy rate is just now starting to rebound very minimally, and there is a small but increasing number of pregnancies occurring in some of our girls who are just entering womanhood. The United States cannot allow these young women to suffer the same infertility fate that their older sisters and mothers did. It would be a disaster for the country, and the president and his administration are advising that everything in our power must be done in order to prevent such an occurrence."

Ryan Stone immediately spoke, "I think the President would be very pleased if I had the opportunity to utilize all my abilities."

Pete quickly replied, "I don't agree. The President would never tolerate the use of your inhuman methods, particularly on an American citizen who has not even been charged with a crime."

Tom Lewis then interrupted, "Okay everybody, that's enough. Ryan, wait outside for a minute. I'll be right there."

Ryan Stone left the room and Tom spoke, "Pete, I can understand your sensitivity in not utilizing Ryan's talents, and at this point that's fine, but depending upon the investigation's progress, I may need him. For now we'll do it your way. Now keep in touch, and if you turn anything up, let me know."

Pete and Emily pensively walked down the hall when Pete suddenly spoke, "Can you imagine the scandal that would arise if the press discovered we were using techniques that Ryan Stone suggested. You and I would receive all kinds of bad publicity, and we would possibly be made the scapegoats for the whole episode. We would probably be fired. I don't want any part of it."

He then continued, "Guys like Ryan Stone make me sick. He should have some of those techniques used on him."

Emily replied, "It's not just guys like Ryan Stone; its guys like Tom Lewis as well. He was certainly willing to have Mr. Stone use his skills, and Tom is a senior man. He should know better."

Pete replied, "Tom is a senior man, but every person has a breaking point, and Tom has a lot of pressure on him. He's being questioned and yelled at every day. His superiors want answers, and nobody has any. The president doesn't know what to do, and he's losing popularity fast. He's stuck in the White House with nothing to say, and nothing to do. There aren't even any disaster sites to visit. Nothing."

Emily spoke, "We don't have the right president in the White House. If President LaBelle was still in there, I'm sure he'd be visiting the current disaster sites. He'd be trying to visit the pelvis of every single young female in this country."

Pete half heartedly started to chuckle, and Emily reacted quickly. "Was that a laugh I heard out of you?"

"Yes, it was," Pete responded. "I guess you haven't heard me laugh much recently, have you?"

"No. As a matter of fact, I haven't." Emily said. You've been pretty somber recently, but I figured it was your stomach pain. Because you didn't say anything, I didn't say anything either. By the way that was pretty quick thinking coming up with that lie about a pulled back muscle. I think Tom bought it for now, but if you continue to walk around all hunched over like that, you're going to be off this case."

"That can't happen," Pete replied. "Cases like this are what we live for. I'll ask the doctor to give me some pain pills until the case is over."

Chapter 23

"Hi Joan," Nancy Holder yelled, as she approached Joan Rosenbloom. "I didn't know you shopped here."

Joan said, "I'm just browsing. I like to shop in different stores every now and then just to see if there is anything unusual on the market."

"I know just how you feel," Nancy Holder responded. "Sometimes Maxwells has some cute little items that you can pick up rather cheaply. By the way football season will be starting soon, and we're going to have a tailgate party before the first game. It's on Labor Day weekend, and, of course, we're expecting you and Steve. Jack says it should be a good season, and we may even get a chance to go to a New Years Day bowl game, perhaps New Orleans or Miami."

Joan sheepishly replied. "Oh, I'm sorry Nancy, but we won't be able to make your tailgate. We're not going to the games this year. I apologize for the miscommunication, but I thought Steve had already told Jack. With college for John coming up, and Carol turning into a young woman, we thought we would spend more time together as a family."

"That's delightful," responded Nancy. "It's always healthy to do things together as a family. I always told Jack that you and Steve had your priorities straight." Nancy

Holder knew "family quality time" was not the reason the Rosenblooms weren't buying football tickets. It was the money. Nancy had heard rumors there were some financial problems, but now she was sure. Nancy had also heard that her friends, the Wilsons, were also having severe financial problems, and to a lesser degree even the conservative Fielder family. *I guess my husband is just very astute financially,* Nancy Holder thought to herself.

Mrs. Rosenbloom left the store in a foul mood. She was angry that her husband had not informed Jack Holder, and certainly had not informed any of the others, that they wouldn't be getting football tickets.

As Joan stomped across the parking lot and approached her car, a small red sports car pulled into the space next to her. It was Patty Rush—Mrs. Frank Rush—the wife of Dr. Frank Rush, Steve's classmate, and the obstetrician from the next town over. How is she still able to drive a car like that Joan thought. The Rushes have to be having financial problems. Steve said all Ob-Gyn practitioners were having trouble.

"Why Patty, how are you? Are you and Frank doing okay?" Joan asked.

"I'm fine.' Patty replied.

"And Frank?"

"He's doing very well, thank you"

They weren't the answers Joan expected. Maybe Patty was unaware of what was happening, or maybe she was too proud to admit it.

Patty continued speaking, "You know Joan, we don't get together like we should. We've got to make an effort. I tell you what. As soon as I get home from getting my hair and nails done, I'll give you a call."

"Hair and nails done," Joan exclaimed. "How can you

afford to get your hair and nails done? Isn't Frank's practice in some difficulty? Steve's is rather slow."

Patty responded, "Frank had a slow spot a few months ago, but after he hired Joseph Moran as his new office manager, things started picking up again. I asked Frank what the difference was, but all he said was that he doesn't interfere with my cooking or shopping, so I shouldn't interfere with his practice. Maybe if Steve is having a problem, he should contact Mr. Moran. He's a real nice guy, and evidently a very good businessman."

"What did you say his name was?"

"Joseph Moran. He's very industrious, and I'm sure he could always use a few more clients. Steve can use Frank's name as a reference if you like."

"Thank you Patty, that's the first hopeful news I've heard in a long time."

"Glad to help. By the way, are you and Steve going to the OB meeting in Chicago this year. It should be a lot of fun. Maybe the two of us could do some shopping, while the men attend those boring meetings. I have to do some shopping for my son. He's going away to Yale next year, and he has absolutely no clothes, and, of course, he won't buy any. I have to do it all for him."

"No," Joan answered, "we're not going this year. We generally don't go to the national meetings."

Patty looked down at her watch, "It's been good talking to you, and I'm sorry I can't talk longer, but I don't want to be late for my appointment. You know how persnickety those hairdressers are if you're even one minute late. If you change your mind about Chicago, give me a call."

CHAPTER 24

John bounded down the stairs to greet his mother. He was completely surprised to see his father sitting there quietly as well. "Hi Dad, I didn't know you were here. Before I forget, you have two messages on the answering machine. Bill Fielder called— he's at the bank and he wants you to call him back today. Some guy from the University Athletic Boosters Club also called. They haven't received your annual donation yet."

He then turned to his mother. "Mom, how was your day?"

She quickly replied, "Oh, I had a few surprises today. I was just getting ready to discuss them with your father, but I'll do it later. How about you?"

"It was pretty good," John answered. "The senior ring sales representative was at school today. We have to pick out the color tomorrow, and then we're going to be measured next Friday. The class officers also talked about our senior banquet. What's a good restaurant to go to?"

"John, let me get dinner. Then I can talk to your father, and you and I can discuss it later."

That was not the response he would have received a year ago. A year ago his mother enthusiastically would have asked for the brochure about the rings, and she would have had six suggestions for the senior banquet right on the tip of her tongue.

"Okay mom," John responded disappointedly. "I'm going back upstairs. Let me know when dinner is ready."

After John disappeared Joan turned to her husband and glared. "Steve, do you know what you did to me today? I ran into Nancy Holder at the store this afternoon, and I had to tell her we weren't buying football tickets this year. Weren't you supposed to take care of that?" Steve didn't acknowledge Joan's question in any way whatsoever, and remained almost completely motionless in his chair. Joan continued, "I told Nancy that we weren't buying football tickets this year because of family reasons, but she knows what's going on. She didn't say anything, but she was just as embarrassed as I was. Now I suggest you get out of my sight."

Steve didn't move.

"Steve, get out of here before I throw something. Go get your phone messages"

"Joan, I have already gotten the phone messages. I can ignore the Athletic Boosters Club, but the bank wants a new financial statement. I wasn't able to make a principal payment on the lake property last month, and all I did was pay the interest. The sale of my motorcycle helped, and I have the boat up for sale, but I think we have to consider selling the lake property itself."

Joan was exasperated, "Steve, I don't understand what is happening here. I also had a conversation with Patty Rush today, and she and her husband aren't having any problems. In fact Patty said Frank is doing better than ever, so why are we having problems? I know I asked you this before, but are you sure you're not having some other kind of problem, because if you are, tell me, and we can work through it together."

Steve replied, "No, I don't have any other problems, and furthermore, I can tell you with one hundred percent certainty that almost all Ob-Gyn practices around the country are doing poorly. Maybe Frank inherited some money."

"No, it's not inherited money. She told me they had a tough time a couple of months ago, but after Frank hired a new office manager, they have been prospering ever since. She gave me his name—Joseph Moran. She said he was excellent, and that he was always looking for more work. Why don't you give him a call?"

Steve hesitated before answering. "Joan, I didn't tell you, but as a matter of fact, I have already spoken to Mr. Moran and his ideas weren't suitable for my practice. I told him I wasn't interested."

Joan replied, "I can understand that, but you can't sit around and let your practice collapse completely. You've got to do something."

"What would you have me do?"

"First of all, you should make some phone calls. Contact the State Health Department, and see what they say."

Steve replied, "Frank Rush did that a long time ago, and he didn't get any satisfaction. He talked to the Commissioner, and the Commissioner was supposed to call him back, but he never did."

"Then contact the chairman of the OB-Gyn department at the university. You've donated quite generously to his department several times. Maybe he can help."

"He won't know what to do. He's not out in the real world like the rest of us. He's mainly interested in research and teaching."

"Contact him anyway. He may realize that if the donations dry up, his research money may dry up, and his job may dry up. Give him a call."

"I don't think it will help."

"Okay then, you said OB practices all around the country are having problems. All those OB doctors can't be sitting around doing nothing. Contact your state Ob-Gyn Society or even the national organization, and ask them what they recommend for both the long and the short term. They should have an answer."

"I don't think so. Those people are still trying to figure out what happened. They won't have any recommendations."

"Steve Rosenbloom, I can't believe that there isn't somebody in the whole wide OB-GYN world who doesn't have a recommendation about this crisis, but if that truly is the case, then you better start looking for another profession. You think about that, and you think about each and every single negative response you just gave me when I was trying to help."

Joan paused for a moment and then focused directly on Steve's face. "Steve, are you depressed?"

"No, I'm not depressed."

"Well, you seem sluggish, and if you are depressed, you should get professional help, and if you're not depressed, you've got to come to some conclusions about what you're going to do."

CHAPTER 25

Steve headed toward the mall. He was looking forward to spending a few hours there, just enjoying himself and getting a break from the constant tension he endured both at his home and at his office. Wandering around the mall would give him a chance to relax; it wouldn't cost him anything, and there was always something interesting to see, particularly in the toy store and the book store. A person could spend hours in just those two stores alone.

Upon entering the mall Steve was flabbergasted. Where were the crowds, and what was that "Space Available" sign doing in the window of the "Just for Baby" store? BINGO! It hit him, a sudden flash of the obvious. The infertility blight and its consequences had hit the sophisticated and prosperous city of Merrion. Steve walked around incredulous. "Just for Baby" was the first to go, but others would soon be following.

A salesman standing at a shop doorway interrupted him. "We've got some outstanding buys. Why don't you come in and look around?" Nobody was in the store except the lone salesman. Steve walked to center court, and looked around. It was eerie. Center court was normally an area of robust activity, but now it was quiet. There were no screaming babies, no running children, no pregnant women and no baby carriages to avoid. The fast food restaurants—normally a hub of activity—were practically empty. There would be more unemployment, and more hardships. He had enough. The mall was just as depressing as his home.

He tried to exit as quickly as he could, thinking and knowing that the mall would soon be closing permanently, but before he could get to the door, he heard a weak and slightly slurred voice calling his name. It was Ben Wilson surveying his quickly deteriorating real estate investment. Ben had been drinking.

"Dr. Steven Rosenbloom, how are you?" Ben said. "Come visit for a while. We haven't had a good visit for a long time. Plus I've got several bottles of good wine back in my office, and I think we should go back there and enjoy them. They're about all I have now. They're bottles I accumulated over the years when I could buy expensive wine by the case and give bottles away. Now I can't afford to buy one single bottle. Come on. Let's go have a drink."

Steve really didn't want to go, but felt obligated to indulge his old friend. Obviously, Ben had had too much to drink, and he probably was depressed, and after what Steve had just observed, Ben certainly had sufficient reason to be depressed. Steve was afraid that a no answer might have been perceived as a personal rejection, and he reluctantly agreed.

It only took a minute to get to Ben's office. Steve was shocked. There were wine bottles scattered everywhere, and no one had cleaned the office in quite some time.

Ben looked at the bottle of wine, exclaimed how expensive it was, and reiterated once again that he couldn't afford such luxuries any more. Ben opened the bottle, sniffed the cork like he was at a five star restaurant, and poured the wine very deliberately into two glasses.

"Steve, what is going to happen to us? I know you're not doing well. Nobody is doing well. Bill Fielder, our loyal fair weather banker friend, called me, and said that if my cash flow didn't improve soon, he would have to foreclose on the mall. I've run this mall for a long time now, and I'm afraid I'm going to lose it. Some of my tenants have to close up shop, plus a number of my apartments are becoming vacant, and I may lose them as well. I don't know what I'm going to do. I'm mortgaged pretty deep on all my properties, and there aren't many options left."

Ben tried to act as serious and sober as he could. He looked directly at Steve. "Steve, have you ever considered suicide?"

Steve jumped up quickly, totally ignoring that his drink had spilled all over his shirt. "Good God Ben, what are you thinking? Let me drive you home. You can come back tomorrow and get your car. You need to get a good night's sleep, and tomorrow you'll have a completely different outlook."

Ben exploded in a horse laugh. "Tomorrow I'll have a completely different outlook? Is my friendly banker going to forgive all my debts, or is all the empty mall space suddenly going to be rented by prosperous tenants? I don't think so. Tomorrow I'll have the same pessimistic—or rather the same realistic—outlook that I have today, except maybe I'll be sober, at least in the morning, but I accept your generous offer to drive me home. Thank you, you're a true gentleman."

Steve drove Ben directly home, walked him to the door and helped him inside. He spoke briefly to Ben's wife Holly, but mentioned nothing about the suicide comment. He believed Ben was drunk, and would forget about it when he awoke the next day. God, Steve hoped so.

CHAPTER 26

"Hey there Ms. Chandler, a little heavy on the gas pedal, aren't you?"

Emily Chandler didn't reply. She was in such deep thought that she was completely unaware that Pete Vangard had spoken to her.

Pete Vangard repeated his question in a louder voice. "Hey Ms. Chandler, you're a bit heavy on the gas pedal, aren't you?"

The sudden noise startled her, and she responded almost before Pete had gotten the words out of his mouth. "Hey yourself! Have you forgotten that we agreed I would drive? Sit back and relax. Enjoy the scenery, or, better yet, close your eyes and go to sleep. I'll let you know when we get there."

"I know you're driving," Pete replied, "but I'm not so sure how responsibly you're driving. We're passing everybody. Plus that last curve seemed a little shaky, and I really don't want my organs splattered all over this county. I like them just the way they are."

"Pete, that's wonderful you can say you like your organs just the way they are, because that's something I *can't* say. I'm a woman in my mid thirties, and neither of my ovaries work. I also have an unused uterus whose only function is to occupy space in my lower abdomen, and the only growth my uterus could possibly sustain is a cancer. What do you think of that?"

Pete started to reply, but Emily continued her diatribe, "Pete, you don't understand. I think about being childless all the time. It haunts me, and it haunts my girlfriends. My female friends and I used to talk constantly about having children, and about how the children would grow up, and where they would go to school, and even who they would marry. Now all we talk about is growing old gracefully. Isn't that wonderful conversation for a group of women in their thirties?"

"God Emily, have you seen a shrink?" Pete replied. "It sounds to me that maybe a shrink could help."

"Yes, I've seen a shrink, and do you know what I learned from those shrink sessions. I learned that in addition to having ovaries and a uterus that weren't working properly, I learned that my brain wasn't working properly either. That's why I went to the shrink in the first place. I didn't need that kind of help, so I stopped going."

"Emily, I don't want to be offensive, but maybe you just didn't click with that particular psychiatrist. Maybe you should try another one."

"What's the matter Pete? You think I'm crazy? Maybe I am crazy, but I'm no different than numerous other childless females in this country. Go to sleep. I'll wake you when we get there."

Pete was happy to get out of that conversation, and quickly closed his eyes.

Emily thought to herself. *Typical male, no empathy.*

Pete Vangard and Emily Chandler arrived at Sun Lee's property about dusk, and Emily immediately thought to herself. Pete was right. This property is out in the middle of nowhere. The two of them walked cautiously around the perimeter of the old warehouse trying to detect anything unusual. There was nothing evident. The windows had been boarded over in order to obstruct the vision of snoopers, and, obviously, there had not been any activity around the outside of the building in quite some time. There were leaves and old papers resting against the main doorway, and the door had not been opened in quite a while.

Pete Vangard was trying to peer in one of the boarded windows when someone behind him spoke, "May I help you?"

Pete jumped, and instinctively reached for his revolver, but stopped short of drawing it. He turned around quickly, and angrily faced the man who had spoken to them. "Who are you, and what are you doing sneaking up on us like that? You could get yourself killed doing that."

"I'm Jack Butler. I own this property. Now who are you two, and what are you doing on my property?" Jack Butler was a grandfatherly old man who apparently dressed strictly for comfort. He was wearing wrinkled pants, unpolished old shoes, and a thinning sweater with a small hole in the right elbow. Fashion was not his concern.

"I'm Pete Vangard, a special agent for the FBI and this is my associate Emily Chandler. We're here on official business." Both showed their identification.

Jack Butler couldn't conceal that he was excited about FBI agents investigating his property, and his imagination juggled images of intense intrigue with those of inquisitive photographers and prying newspaper reporters.

The voice of Emily Chandler quickly returned him to real time. "I understand this building is rented to Sun Lee. What does he use it for?"

Jack Butler flashed a satisfied smile, "You are right on one count. Sun Lee rents this building, but on the other hand he doesn't really use it. Leasing to him was a good investment for me. Around here people don't have much money. In fact, financially some of them are really hurting, but I'm fortunate. I get a check from Sun Lee the first of every month, right on time. Don't have to worry about maintenance, and there aren't any phone calls in the middle of the night. Like I said, he mails in his rent check every month. Right on time. No hassles. Ideal tenant as far as I'm concerned. As far as I can tell, he only used this place for three days and three nights, all during the same week. Kind of strange, huh. Three days in a row, and that was it. Been vacant ever since. Hadn't even seen him since until he showed up here last week. He said he was just checking it out. Wanted to make sure there weren't any problems with the property."

Emily persisted, "When Sun Lee originally rented it, what did he say he was going to use it for? You must have asked him that."

"I'm sure I did, but I don't remember what he said."

"Is Sun Lee the one who actually rented it, or did someone else actually rent it?"

"No, no one else. Sun Lee was the one who rented it. I remember him signing the papers, right over there in my kitchen. We spread the papers right out on the kitchen table, signed them and that was that."

Emily Chandler was getting impatient, "Mr. Butler, what did Sun Lee use it for on the three days he used it?"

"What did he use it for? I don't know. All I know is that your man Sun Lee drove a truck right into the warehouse. Soon after another truck arrived, and this second truck also drove into the warehouse. After a while both trucks left, and the exact same thing happened the next two days. I never saw any activity after that, and like I said, you can't ask for a better tenant than him."

Emily wanted to make sure she had heard right, and followed up, "Who was driving that first truck? Was Sun Lee driving?"

"Yes, Sun Lee was driving. That's what I just said. He had one passenger with him, rode in with him and rode out with him. I never saw that passenger before, and I haven't seen him since. Same with the two men in the other truck. Never saw them again either. Other than Sun Lee I really didn't get a good look at any of them, but I do know they were foreigners. They were Orientals, just like Sun Lee. I also remember that Sun Lee's passenger was kind of scary looking. It reminded me of an old western movie where some mean old cuss was riding shotgun on a stagecoach. One thing did seem a little odd to me that day though. Sun Lee drove one truck coming in, and drove the other truck going out. The two drivers switched trucks. I thought that was peculiar."

Emily persisted with a machine gun volley of questions, "What kind of trucks were they? Big trucks, little trucks? What color? Any special markings on them? Is there anything you can remember about them, anything at all"

Mr. Butler was proud that he could remember one of the trucks. "Sure can, that's my business. The one truck was a Ryder truck. I remember that. I really don't like to see people drive those rental trucks up here, on to my property I mean, not unless I really know who the people are. You never know what some stranger could be transporting. It could be hazardous materials, explosives, guns, drugs, you never know. I always make a note of those kinds of trucks. Like I said, don't like them. Plus these foreign guys were driving. We don't see many foreigners up here, rarely any Chinese. I was kind of suspicious, but I guess I was wrong. Haven't had one bit of trouble, and like I said I get my check right on time. No problems. Now lets see, the other truck, I don't remember. I didn't make a note of it, but it wasn't a rental. I would have noted that. That Ryder truck, I wrote down the license plate. I've been doing that on those rental trucks ever since I can remember. I don't want to be blamed for any crime committed on my property."

Pete and Emily both choked with amazement, but it was Emily who spoke first, "Do you still have that license plate number? That could help tremendously."

"Sure I've still got it. I wrote it down in my faithful notebook. I keep that notebook right on my kitchen table. You two come on over. I'll get it for you."

Jack's kitchen had the same appearance as Jack. There was stuff piled all over, and there was no semblance of any organization. However, his notebook was right on the kitchen table, and Jack found the number without any difficulty. "Here it is. Hope it helps."

"I am sure it will," Emily replied. "Thank you."

After a few more brief unproductive questions, Pete and Emily figured they weren't going to get any more information from Jack Butler, and they decided to leave. Emily gave a few departing comments.

"Mr. Butler, I want you to watch for any future activity whatsoever around this warehouse, and if any occurs, call me as soon as possible. If you remember anything else about Sun Lee, his associates, the trucks, anything, call me. If you happen to think of something that might help us, give us a call right away. If you can't get in touch with us, write everything down so you don't forget. Write down everything, even the slightest little detail, every name and every identifying characteristic. Write it in that notebook of yours."

Pete listened politely, but definitely not enthusiastically as Emily concluded her parting remarks. He certainly didn't expect to be receiving a call from Jack Butler, but he realized he had to listen as Emily finished her exhortation. When Emily finished talking, Pete added, "I realize Sun Lee pays you well, but he can not know the FBI was here. He may have been involved in a crime, and we need your help. Here is my card."

Jack Butler became wide eyed and apprehensive, "What kind of crime was it? Am I in any kind of danger?"

Pete thought for a moment, and then answered in the affirmative. "Yes, if Sun Lee knows what you are doing, you may be in some danger, so just stay out of his way, and if he or anybody else shows up around your warehouse, call us as soon as possible."

Pete and Emily walked slowly to their car, all the while carefully observing for any signs that might help them. None were there. It had been too long.

As soon as they took off, Pete said, "Do you really expect to learn anything from that old geezer? He likes the attention and excitement, but while we are dealing with crimes and criminals, he's acting and talking like it is old home week or his high school reunion or something. What do you think?"

Emily responded, "What do I think? I think Sun Lee is not an innocent man. When did you ever know a doctor to drive a truck like that, sit around for a couple hours, and then set out driving the truck again? Unless it is his wife's dead body, a doctor doesn't do that, much less three days in a row. Doctors hire people to do it. Those arrogant snobs don't want to get their hands bruised. It might interfere with their golf game."

Pete replied, "This guy is a Chinese doctor. Maybe he's different."

Emily responded, "Not a chance. He wasn't educated in China. He received his medical degree right here in the United States. All these guys get A plus in Arrogance 101. They teach it in medical schools."

Emily then quickly returned to the case. "Now why would the two trucks go into the warehouse together? I assume there was a transfer of goods from one truck to the other. We need to check on that truck that Sun Lee was driving, where it came from and where it went. The same with the other truck. In this computer age we should be able to track down Sun Lee's truck in two minutes, particularly since we have the license plate number."

Pete knew exactly what Emily's next statement was going to be, and quickly interjected, "And since we can track it down in two minutes, we can relax for a while. Let's go home and unwind. Tomorrow is going to be a full day."

"Why don't we check right now?" Emily said.

Pete answered, "Because we've both had a long day and we're both tired, and I'm a firm believer in not working when you're tired. That's when you make mistakes."

Emily questioned him, "Are you sure it's just because you're tired, or is your stomach acting up again?"

"My stomach acts up all the time. Some nights I can't even sleep, but you'll be happy to know that I have an appointment with the doctor."

"I've heard that before. Keep the appointment this time, will you?"

"Don't worry. I will."

Early the next morning Emily arrived in the office eager and ready to go, while Pete drifted in about fifteen minutes later. Even before he had a chance to remove his coat, he was essentially assaulted by Agent Chandler, "Alright Pete, let's track down that truck of Sun Lee's."

Pete responded, "We'll get to that, but first I think we should revisit the Institute for Population Demographics. There has to be information floating around those walls. That's their business, their livelihood. Someone has to know something, or, at least, they have to have some ideas. We'll start with your old friend, Kirby Wadsworth. The more we visit him, the greater the chance he'll slip up…but first I need to ask you a question. Do you think you can control yourself over there, or should I go myself? We don't want any misconduct charges brought against us. Remember, if we really need some muscle work, we can always call in Ryan Stone. I am sure he's much more effective at it than you are."

"Yes, I can control myself. Remember, I'm a professional just like you, although I suppose it wasn't very professional when I told the Professor I'd like to jump over that desk of his and bash his head in. On the other hand, I don't regret saying it one bit, and I'm still hoping I get the opportunity."

"Emily, I don't think I should be listening to this, and because of what happened the last time we were there, I think I'll just position myself between you and the Professor. You stay in the background a little bit. I should probably do all the talking as well. Now let's get going. We're also going to call on President Malone to see if he has remembered anything we could use. He may be the most difficult to find, so let's begin with him rather than the Professor."

"Do they know we're coming?" Emily asked.

"No, and I don't think we should notify them. Surprise is always better. You never know when something significant will be in plain sight on somebody's desk, and if you notify the person, it will certainly disappear."

President Malone immediately came out from his office upon receiving his secretary's announcement that FBI agents Peter Vangard and Emily Chandler were in his waiting room. "Tragic, isn't it?" President Malone said. "Professor Wadsworth was such a scholar, and so dedicated to his work. I would say he was more dedicated than anyone else here at the Institute."

"What are you talking about?" Pete replied.

"Haven't you heard? Professor Wadsworth passed away a few hours ago, apparently a heart attack or a stroke or something. So sudden, so unexpected. I just heard the bad news a few minutes ago myself. His death will be a big loss for this Institute."

"How did it happen?" Agent Chandler excitedly asked

"What do you mean? It just did. How do heart attacks, or strokes, or any of those sudden death events happen? They just do."

Emily quickly turned to her partner. "Pete, now what do you think? You must admit it's very peculiar that Professor Wadsworth just up and died. Here we are in the middle of a national investigation, and one of our central players suddenly expires. That sounds awfully suspicious, and I think it's now pretty obvious what type of case we're dealing with, and I believe quite strongly that we're moving much too slowly."

"Emily, let's not do anything rash. Whether it was terrorism or not, the deed has already been done, and if our national security was breached, it was breached months ago, and not just recently. Let's work through this logically, and make sure we do it correctly. Perhaps if we do something right for a change, we can prevent a future catastrophe. As it stands now, despite the multiple catastrophes that our country has experienced recently, I do not believe the United States is capable of reacting appropriately, either in a preventative or a reactive mode."

"Okay," Emily said, "but we need to get the crime scene investigators and the fingerprint people in here as soon as possible. We also need to get the medical investigators and the lab people over here. I assume our colleagues have already been over to the Professor's house, and I assume they have already performed an autopsy or they are about ready to perform one. The computer experts should also be here, and while all those people are doing their job, you and I need to check on Sun Lee's truck."

CHAPTER 27

Agent Chandler phoned the Ryder truck headquarters right away, and after a few brief conversations consisting of "I'm not sure I'm allowed to provide that information, and who are you again," Emily Chandler's call was finally put through to Joe Fleming, the Director of Operations. "Mr. Fleming, this is Emily Chandler. I'm a special agent with the FBI and I need some information about your rental trucks. I need to know if a Doctor Sun Lee rented any of your trucks, and if so, when and where. You will need to go back in your files about a year or so, maybe a little longer. Secondly, I want to know who rented the Ryder truck with the Michigan plate W643197. I'm pretty certain it was rented by the same Sun Lee, but double check it. I would like your people to start working on this immediately, and my partner and I will be in your office tomorrow. You can check our identification if you wish. Just call the Federal Bureau of Investigation or check with the local police. They'll verify our credentials."

Mr. Fleming responded in a pleading voice. "Ms. Chandler, we have a lean operation here. We've had to cut way back with the economy the way it is, and I can't spare anybody for a project like that. Why don't you call back in a few weeks and I'll see what I can do?"

Emily Chandler answered, "Mr. Fleming, my partner and I are coming to your office and I want the information ready when we get there. If not, I will shut your operation down, and it will stay shut down until I get the information. You be there, and you have someone else there who can provide us with any other information we may need. Do you understand?"

"Yes, I understand. I understand the government is once more hindering a business that is desperately trying to survive. I also understand that neither you nor your partner has to worry about meeting a payroll or making expenses. But don't worry, Ms. Chandler, I'll get your information. Good bye."

Agents Vangard and Chandler arrived right on time. Mr. Fleming was there and so was Mrs. Alice Jones, one of the computer experts for the company. Mr. Fleming wanted the meeting to be as short as possible and began speaking, "We checked on Sun Lee. He never did any business with us. We examined our records for the past eighteen months, and his name never popped up." For emphasis Joe Fleming repeated, "No, Sun Lee never did any business with us." Then he added, "Why don't you help our competitors for a while? Have them check their records for the past several years." He paused just long enough for his words to sink in, but not long enough to give Pete or Emily a chance to speak. "That license plate you gave me. That truck was rented to Joseph Kim. He rented it for four days in Acton City, putting about twenty four hundred miles on it. Joseph Kim checked the truck out, and Joseph Kim checked the truck in. Uneventful. No complaints. Anything else you people need?"

Emily was surprised to learn Sun Lee's name was not in the record and questioned Joe Fleming further, "Are you sure about Sun Lee? I was certain his name would appear."

The intonation in Joe's response purposely revealed his irritation. "Yes I'm sure."

Emily wasn't satisfied. "Who checked the records? Was it somebody reliable?"

"It was somebody reliable," Joe sarcastically replied. "It was me, plus I had Mrs. Jones double check the records as well."

Pete was astonished. Normally Emily Chandler was quite astute. Pete Vangard figured it was Agent Chandler's emotional investment in the case that had affected her thinking, and it concerned him. What would she do in a more critical situation?

Emily started to speak again, but before she could embarrass herself further, Pete Vangard confidently and casually seized control of the conversation. "Sun Lee's name isn't there because he didn't want his name on any documents. That's why Joseph Kim's name is there. Mr. Fleming, I want you or Mrs. Jones to compile a list of every single person who rented a truck from your organization from a year before to six months after the date Joseph Kim rented his truck. Specifically, check for any people with Chinese names."

Joe Fleming exploded. "Do you know how long that will take, how much time it will consume? This isn't a government agency. This is a private business, and we don't have that kind of time. Besides, that sounds like discrimination to me. We don't separate our customers into Chinese, Blacks, Whites, Hispanics, whatevers, or any of the above."

Almost nonchalantly Pete replied, "I tell you what, Mr. Fleming. You cooperate with us and I'll guarantee nobody from the Treasury Department comes around investigating your tax records, and nobody from the Department of Transportation demands the safety records for your motor vehicles, and nobody from the Department of Labor investigates your employee records or your retirement plan records. Otherwise I can't guarantee anything. In fact, I wouldn't be surprised if an agent from one of those agencies called you tomorrow. What do you say? Do you think you can help us?"

Joe Fleming angrily responded, "Mr. Vangard, is this the FBIs normal procedure for obtaining information—using extortion."

Very calmly Pete replied, "Mr. Fleming, I'm not sure what you're referring to, but I thought you would appreciate my efforts to safeguard your records from some prying government agency. Let's look at it pragmatically. You're going to save a lot of time doing the minor research I requested rather than explaining all your tax records to the Treasury Department. Sometimes those investigations take forever."

Joe Fleming remained angry. "Mrs. Jones, get these people the lists they need. Print them out, and get them to these fine upstanding, law abiding government officers as soon as you can."

The two agents didn't appreciate the hostility, but didn't comment. They believed Mr. Fleming had been pushed as far as he could for one day. They acted very politely, because they might need more information later on. After some assurances from Mr. Fleming that none of his other records contained any other worthwhile information, and after a few more computer runs by his assistant Mrs. Jones, the two agents left.

As they walked toward the car Emily spoke, "Pete, you've changed your interviewing technique."

"What do you mean?"

"I mean using extortion to obtain information from Mr. Fleming. Have you been talking to Ryan Stone?"

"No," Pete replied as he chuckled to himself.

There was a brief pause before Emily spoke again, "Pete, you did very well in there. You must be going through one of those pain-free periods, right?"

"You're right, and maybe it's the pain medications the doctor has me on, but who knows. When he examined me, the doctor wasn't sure whether he could feel a mass in my pancreas, or whether it was just normal intestine so he ordered a CT scan and an ultrasound examination. He's worried about a pancreatic tumor."

Emily spoke, "Well I hope those studies clarify the situation, because you're starting to look different. You look a little pale, and you look like you're starting to look a little thin."

"Thanks Emily. That's one of the finest compliments you ever paid me."

Emily spoke again, "I'm not finished yet. Are you able to stay on this case?"

"Sure can. I'm as physically and mentally capable as you. Some team, huh?"

"Pete, I also have to ask you another question. Did that doctor prescribe narcotics?

"Don't worry Emily, no narcotics."

CHAPTER 28

Going through the lists delivered by Joe Fleming was very tedious and very time consuming, and Pete and Emily were thankful for the assistance from several FBI newcomers. Normally the veterans considered these newbies a nuisance. When it was all finished, twenty-seven Chinese names had been extracted from the files. They were scattered throughout the eighteen-month period, but there was a concentration of six China rentals within three weeks of Joseph Kim's rental.

Emily Chandler was back on the phone, "Hello, this is Emily Chandler from the FBI; I need to speak to Joe Fleming or Alice Jones." Because she was lower in the chain of command, the call was forwarded to Alice Jones.

Agent Chandler said in a friendly voice. "Ms. Jones, I've selected five names from the list you gave us. If you could, I would like their phone numbers and their addresses, plus I would like the total mileage each of these people put on the trucks they rented. I would like the same information about Joseph Kim."

"No problem Ms. Chandler, I will call you right back," replied Mrs. Jones.

It was less than an hour before Emily Chandler received the information. She retreated to her office, closed the door, and sat at her desk with pages full of numbers, some maps and a computer. She was tabulating different mileage totals from International Pharmaceutical to the four warehouses that Sun Lee had rented or purchased. She calculated the mileage every which way, from warehouse to warehouse, round trip distances, using back roads, using turnpikes, from International Pharmaceutical to each warehouse, and every combination of the above.

She finally called over to Pete Vangard. "Pete, this looks pretty straight forward. I obtained information on six people from Alice Jones. Of those six it looks like there are four players. Of course one is Joseph Kim, and of the remaining five, there are three who I believe were working with Sun Lee. I was able to eliminate one of the five because he didn't go anywhere. He must have stayed right around town. I eliminated another gentleman because the mileage on his truck didn't fit. The mileage for Joseph Kim and the other three fits perfectly. There was one man for each warehouse, and the total mileage on the odometer of those Ryder trucks matches very closely with the recommended travel directions from my computer. Sun Lee took the shortest route right off the computer, and followed it exactly. He personally transported something from International Pharmaceutical to each of the four warehouses, loaded it on the other truck, and then drove the other truck to its final destination. One of these four accompanied him on each trip."

Pete Vangard replied, "Good work Emily, but we still don't know what really happened. All we know is that Sun Lee exchanged the contents of one truck with the contents of another truck, but that doesn't really tell us much. We need to know what was exchanged, how it was spread throughout the United States, and most importantly how we can prevent it from happening again. One truckload or three truckloads can't spread a poisonous agent throughout the entire United States. Furthermore the mileage on the trucks indicates that the trucks remained relatively local. They never traveled far enough to distribute anything nationwide, and if we're trying to explain the nationwide infertility crisis on the movements of those trucks, we can't do it. It just doesn't make sense. All the pieces aren't here, and those that are, don't fit together."

There was a brief silence until Emily spoke, "Let's start interviewing Sun Lee and his associates right now."

Pete answered, "Do you think we'll get any information from them?"

"I don't know, but I'm sure we definitely won't get any information unless we try."

Pete and Emily decided to leave Sun Lee for last. They would pursue his four companions first, obtain as much information as they could, and then go after Sun Lee. First on Emily and Pete's list was Joseph Kim. On the Ryder truck application Joseph Kim had listed his address as 106 Second Avenue, Albany, New York.

Pete and Emily flew to Albany, rented a car, checked their directions, and were off. At first the ride took them past a few successful commercial establishments, but this gradually changed. As they progressed closer to their destination the businesses were obviously less successful, and more and more stores were closed. The neighborhoods became poorer and poorer. They turned on to Second Avenue, a residential neighborhood, or, at least, a former residential neighborhood. There were run down houses with boarded up windows, vacant lots with an occasional drunk sleeping in the corner, and several disheveled people wandering aimlessly on the sidewalk. 106 was one of the vacant lots. Emily glanced at the "Dead End" sign at the end of the street. Boy, isn't that sign appropriate, she thought.

Emily suggested asking some of the people if they remembered a Joseph Kim. That proved unsuccessful. None of them had ever heard of Joseph Kim.

"Let's go to the post office. We'll see if this Joe Kim really lived there. If he did, we'll see if he left a forwarding address." That approach provided some information. "Yes, yes, Joseph Kim lived at 106 Second Avenue. No, he never left a forwarding address. Just moved away, address unknown. Sorry."

Pete and Emily climbed back into the car, both totally discouraged. Pete spoke first. "Let's go back to headquarters for a while. We need help. You and I will continue with Joseph Kim, and we'll also take Bin Liu, and we'll assign the other two gentlemen to Agents Jordan and Wiley. If justified, we're supposed to have as much assistance as we need—and I think it's justified."

Bin Liu listed his address as Twelfth Street in Atlanta. Pete and Emily took an early flight, rented a car and set out for Twelfth Street. It was a relatively nice neighborhood with cars parked on the street, and people strolling happily on the sidewalk. Pete and Emily were optimistic as they approached his apartment. Someone was living there. Unfortunately it was a middle aged white couple.

Most of the neighbors didn't remember Bin Liu, and those that did, had only a vague remembrance. They said he stayed pretty much to himself. They didn't know what happened, or where he went. He just moved away. He never caused any problems, never bothered anybody, and as far as they knew, he didn't really associate with anyone.

The information from the post office was the same. "Yes, Mr. Liu lived there, but he moved away, and never left a forwarding address."

As agents Jordan and Wiley joined agents Chandler and Gardner in Pete's office, Pete spoke to the two of them. "Well, how did it go? Let me guess. You didn't find out one thing about either of them. Nobody knew anything. Nobody knew where they went and there was no forwarding address. You drew a big zero, same as us."

Agent Jordan responded with a smug smile on his face. "Oh, not so fast. You're only right about one of them. He was a ghost. Vanished without a trace. But the other gentleman had a girlfriend. This girlfriend was almost one hundred percent sure her former boyfriend went back to China. She said that just before he disappeared he went on a three day business trip. He then came back for one day, and then left forever. She thinks he went to China, and she also thinks he was promised that he would be well taken care of over there. She doesn't know where he lives in China, and she really doesn't care anymore."

Emily was exasperated. "Now what do we do? We rely on tips from friends and relatives to solve crimes, and we rely on answers from neighbors. How many tips do you think we are going to receive about these four gentlemen? I suspect all four of our disappearing friends went back to China. They are now just four little yellow guys living in one of the largest countries in the world, and they are mixed in perfectly with one billion other Chinese."

CHAPTER 29

Tom Lewis, Glen Hardy, Pete Vangard, and Emily Chandler were once again in their favorite conference room, and once again Tom Lewis began the meeting. "Alright someone, tell me why our women aren't getting pregnant. What happened to them?"

Emily Chandler immediately began to speak, but Tom Lewis cut her off and continued speaking, "That statement and question I just used are the same statement and question with which President Freeman begins all his meetings, and so far no one has been able to give him a satisfactory answer, and that includes us. We have to change that."

Tom Lewis paused for a moment before continuing, "Now what were you going to say Emily? You seemed quite eager to speak. What's on your mind?"

Emily answered, "I think we're starting to make some headway on this case. It seems to me it's rather obvious that the Chinese, or at least some people of Chinese ancestry are behind the whole scheme. However, I am not sure whether they're Chinese government agents, or they're independent operators."

Tom interrupted, "Emily, stop for a minute. Are you relying on concrete evidence for this opinion of yours, or are you just speculating. At our last meeting we discussed some facts that could possibly indicate the Chinese were involved, but we have to be sure. You've taken us down the wrong road on several occasions already, and the President and his close advisors are getting rather testy about the lack of progress on this case, and particularly about all the false information they have received. Remember how everyone first operated under the theory of a viral etiology, and then this was subsequently disproved."

Emily quickly interrupted Tom, "I never operated under a viral etiology theory, and maybe you should remind the President and his advisors that the viral etiology theory came down from them to us, and that it did not go from us to them."

Tom responded, "Thanks for the observation Emily, but I think I'll pass on that assignment. I'm really not too eager to remind the President that it was his mistake, even though it's true. I know that it was their theory and not ours.

"Later on we talked about religious cults and secretive religions being the cause of the infertility problem, and even al-Qaida was brought into the discussion. I believe they were your concepts Emily, weren't they?"

"Yes they were, but the al-Qaida subject matter was introduced for informational purposes only."

"And the cults and religions."

"No, I truly thought they could be the cause."

"Well then, you can understand why we have to be sure, and I have to be especially careful before accusing any other person or organization of this heinous act."

"I know you have to be careful, but you have to admit there are some suspicious signs that are pointing to the Chinese."

Tom replied, "Yes, I'll admit there are some signs, but there is no solid evidence to actually confront the Chinese, or even to ask for their assistance. Officially the Chinese government is denying any knowledge of anything pertaining to the problem. Their leaders maintain they don't know what happened, or how it happened, or why it happened, and they claim they are just as ignorant as we are. They also gave an official expression of sympathy and pledge of support."

Pete replied, "Well, we couldn't have expected anything but that type of response from the Chinese government, and as for the investigation, I believe it's a step in the right direction. Even though it's a baby step, at least it's a beginning."

Tom spoke, "Unofficially, however, the Chinese are admitting that they may be developing a similar infertility problem in their own country. Their leaders are privately admitting that many of their young women are suffering from the same inability to become pregnant as are the young women of the United States. They are very concerned, and are actually asking for any assistance we might be able to give them. Although the number of their affected females is still low, they are afraid that pretty soon their entire country might be involved. Our President is very sympathetic to their plight, and wants to help them in any way possible."

Emily exclaimed, "I don't believe them. They're lying."

Pete immediately replied, "Emily, you don't have any evidence they're lying, and until you do, you cannot make such an accusation, and you probably should never make an accusation like that anyway. Never say somebody's lying. That's bad public relations. It also puts you in a position where you may have to defend yourself, not only publicly, but also privately to your governmental superiors. You should always say something like 'my interpretation of the facts is somewhat different.' It is much less likely to cause offense. Do you understand?"

"Yes, I understand."

"Good," said Tom Lewis, "and now that everyone understands, what does everyone think of an early stage infertility problem developing in China?"

Pete replied, "I think we need to brainstorm here for a while, because this China development opens up a multitude of possibilities. It could mean that the same natural affliction which previously struck the United States is now in the early stages of hitting China. It could also mean that both countries are affected because of a deliberate act by a third party, and that third party could be another country acting alone, or it could be using highly paid foreign mercenaries to do their dirty work. Since we think there might be some Chinese involvement, perhaps it's some ideologue renegade Chinese group, or perhaps the Chinese individuals are the mercenaries."

Emily spoke, "I bet that somehow someway Professor Wadsworth had something to do with it. I'm sure of it. If he were alive today, I'm sure he would be ecstatic."

Tom spoke, "I guess there are a multitude of possibilities, and they all need to be pursued, but until we get more information, let's review our most recent investigations. I heard from the men who are investigating International Pharmaceutical, and they haven't come up with much. They really don't have anything substantial. They have conducted covert physical searches of all the employees' homes, and they have found nothing. They have been monitoring their telephones and their fax communications, and there is nothing. Nothing suspicious was sent by e-mail, and there is nothing on their home computers."

"How about sleeper cells of Chinese Americans aiding them?" Emily asked."

"No evidence of that," Tom Lewis replied.

Pete then spoke, "Chinese American is not a term Chinese officials recognize. As far as they're concerned, they're all "Overseas Chinese" so I wouldn't be surprised if the perpetrators are receiving some assistance from people we call Chinese Americans."

"And the building task force people?" Emily asked.

"A little bit of progress," Tom replied. "Of course they couldn't do a physical search of the place, but the phone records of the company indicate some calls from that building went to Sun Lee, while other calls came from Sun Lee, and went to International Pharmaceutical, but that's all we have. All those calls took place months ago, and we have no idea of their content. We've monitored all the trucks going in and out, and we've examined the products after they've been delivered to their destination and there's nothing. Every single container of every single truck has been completely true to its label. Nothing nefarious or contaminated has left that plant since we've been on this case, so even if we postulate that these Chinese characters did it, we don't know what they did or how they did it. I'm completely frustrated with this case, not only because I haven't been able to solve the case, but also because I'm being tormented down at headquarters every day. Those guys down there are all over me, just as their superiors are all over them. The President is constantly harping on the negative economic news, and the worsening economy, and how it is starting to really impact our society. I have some newspaper summaries which the President has instructed his assistants to distribute. Here you are, for your reading entertainment."

Depression Will Hit. The often quoted phrase, "It was the best of times, it was the worst of times" is not applicable. It is becoming the worst of times, and there is no doubt it is becoming the worst of times. The country's entire social and economic orders are being disrupted. Whole industries comprised of major companies are plunging into a depression. Baby food companies, toy companies, infant clothing companies, and other related companies are closing. There are no expenditures on new equipment. Family income is down. Unemployment is up. Optimism is down, pessimism is up. Family wealth is down, suicide is up. The stock market is plunging, and it is predicted it will be worse than the Great Depression. It will be the "Greatest Depression," and there does not appear to be any hope for a reversal.

Through the years people have often spoken how the future of a country is in its children. How obvious this has become. There are no children and there is no future.

The social order is being disrupted. Some facts established long ago are changing or being challenged. Roe v. Wade is in danger of being overturned. Moralists and economists are arguing that an unborn baby is a person. It is wrong to kill such a person. Every person is necessary to help the United States survive. The opinion promulgated by some, even some women, is that no female capable of giving birth, whether married or unmarried, has any right to birth control. It is Un-American. The closet door is closing once again. Prejudice against homosexuals is surfacing, particularly female homosexuals, unless they're willing to carry a fetus. Persons should be in a relationship where a child, if at all possible, can be produced.

Economic pundits are pontificating about how bad the depression will be. Unfortunately there are not many of these economic pundits left to pontificate. Remaining companies can not afford to have people on the payroll that sit around and issue opinions. They need workers to be real workers. More people are unemployed and more business failures are being reported than ever before. No hope for change is visible in the foreseeable future. Personal and business bankruptcies are no longer news. Because bankruptcies are so commonplace, there is just a small wisp of pity for those declaring bankruptcy. The wealth meter, the gauge which reports total national wealth, continues to drop. The "Greatest Depression" is the proper moniker.

Persistent pessimism is gripping the entire nation. The recently released economic data verified what the entire country already knew. The economy is progressively getting worse, and the future outlook continues to be bleak.

CHAPTER 30

Steve stayed at the office after everyone had gone. He had had a bad day, but now all days were bad days. The office staff was becoming progressively angrier each day. Dr. Rosenbloom already had to terminate a nurse and a secretary, because the prior salary reduction had not been sufficient. Neither termination had been amicable. His secretary, Mrs. Ferguson, had been with Dr. Rosenbloom for about eight years, and she had no place to go—there weren't any jobs. She screamed at Dr. Rosenbloom. "My husband just lost his job too. What am I going to do, and how is my family going to survive? I gave you eight years of my life, and what do I get? Nothing, I'm put out on the street. You have no loyalty, and I hope God gives you the justice you deserve."

Steve responded sadly with what had become his most common phrase, "I'm sorry. I'm sorry."

Mrs. Ferguson snapped back, "You're sorry. You're sorry. What does that do? That doesn't help me one bit. You're an ungrateful selfish man."

The termination of his nurse Ellen Nash was just as unpleasant.

The former camaraderie in the office had been replaced by an antagonistic atmosphere, and Dr. Rosenbloom no longer enjoyed being there.

Steve sat at his desk and contemplated his future life. What would it be like tomorrow, next month, next year, ten years from now? His life was miserable. His office staff yelled at him; his wife yelled at him, and his children yelled at him. All his toys were gone: his motorcycle, his boat, they were all gone.

And he still had to tell John about next year. Steve had tried to hold on to the lake property by spending what remained of John's tuition money. Now John wouldn't even be able to attend Holmesdale Community College. John would have to get a job. Of course Steve fully realized how ridiculous that concept was. There were no jobs.

Steve thought to himself. What difference would it make if he left the world now, or he lived a few more years and died naturally? What's an additional ten years on earth when you consider the length of eternity? Why spend an additional ten miserable years on earth when there is an easy way out? He opened his drawer, and looked at the handgun in the back. He kept it there for protection when he was alone in the office late at night. He stared at the gun, repeatedly picking it up and putting it down. He thought about Ben Wilson, and how Ben seemed to think that suicide was a legitimate alternative. Steve picked up the gun once again. But then he didn't put it down. He loaded it, placed the barrel in his mouth and pulled the trigger.

CHAPTER 31

Wakes are always awkward occasions. People are very uncomfortable, don't know what to say or do, and in general stumble and stutter when facing the grieving parties. For the deceased's family, some consider a wake to be cruel and unusual punishment. Half the people are crying. Estranged relatives come in the hope of being treated amicably. Traitorous friends come not knowing whether they will receive a kind reception, or a reception they truly deserve. Betrayed former friends don't come at all, and unsuspecting others wonder why such friends are no where to be seen.

When suicide is involved, the discomfort is worse. Family members are embarrassed, while hate and anger permeate the atmosphere. Among those attending, the question of "why suicide?" is whispered over and over again, but never to the spouse.

John Rosenbloom confronted his mother. "Dad doesn't deserve a wake. He abandoned us. He let us down, and he deliberately chose to leave us. His last conscious thought was a choice to be away from his family. I don't want to go to his wake, and I don't want to face the people who will be coming to the visitation."

Mrs. Rosenbloom held her temper and spoke in a calm voice. She recognized all the anger and hate and depression in her son. "John, be quiet, and get control of yourself. Your father was under a lot of pressure, and he did the best he could. I should have recognized what was happening, and I should have helped him."

John acquiesced because he recognized the guilt and depression his mother was feeling.

The wake was scheduled from seven to nine PM, but the mourners actually began to arrive a few minutes before seven. The early ones wanted to get in and get out before the real crowd arrived. There weren't many flowers. People couldn't afford them.

Mrs. Mary Custer, a neighbor down the street was one of the early ones. "Joan, I am so sorry. I don't know what to say, but if there is anything I can do, let me know. My sympathy is with you." Joan felt relieved. She believed Mary Custer was truly sincere, and genuinely interested in helping. She was a sophisticated old lady and knew just what to say. She was a comfort.

For about a half hour Mrs. Rosenbloom heard only about the good old times from the different mourners, but all the while she could perceive the soft whispering in the background. "Why did he do it? His wife must feel awful. And the children. They have to live with it the rest of their lives."

Holly Wilson was the first of Joan Rosenbloom's real close friends to arrive. "Joan, I'm sorry," Holly said. "I'm sure you feel terrible. Is there anything I can do?" Then her voice broke, and she couldn't continue. She had to pause and take a deep breath before finishing her sentence "but at least you know where he is." The statement stung Joan Rosenbloom's mind and body. She froze for a second and then quickly recovered. "Thanks for coming Holly. Where's your husband? Where's Ben?"

Holly openly began crying and almost imperceptibly replied, "I don't know where Ben is. When I came home yesterday, he was gone. He left a note for me saying it was best for everybody if he left, and that he would come back when conditions improved. He didn't say where he was going."

Joan Rosenbloom broke down crying, and needed Jack Holder, another of her close friends to quickly step forward, not only to comfort her, but also to support her physically.

"Thank you, Jack. I guess I'm not doing very well, am I?" Joan said as she gradually recovered her composure.

"You're doing fine Joan. Please accept my sincere condolences."

Jack Holder then approached John Rosenbloom who was standing close by. "John, take care of your mother. Your father would want you to be strong. Make him proud of you."

"What do I care if I make him proud?" John responded. "I'm not proud of him. He ruined our family, and I'm here only because of my mother. I don't care about my father."

Carol Rosenbloom was crying and tugged on John's sleeve, "John, stop. You are embarrassing everyone." John looked at Carol's face. He looked at her tears and uttered "I'm going outside."

Everything was calm for a while as friends calmly and appropriately paid their respects. Joan Rosenbloom seemed to strengthen.

Tom Jackson, another neighbor, whom her deceased husband Steve had formerly described as a crusty old guy who spoke too bluntly without regard for other people's feelings approached Joan. "I'm sorry Joan, but don't worry too much. He's probably better off than the rest of us."

Joan broke down again. This time it was Bill Fielder, the banker, who came to her aid. "Hang on Joan, maybe you should rest for a while. Here, I'll help you."

"I don't want your help," Mrs. Rosenbloom replied. "You are the cause of all this. You and your bank literally broke my husband. You didn't have any faith or trust in him. Look up there. Look at that casket, and look what you did. You killed my husband. You also ruined Ben Wilson. Ben Wilson ran away from his family because of you. It's your fault. You ruined our family, and you ruined their family. Get out of here. Get out of this funeral parlor."

Fortunately Jack and Nancy Holder had stayed to make sure Joan was able to make it through the evening. They rushed to the front of the room, turned Joan away from Bill Fielder, and pushed her to one of the side rooms.

Jack Holder spoke, "Joan, don't go back out there. It's too strenuous."

"Jack, I have to," Joan replied. "These people came to pay their respects."

"Joan, listen to me," Jack said. "It's too strenuous for you, and probably dangerous to your health. Stay here until it's time to go home. The people will understand, and I'll have Nancy stay with you."

"Jack, you're probably right. Thank you. I don't know what I would have done without you."

CHAPTER 32

Joan Rosenbloom was sitting in the living room chair, staring at the unopened envelope she had just received from North Central Life Insurance Company. She was sitting all by herself in a living room that had changed considerably since her husband's death. The Oriental rugs had been removed and sold, and so had some of the wall hangings and most of the knickknacks. Even some of the furniture had been sold. There was no longer the ostentatious display of the nouveau riche. Now every item in that room was necessary and practical.

Joan had anxiously been awaiting the letter, and had pushed very hard to obtain Steve's death certificate and all the other papers required by the insurance company. Fortunately her friend Jack Holder had functioned as her attorney. He handled everything very efficiently, and all Joan had to do was sign the papers. She was very grateful, but now she was afraid to open it, and she sat there trembling in fear of what it contained. Would it be a denial of her husband's death benefit claim, or would it contain a check? Joan had fretted for a long time that the insurance company would reject the claim for the death benefit because he had committed suicide. She had heard somewhere that suicide nullified a person's claim to the financial benefit of a life insurance policy, and she was worried the claim would be denied.

She held the letter up to the light, but she couldn't tell. It was one of those opaque envelopes that didn't let you see inside. She sat there longer, essentially motionless and staring at the envelope. *This is crazy,* she thought to herself. *I've got to open it.* She flipped the letter over into her left hand, and slid the finger of her right hand under the sealed flap on the back. She slowly peered inside until it became patently obvious. There was a check inside. Thank God, she sighed as she emotionally and physically disintegrated into the chair.

Mrs. Rosenbloom needed the money. She felt guilty because it was her husband's death that had improved her family's financial condition, but she was relieved because now she was better off financially than she had been in a long time.

Joan was happy but didn't think it appropriate to show it in front of her children. Despite the children's feelings toward their father, she felt John and Carol would think a display of joy at receiving the insurance money would be crass and disrespectful. She tried to act as normal as possible but at the same time wanted the children to enjoy some happiness themselves.

Joan yelled upstairs. "John, come on down here for a minute. I have some good news for you." John wasn't sure he had heard right. Good news. It must be a mistake. There was never any good news in this house. John was skeptical, but he was at least curious enough to walk down the stairs. His mother was standing in the kitchen waiting for him. "John, I really do have some good news for us. Your father at least provided us with some life insurance money. There should be enough to last for a few years, and I think you should take some of it and go to school. We can't afford the Ivy League, but go to Holmesdale and get your degree. Who knows what will happen after that?"

John tried to conceal his excitement, but he just couldn't. "Mom, are you sure you can afford it? I have already mentally accepted the fact that I won't be going to school next year, so you don't need to send me. I'm sure you can put the money to better use someplace else."

"John, I want you to go to school; it'll make me happy"

"Are you absolutely sure?"

Joan had tears of happiness in her eyes. "I'm absolutely sure John. Go to school. I don't want to say your father would have wanted it, because I know how bitter you feel toward him, but truly, your father would have wanted it. Come on John; give your mother a hug. This family hasn't had many hugs recently."

John was in a happy mood. He had just come back from Holmesdale, and everything was all set. He was eager for classes to begin, and he was also happily daydreaming about participating in some extracurricular activities. Perhaps he could get a part time job to help pay some of his expenses, and maybe even help his family a little.

He briskly walked up the steps and opened the front door to his house. He went to the kitchen where he expected to find his mother. John was eager to tell her he had enrolled at Holmesdale, and how grateful he was to be going. "Mom, everything is all set," he beamed, as his mother sat expressionless at the table. "My enrollment is complete," John said proudly.

Suddenly Mrs. Rosenbloom started crying uncontrollably.

"Mom, what's the matter? What happened?" John said.

Mrs. Rosenbloom pounded on the table, threw the coffee cup across the room and yelled. "Your father! How could he do this to us?"

"Mom, what is it? What did dad do?"

Mrs. Rosenbloom didn't answer and pounded her fist on the table once again before exclaiming, "How could dad do this to us?"

John responded, "Mom, are you all right, or should I call for help?"

"John. No. I'll be all right. Give me a minute." She was now sniffling and stuttering as she spoke to her son. "John, your father's accountant, George Johnson, called this morning, and apparently your father hadn't been paying his taxes recently. Mr. Johnson said that in order to wrap up your father's financial affairs, the estate would have to pay his back taxes, plus pay the omitted social security and medicare payments. There are some penalties, and some fines that have to be paid, and there are also some other unpaid bills, which will also take some money, and…"

John suddenly screamed. "That's great. That's just great. My dad is a criminal. Yesterday I was glad he was dead, and now I wish he was alive. I wish he was alive and suffering. I hate him." John stopped only briefly, and then continued screaming, "Is this going to be in the newspapers? If it is, I want to move away from here? I'm going out, and I don't know when I'll be back."

Mrs. Rosenbloom quickly moved toward her son. "John, don't do anything rash. Stop and think for a while before you do something foolish."

John yelled back at her. "How much of the money is gone? I'm not going to Holmesdale, am I? I think dad really did hate us—to do so many things to us."

Mrs. Rosenbloom started to weep once again. "The

accountant said that after all the legal matters are taken care of, and the fines and penalties are paid, there won't be much left. I don't know what we are going to do. And you're right—you will have to postpone Holmesdale for a while."

"You know it's not just for a while. You know I'll never go to school. Just say it. I *hate* him."

CHAPTER 33

Mrs. Rosenbloom sat in the kitchen waiting for the clock to tick a few more times before she called the children to dinner. At the same time she was deep in thought pondering the future of her son and her daughter. She thought their personalities had changed.

Carol had become more quiet and reserved, and was starting to become withdrawn. Joan Rosenbloom was concerned. A mother is always concerned about her daughter's welfare, but Mrs. Rosenbloom was beginning to worry that her daughter's behavior was becoming pathologic.

Mrs. Rosenbloom was also concerned about her son John, although John's attitude had actually become more upbeat. Mrs. Rosenbloom worriedly chuckled to herself about her children and her own state of mind. She worried about her daughter Carol, because Carol seemed too sad, and she worried about her son John, because John seemed too happy.

John was in a better mood than he had been. He was moving at a faster pace and had a little bounce to his gait. His interests were expanding and he was venturing outside the home again. Maybe he had a girlfriend. Mrs. Rosenbloom hoped it was a girlfriend, or John's strong personality, rather than drugs or alcohol which were giving him this temporary boost.

At 5:30 PM Mrs. Rosenbloom called to her children. "John, Carol, dinner is ready. I'm getting ready to put it on the table."

John came down first, glanced at the stove, and sarcastically remarked. "Beans for dinner. That's a change. We haven't had beans in two days. Let me see. What will we have tomorrow?"

Mrs. Rosenbloom quickly replied, "John, you know how tight things are around here. It's tough to feed three people when you don't have much money."

Taking crumpled twenty dollar bills from his pants pocket, and throwing them on the table, John snapped at his mother, "I know how tight things are around here. Here is some money. Maybe this will help."

Mrs. Rosenbloom glared at her son, "Where did you get that money? You don't have a job."

At that moment Carol entered the room, and seeing the panicked expression on her mother's face, fearfully asked, "What are you two talking about? What is going on?"

Mrs. Rosenbloom tried to be nonchalant and responded, "Oh nothing special" and then in a subdued voice added, "But I do want to meet with the two of you after dinner."

Carol whined, "Now what? I don't want to have a meeting. I don't want to have any more meetings. Anytime we have a meeting it is because something bad has happened, or is about to happen. We never discuss anything happy. I'm not hungry. I'm going upstairs."

Mrs. Rosenbloom quickly spoke, "Carol, wait. We've got to talk; it's important. Let's talk right now." Out of respect for their mother both children turned to listen.

Mrs. Rosenbloom took a deep breath and began, "You both remember Mr. Edison, don't you?" He's a real estate agent, and he's going to come over tonight to appraise our house so we can get it ready to sell. We cannot afford it any-more. We are going to move to Crossville, my old home-town. Oh, I had such a good time there when I was growing up. We're going to move in with gammy and granddad. They are really excited for us to come. It will be great."

Carol spoke, "It will *not* be great, and you know it. It will be a disaster, and I don't want to go."

John also answered, "The last time I saw Mr. Edison, dad was going to buy a farm. It was supposed to be an investment that we all could enjoy while it appreciated in value. Now we can't even afford a house of our own. I agree with Carol, and I don't want to go to gammy and grand-dad's either. It will be awful, and you always told us you couldn't wait to move out of Crossville. This conversation has completely ruined my appetite. I'll be up in my room."

Mrs. Rosenbloom, pleading, spoke again, "John, Carol, wait. Dinner is all ready to be served. Sit down and eat."

Carol replied, "Mom, the dinners just aren't as good as they used to be. I used to like it when we had steaks, or pork chops, or salmon, or things like that. Now we have beans and spaghetti all the time."

"Carol, we have good dinners. They are much healthier now. All that red meat was bad for you."

"Mom, it's not just the food. It's the entire atmo-sphere. I used to sit in my kitchen chair and look through the door into the dining room. I could see the mahogany breakfront against the wall, and I could see the sparkle from your Waterford collection. You always said the Wa-terford collection would be mine some day, and I always dreamed of my children enjoying that same sparkle that I did, but now where is it? The Waterford is completely gone. It disappeared piece by piece, and now the break-front is gone too."

"Carol, they were just luxuries. We really didn't need those things."

Carol replied, "But everything is disappearing. Look in the living room. Dad's favorite chair is gone. And I lost the television set from my room."

"Carol, listen, what family needs three televisions? A family can certainly get by with two televisions and probably even one."

Carol replied again, "That was my television. It was in my room, and I could watch the programs I wanted. And who are the people who bought all our things? Why do they have money and we don't? It's not fair."

"Carol, you will learn as you get older that a lot of things in life are not fair. But to answer your question, everything was bought by wealthy people or dealers who represented wealthy people. They are people who have more than enough money to survive for years. Other pieces were sold to people who exist by profiting from the hardship of others."

"Mom, that isn't right. We deserve to be one of the wealthy families."

"Carol, I'm not sure who deserves to be among the wealthy, and I think it's even difficult to define the word "deserves" when it comes to money. Does Mrs. Jones deserve to be wealthy? She didn't do anything her entire life except go to luncheons and get her picture in the paper. She's wealthy because her grandfather worked hard all his life, and then when he died, she inherited all his money."

Carol spoke, "Dad deserved his money. Look how long he went to school, and then look how hard he worked after he graduated."

Mrs. Rosenbloom responded, "Carol, I married a doctor and I supported your father and his profession completely, but I always wondered about those doctors and those lawyers who felt they were entitled to large salaries just because they were doctors and lawyers. That degree they obtained didn't entitle them to large salaries. It only provided them with the opportunity to work hard as a doctor and lawyer, so that they might earn an appropriate compensation."

"Mother, I don't understand what you're saying, and I don't care what you're saying. This shouldn't be happening to us."

Obviously Mrs. Rosenbloom wasn't getting through to her daughter. Both were becoming frustrated. "Carol, maybe we can talk about this later. Remember, Mr. Edison is coming to look at the house. Now let's sit down and eat. We should be thankful we have dinner. Some people don't even have that. John, why don't you give the blessing?"

CHAPTER 34

Moving in with the grandparents was a depressing day for everyone. Mrs. Rosenbloom hated returning to Crossville, the town which she had struggled so hard to escape. Crossville was a dingy, dying town with no industry. The mills had gradually all dried up, and no new industry had come in to take their place. Unemployment was already a problem before the infertility debacle had even begun.

Moving back into her parents' house was the worst blow of all. She knew that she and her children were an inconvenience to her parents, and she also knew that her parents knew how she felt about Crossville. She was humiliated.

The house itself functioned very well during the town's heyday, but that was years ago. It was certainly below Joan Rosenbloom's standards. It was a small row house—an old blue collar house in an old blue collar neighborhood

Mrs. Rosenbloom's parents were very cordial, but they really didn't want these three intruders. The grandparents had their own lives and their own habits.

Mrs. Rosenbloom felt sorry for her children. Carol was now in the same position she herself was in years ago. How would she ever get her daughter out of Crossville? Mrs. Rosenbloom worried about John. This was yet another setback for him, plus he had the worst living accommodations. It was a three bedroom house and John didn't have one of the bedrooms. He had to sleep in a makeshift bedroom in the basement. Plus, where was he getting his money?

Mrs. Rosenbloom had tried several times to talk to John about his lifestyle, about how he was able to obtain money without a job. She accompanied John downstairs, not to yell at him but to counsel him. "John, I understand this is a letdown from what we had, but we will all pull through. We have to be strong, and look to the future."

John didn't respond. He knew what was coming. His mother had tried the same approach before.

"John, you are a young man now, and you are responsible for your own actions, but I am your mother, and I don't want to see you in trouble, and whatever you are doing, the money isn't worth it."

John didn't say anything.

"Well, don't you have anything to say?"

"No, I don't have anything to say, and I would appreciate it if you didn't pry into my affairs."

"John, I'm older than you and I have much more experience. Why don't you tell me about it?"

"You don't even know what I'm doing."

"No, I don't, but I have a strong hunch. John, you think your parents don't know anything, but youngsters are no different today than they were when we were young."

John interrupted, "Mother, I don't have anything to say. Now let me settle into my dungeon."

Mrs. Rosenbloom started to cry. She turned sharply and started up the stairway, but half way up she stopped and sat down on one of the steps. She was trying to camouflage her tears before entering the main portion of the house.

John spoke to his mother in a loud voice. "Mom, what

are you doing sitting on the stairs like that? You're driving me nuts."

Mrs. Rosenbloom was hurt. Still crying, she slowly rose from the step and headed upstairs towards her bedroom, all the while moving stealthily so as not to encounter her own parents. Luckily she made the passage to her room without being discovered, and being completely exhausted from the day's emotional events she laid down quietly to take a nap.

Before long Mrs. Rosenbloom heard a commotion downstairs, and she rose to determine the cause. She opened the door slightly and immediately closed it. She recognized the two plainclothes policemen downstairs, and once again fear overcame her. She flopped on the bed, and she hoped. She hoped they weren't after her son.

A knock on the door rattled her even more, and she remained silent until Carol spoke from the other side of the door. "Mom, there are two policemen downstairs who want to speak to you."

"What do they want?"

"They want to speak to you."

"Did they ask for John?"

"No, they didn't."

"Do you think they know John lives here?"

"I don't know. Why? What has John done?"

"Nothing. I just thought they might want to talk to him."

"They didn't ask for him; they asked for you."

Mrs. Rosenbloom was afraid. She rose from her bed, descended the stairs very slowly, and spoke to the two men. "May I help you?"

The senior of the two men responded. "I'm Detective Collins and this is Detective Howard. We need to ask you some questions about your attorney Jack Holder. Apparently Holder defrauded some of his clients, and I believe you were one of those clients he defrauded. It seems he preyed on people when they were particularly vulnerable; for example, when their spouse died. Our investigation has revealed that he may have swindled you out of some of your deceased husband's funds. I don't think there is any chance of recovering your money, but if we put him away, he won't be able to prey on any more people. We need your help."

What an ambivalent announcement. Joan was angry that Jack Holder, the longtime and trusted friend of the entire family, might have stolen from them. She felt nauseous over the betrayal. At the same time she breathed a sigh of relief that the detectives were not in search of her son. Elatedly she replied, "Of course I'll help. What do you want me to do?"

Detective Collins spoke, "Answer our questions as candidly and completely as possible. Tell us everything you can, because the more information we have, the greater the chance of putting Jack Holder where he belongs, namely, in prison"

Joan tried to recollect every detail that would help the detectives convict her old friend Jack Holder. The session lasted about forty-five minutes before the detectives completed their questions, thanked Mrs. Rosenbloom for her efforts, and politely promised her that Jack Holder would receive his appropriate punishment.

John Rosenbloom observed the entire process. He secretively watched and listened to make sure his name was never mentioned. It never was, but he was scared. He was surprised at the efficiency and the thoroughness of the two policemen. John panicked for a moment, and thought about bolting right then, but he decided against it. The policeman weren't looking for him, and maybe they didn't even know about him. He figured he had at least a little time, maybe a lot of time; maybe they would never come back.

CHAPTER 35

Carol sat quietly at the kitchen table listening intently to the conversation between her mother and Holly Wilson, both of whom were also sitting at the table. Ever since Joan Rosenbloom lost her husband to suicide, and Holly Wilson's husband disappeared, the two women had become close friends. They both realized that previously they were just two snobs who went to the same events.

Joan Rosenbloom now let Carol participate in, or at least listen to some of her semi private conversations. She wanted Carol to hear about all the sinister aspects of life, and how to deal with them. She no longer cared that Carol meet the right people, for meeting the right people and relying on the right people were a formula for disaster. She wanted Carol to succeed completely on her own.

Holly was describing what had happened to Jack Fielder, "He was at home on Saturday afternoon when it all started. Supposedly he had had a rough week at the bank, where there was just one foreclosure after another. People were asking the bank for more time and more money, and he had been ordered to say no to all of them. People yelled at him, cursed him and threatened him. Some even suggested that he make sure his home was secure, and that his family was protected. The pressure was too much for him, and his mental state progressively deteriorated over the weekend until he was paranoid, delusional and completely non-functional. He even believed his wife and children were against him. He locked himself in the bathroom and the police had to forcibly take him to the hospital."

Holly sipped her coffee and Joan asked, "How long will he be in the hospital?"

Holly replied, "I don't know. It depends on how well he responds to therapy. Right now his psychiatrist has him in a locked room and on medication."

Holly continued, "I don't feel sorry for him; it serves him right. He had the breakdown because he was under stress, but his situation wasn't unique. Everybody is under stress these days. Look at our husbands. They were under stress, and that stress was primarily caused by Jack Fielder and that bank of his. I think the bank should have stuck by our husbands a little longer. They would have pulled it out. I'm sure of it. Don't you agree?"

Joan answered, "Well, there were other contributing factors, and I suppose our husbands were partly responsible because of their lifestyle and their debt, but yes, I agree. I believe the bank should have been more accommodating, but banks are like that. They're friendly and neighborly when you're riding high, but not so friendly and neighborly when you're being dragged on the ground. That's their business, isn't it? Business always trumps friendly and neighborly."

Holly spoke, "I wonder how that friendly and neighborly bank is treating its very own Jack Fielder. I bet those bank board officers don't treat him any better than they treated our husbands. They're merciless."

Joan responded, "I'm sure those board members have a completely different perspective than we do. I'm sure they consider themselves to be good businessmen and good citizens just executing their responsibilities. I'm sure their consciences are clear."

Holly snapped, "Joan, how can you sit there and defend those people after what they did to us? Our husbands are gone because of them. Do you really….and I'm sorry for saying this but it's true…but do you really think your Steve would have committed suicide if the bank had been more understanding? I don't think so, and poor Ben, he would still be home with me if the bank had acted more appropriately. I wake up every morning with tears in my eyes, and the first thing I say to myself is, 'Where are you Ben? Please come home.' After all these years there's no one beside me in that bed, and I don't know where he went. I don't know whether he's coming back, or whether he's gone forever. I'm not sure I can take this, and it's all because of Jack Fielder and his bank. I don't feel sorry for Jack's wife either. Now she'll know what it's like to have your world shattered, and to be ostracized by your former friends. I hope she knows she can't come around here for sympathy."

Joan responded, "What are you going to do if she calls and asks if she can come over for a cup of coffee?"

"I'm going to tell her no. I'll tell her to go down to the bank and get a cup of coffee, or I'll tell her to go have coffee with her husband up on the loony ward, I certainly don't want to have coffee with her."

"Holly, it wasn't her fault, and she probably didn't even know what was happening to our husbands. Maybe we should even invite her over for a cup of coffee. I'm sure she could use some comforting."

Holly stopped and stared, "Joan, you're certainly acting mighty gracious for what's been done to you. Are you okay?"

"Yes, I'm managing. It's hard, but I'm managing, and I suppose it's good for you to let some of that anger out of your heart. Isn't that what the psychiatrists say? Talk about it and don't keep it bottled up inside, although that theory never made much sense to me. I always felt better when I talked about happy events rather than when I talked about sad events, and let's be thankful Holly, we certainly had a lot of happy times over the past few years."

"I'll concede that," said Holly. "We had a lot of good times,"

Joan and Holly then began to reminisce. They alternately laughed and cried and laughed and cried until they were emotionally empty. It was all part of the catharsis and the realization that the good old days were just that, the good old days, never to be seen again. For them the good old days were dead.

Holly instinctively checked her wrist, but her watch had been pawned, just like that fancy pendant from Tiffanys, and all of her other valuable jewelry. The two women chuckled knowingly, and simultaneously glanced at the wall clock. "Look at the time," Holly exclaimed. I have to go, and don't bother coming to the door. Sit there and finish your coffee. I'm leaving. Good bye." Holly was out the door.

Carol and her mother sat at the kitchen table for a brief minute until Mrs. Rosenbloom arose and took her coffee cup to the sink. Suddenly Carol spoke. "Mom, what was your father like when he was younger? I don't mean now. I mean before he retired, when he was out in the world. Was he a good man?" Joan was surprised by the second question. It sounded like there was doubt in her voice. Perhaps Carol had heard a rumor.

Without flinching Mrs. Rosenbloom responded, "Dad was always a good man, and he is still a good man. He was always a hard worker, and he was an honest man. He worked every day, and he came home every night. He never made much money, and he never became famous, but on the other hand, he never got into trouble. He was proud of his family, and he was always good to your grandmother, and he always treated us children like we were special. I remember our vacations very well. They weren't elaborate or exotic vacations, but they were fun, and we always had a good time. Now what is this all about Carol? Why are you asking about your grandfather?"

Carol didn't answer that question but asked more of her own, "Mom, why did you get married, and do you think that I should ever get married?"

Mrs. Rosenbloom was flustered, and momentarily paused in order to conceal her discomfort from her daughter.

Carol continued talking, "As far as I can see, all men do is cause grief. Look at the men I have known. Our good friend Jack Holder stole from us. Ben Wilson ran away from his family. Bill Fielder is crazy and in the hospital. Dad committed suicide, and even my own brother John is doing something wrong. Women can't have children anymore, and there doesn't appear to be any reason to get married. There's no value in it, and I don't think I will ever get married. I'm going to be completely on my own."

Mrs. Rosenbloom was stunned, but outwardly still maintained her composure, and responded in a very loving and a very dignified voice. "Carol, I think we need to have a little talk here, because you're being much too negative about life, and your attitude toward men is much too harsh. Carol, you're young, and haven't had enough experience yet, but there are an awful lot of good men out there. You'll see that when you get older, and your horizons widen, so don't be so pessimistic. I'm not sure what John is involved in, but I pray that it's not too dangerous, and that he turns his life around."

Joan Rosenbloom then started sniffling as her eyes and nose all began to run. "As far as your father is concerned, I believe it was a combination of circumstances which caused him to commit suicide, and I believe all those men you mentioned had similar faults. Your dad's focus was too concentrated on accumulating material things, but so was mine. His damaged male ego was also a major contributing factor, but truly, your dad was sick, and he didn't get any help. I should have been more cognizant of his depression, and insisted he see a psychiatrist, but I didn't. Your dad had a severe unrecognized depression which finally got the best of him. It was mental illness that killed him."

There was complete silence for a moment, and then Joan Rosenbloom continued, "I'll admit it's not like the old days when men were mythically supposed to be a woman's Price Charming or her White Knight and they never did anything wrong. It's different now. Women now realize, or at least they admit, that their men very often prove to be an embarrassment, and that they probably receive too much guidance and too much forgiveness than they deserve, but men are now portrayed as they really are—equal to women, nothing better, nothing worse."

There was another long silence, and this time Carol finally spoke, "I guess I never understood. I feel terrible—even worse than before."

Mrs. Rosenbloom responded, "Don't feel that way Carol, and don't dwell on the past. You're young, and you have a lot of healthy living to do, and with all your talent, there's no one who can stop you from living life to the fullest."

CHAPTER 36

Carol descended the stairs more rapidly than usual. She was also dressed differently. Instead of the standard uniform of sweatshirt, worn jeans and sneakers, she was dressed in her good blue blouse, matching sweater, black slacks and real shoes.

At first Mrs. Rosenbloom only looked, but because Carol didn't volunteer any information, Mrs. Rosenbloom finally asked, "What are you doing today? You certainly look nice."

"I'm going to work. I'm starting a new business, and I'm going out to recruit my first clients." Carol was bursting with confidence and enthusiasm, but she controlled her emotions admirably. She was trying to act very businesslike. Mrs. Rosenbloom was proud of her daughter's ambition, but skeptical of her possible success. She didn't want her daughter to suffer any more disappointments and questioned her further, "Tell me about it. I want to know all about your new business. Maybe I can help."

"Okay", Carol said excitedly, "I'm going to visit all those people in this town who have more than enough money to live on, particularly the older ones. They will be my clients; at least they will be my first clients. Of course senior citizens won't be the only niche market I'll be going after, but I will start with them. They are the most vulnerable and I think I can help them.

My cards are all printed, and I'm ready to go." Carol proudly showed her mother her business cards, SENIOR CITIZEN CONSULTATION SERVICES, CAROL ROSENBLOOM, PRESIDENT. "Maybe if you can call some of the names on this list, it will help get me in the door. You were a resident of this town years ago, and your parents have lived here forever. I think some phone calls from you would be a tremendous help.

"Okay, I'll help," Mrs. Rosenbloom responded, as her heart agonized that her daughter would succeed. "I should be able to get you a few appointments. After all, like you said, I lived in this town for years."

"Fine," Carol said enthusiastically. "I'll check in later. Now I've got to be on my way. And Mom, I'm finished relying on other people for my wants and needs. I'm going to succeed strictly on my own."

"Carol, I hope you do succeed, but it is a rough world out there, and I hope you won't be too disappointed if things don't work out like you imagined, but no matter what happens, I'm proud of you."

"Mom, I won't fail. I've never failed before, and I won't fail now. You know as well as I do that I always succeeded in everything that I ever attempted, and I will succeed now. And I didn't just imagine, I planned. I'll be home for dinner."

Carol was extremely confident as she walked up the steps over on Grape Hill. Grape Hill was a well-to-do older neighborhood. Although they were not considered the real wealthy, the residents of Grape Hill were older, and, despite the economic problems, it seemed they had accumulated enough money over the years to provide a comfortable living for themselves.

Carol rang the bell and was greeted courteously by Mrs. Joan Finn. Mrs. Finn's husband had died about six years ago and her two children were already grown, married, and living as far away from Crossville as they could. They rarely came to visit.

The polite preliminaries were over quickly, and Carol was poised, and came directly to the point. "Mrs. Finn, I think I can make your life more comfortable and more fun. First, the fun part. Do you own a computer?"

Mrs. Finn replied, "No I don't. I have always wanted a computer, but I never got around to buying one, and for years I've always wanted to go to a computer class, but I never did. I always put it off, and I never went."

"Mrs. Finn, that's the answer I was expecting. Mrs. Finn, I've got a portable computer, a laptop computer. You can learn to use a computer right here in your own home. You won't have to enroll in any outside classes, and you won't even have to buy a computer. I will come to your house with my laptop, and I will give you lessons right here. I guarantee you will learn how to use a computer, and you will have fun learning. If you want to invite a friend, the two of you can learn together. That may be even more fun. Think about it. Talk to your friends. Tell them how Carol Rosenbloom is going to teach you how to use a computer." Carol was rolling. Everything was going as planned, and she was gaining more and more confidence every minute.

"Now for the business part. Mrs. Finn, there are a lot of areas in your life that I can make easier for you; for instance, medical bills. Hospitals make a lot of mistakes in their billing. They don't always itemize the bills, and you can't always determine whether it is really a bill, or just some kind of notice. I can come to your home and monitor your medical bills for you. I'll make phone calls to the hospitals, doctor's offices, pharmacists and anybody else that you think necessary."

Mrs. Finn responded enthusiastically, "Why that sounds wonderful. That would be a big help. I get confused all the time with all the literature that hospital sends me. Most of the time I can't tell whether it's a bill, or whether they're just filing the insurance, or whether the insurance company has paid or it hasn't paid. It's so confusing. I believe there would be a lot of older people who would be interested in that service."

"Good," Carol replied, "and the medical arena is just one area. How about charitable requests? There certainly are a lot of requests for charity these days. Some are legitimate, but others are not. Before you donate anything, I will verify whether it is a legitimate charity, or it's a scam."

Mrs. Finn clapped her hands, smiled widely, rocked back and forth in her chair, and then spoke, "That's another good idea. I hate it when these scam artists take advantage of the kindness and charity of compassionate people. I'm with you on that one."

"And how about salesmen? Sometimes you just can't tell whether they are on the up and up. I will advise you on phone solicitations of any kind, and if some salesman wants to make a pitch about a vacuum cleaner or something, call me and I'll be there. I won't let him get away with anything."

"Carol, you have certainly put a lot of thought into this business of yours. I'm sure you're going to be a big success."

Carol was beaming and continued speaking, "I will come to your house to provide all this assistance, and you won't have to leave your premises. Mrs. Finn, think about what I have discussed with you today, and give me a call when you are ready to begin. I would like to help you. If you have any questions, call me. Here is my card. Thank you for your time."

Carol spent about a week canvassing the Grape Hill neighborhood. She gave her spiel enthusiastically and hopefully. She believed both her business and entertainment services were worthwhile, and that they would truly benefit the residents of Grape Hill. She couldn't wait to enroll her first clients.

Approximately a week went by and Carol didn't receive any positive responses. She hadn't received any responses at all. Carol was still hopeful, but was gradually becoming discouraged. A few more days went by and Carol couldn't wait any longer. She was obviously disappointed and her anxiety was increasing.

She decided a follow up telephone call might be helpful. The calls were disastrous. Carol became more and more despondent as she talked to several of the people she had visited. They all mentioned that her ideas were good, but the timing wasn't quite right. Perhaps she should call back in six months.

She called Mrs. Finn. "Mrs. Finn, how are you doing today?" Without giving Mrs. Finn a chance to reply Carol continued, "I thought I would call, and ask if you had any questions about our discussion the other day. I thought I would have heard from you by now. You sounded so positive."

Mrs. Finn hesitated a moment and then spoke, "Carol, I think learning how to use a computer would be fun, and you are right about the number of scams aimed at older people, but the truth is, I don't have the money. Most people think the residents of Grape Hill have a lot of money. We don't. Years ago there were some who had a lot of money, but most of us just had a comfortable living, and even that is no longer true. At this time I don't have the money, or I would sign up right away. This recession is quite severe, and it is even affecting us, the snobby residents of Grape Hill. The stock market has plummeted, and if it is true that the stock market predicts the future economy, then the United States is in for a long hard economic siege. This recession has stolen our life of luxury, and even our life of comfort. I'm sorry, Carol, and I wish you the best."

Carol very politely and very quietly said thank you, and hung up the phone. Her great idea was a failure, and she started to cry. She reflected on how Mrs. Finn said that the recession had stolen her luxury and her comfort. Carol had even worse thoughts. She felt the recession had stolen not only her luxury and her comfort, but her entire life. It had taken her father, her family's house, her family's resources and her family's future. She felt destined to a miserable and hopeless life in the town of Crossville, the town that both she and her mother had tried to escape. There would be no escape for either of them.

CHAPTER 37

Jack Butler was startled by the sound of a moving vehicle, and as quickly as his old body would allow, he scrambled to his feet and watched intently as Sun Lee drove the Ryder truck into the warehouse. Just as quickly he was on the phone calling the FBI. "Hello, this is Jack Butler. I need to speak to Agent Vangard right away."

"Good morning Mr. Butler. I'm Catherine Parker, Mr. Vangard's secretary. Mr. Vangard is not in his office right now. Is there any message?'

"Yes, yes there is. Tell Agent Vangard that Jack Butler called. Have him call me. He'll know why."

"Thank you Mr. Butler. I'll tell him you called. Have a good day."

It had been a long time since the first delivery, but once again Sun Lee had driven a truck laden with Ovamort from the International Pharmaceutical plant to Jack Butler's warehouse. Chou Chang had decided that another dose of Ovamort was necessary. For Chou Chang there were too many possible American children on the horizon, and he deemed it necessary to sterilize the remainder of the young American females. If delivered as before, Chou

228

Chang felt success would be guaranteed, but if the second Ovamort delivery was unsuccessful, Chou Chang knew the American population would rebound, and Project Mao would fail.

Meanwhile Pete Vangard was slowly driving through the heavy traffic to his office. It was mid Friday morning and he was anticipating a short, easy day and then a quiet, restful weekend, but these thoughts were abruptly terminated by a phone call from his secretary. "Mr. Vangard, this is Catherine. Mr. Jack Butler called a little while ago and wants you to call him. No, he didn't say what it was about….. No, he didn't say it was urgent or anything. He just wants you to call him."

Pete Vangard replied, "Catherine, I'm sure what he wants isn't important. I'll call him on Monday."

Catherine Parker responded "Mr. Vangard, one more thing, I'm seriously concerned about Agent Chandler. She's not herself, and other than this case you're working on, she doesn't seem able to concentrate. Her anxiety level is way up, and I'm afraid that if you weren't around, she might do something rash."

Mr. Vangard's tone changed considerably, "Catherine, thanks for the call, and thanks for the information about Agent Chandler. She's been working extremely hard on this case, and she probably needs a little rest and relaxation. I'll speak to her about taking some time off. That should fix the problem."

Pete thanked his secretary, hung up the phone, and continued navigating his way through the traffic. He was tired, and his stomach hurt, sometimes excruciatingly so, and he was eagerly anticipating a weekend of some much needed relief.

After arriving at the FBI building, Pete fumbled around his office for a while. He gently and guiltily tapped on his desk. *This better not ruin my weekend, but I guess I'm obligated to give Jack Butler a call.*

Just then Emily Chandler knocked and entered Pete's office. "How is everything Pete? Anything new?"

"Jack Butler called, but I'm not sure how significant that is. As a matter of fact, when you walked in the door I was trying to decide whether to return his call, or go to lunch. He didn't say what he wanted, except that he wanted me to call him."

Emily interjected rapidly, "How long ago did he call?"

"Oh, it's probably been a couple hours now."

"And you didn't call him back."

"No, I didn't, and I've decided I'll call him later. Now how about joining me for lunch?"

Emily angrily replied, "You go to lunch. I'll call him."

"Emily, don't. He asked for me, not you. I will call him." Pete then paused briefly. "I tell you what. Meet me here after lunch, and we'll call him together. Now go relax. Get out of the office for a while. Walk around the block a few times, or go look at the birds. From what I understand you've been bugging everybody in the office about this case."

"Pete, that's not fair. Whoever did this ruined my life, and also ruined the lives of millions of American women, and what are you doing? You're going to lunch or you're worrying about your weekend being ruined. Pete, you just don't understand what is going on here."

"I understand what is going on here, and so does everyone else in the office. You have the wrong focus. Supposedly this case is important because of national security, not because some American women can't have children. You're the one whose reasoning is faulty. Now I'm going to lunch, and I'll call Mr. Butler when I get back."

"Pete, it's your stomach, isn't it? It's changing your entire personality, and it's definitely interfering with your thinking. I don't want to be uncharitable here, because I know how important this case is to you, but I believe you need to reevaluate your role in this case. Maybe you need to take a medical leave of absence."

"Emily, stop it. Any time I say something or do something you don't like, you ask me how my stomach is doing. I'm doing fine."

"Pete, I don't think you are, and I can tell by the way you carry yourself. What's the status of your medical work up? What did the CT and ultrasound show?"

"For your information they both showed a mass in the pancreas, although neither study could determine whether it was benign or malignant. I'm scheduled for a needle biopsy."

"Well, how can you say you're fine then? You're not. You've got a mass in your pancreas, and it's affecting your life."

"Emily, you're wrong. It's not affecting my life."

"No Pete, I'm not wrong, and do you know how I know it's affecting your life?"

"No. Please tell me. I can't wait."

"Because you're possibly passing up a lead that could enhance your career, and Pete Vangard doesn't pass up leads like that."

"Emily, please. Be quiet. We'll call after lunch. That's an order."

Sun Lee didn't have to wait too long. After a short time a truck pulled up and was immediately admitted to the warehouse. In a short time both trucks would be ready. The exchange would have taken place, and the Ovamort would be ready to be delivered to the supply terminals.

Sun Lee was starting to feel a sense of satisfaction settle throughout his entire body. He was approaching the finale of the Ovamort distribution. The program had been tremendously successful the last time, and Sun Lee projected it would be just as successful this time. The Ovamort had already been delivered from the other three sites and this was the last. He called to his companion, "Charlie, you transfer the boxes. I have to cancel the lease on the warehouse. Do the best you can, and I'll be right back."

Sun Lee walked briskly to Jack Butler's apartment. The door was open and Jack Butler was sitting at the kitchen table alternately thinking and writing. Sun Lee's knock on the door completely surprised him. Jack quickly rose from his chair, and awkwardly knocked some papers on the floor. Even more awkwardly he tried to retrieve them, and obviously tried to conceal their content. Sun Lee immediately was aware something was wrong, and rapidly walked across the room to investigate. Jack realized Sun Lee's intent, and tried to prevent him from reaching the papers, but Jack was too old and too slow. Sun Lee grabbed the papers and started to read. Sun Lee saw his name, his actions and the actions of his associate described in complete detail. He saw the license number of the Ryder truck.

"What is this?" Sun Lee demanded.

Jack Butler did not answer.

Sun Lee pressed Jack Butler not only verbally but also physically, pushing Jack little by little until he was pinned against the wall. All the while Sun Lee was asking questions. "Why are you writing this information down? What are you doing? Answer me!"

Jack Butler's phone rang, and both Sun Lee and Jack Butler stared at it, with Sun Lee hoping it would stop, and Jack Butler wishing it would keep ringing until the caller realized there was something wrong.

It was Pete Vangard who was calling. Pete was back from lunch, and fulfilling his obligation to return Jack's call. Pete thought to himself, *I didn't want to talk to him anyway. I'm sure he doesn't have any new information.*

Pete turned to Emily and jokingly said "No answer. I told you it wasn't important. If it had been important, he would have been sitting right by the phone waiting for me to return his call." He then turned serious again and said, "I'll call him later. Why don't you check back in a couple of hours?"

"Fine," Emily replied harshly. "And Pete, I still think you have to seriously consider your role in this case. That stomach of yours is interfering with your judgment, and this is a case that is just entering phase two. It's like a football game, and I believe the second half is just beginning. Why else would Sun Lee have visited Jack Butler's warehouse recently, and why is Jack Butler calling us at this time? Something has just happened, or is about to happen. If anything turns up, call me. I don't care whether you think it's important or not. I'll be in my office."

Pete thought that Jack Butler might call him right back but that didn't happen.

Pete called his secretary. "Catherine, I just called Jack Butler and wasn't able to reach him. He might have been at lunch, but why don't you wait a few minutes and give him another call?"

"Okay Mr. Vangard, I will."

Catherine Parker had worked with Mr. Vangard for a long time now, and she knew exactly what that conversation meant. She was to call Mr. Butler immediately, and continue calling him until she made contact.

Later, she rang her boss. "Mr. Vangard. I've called several times, but I still haven't been able to reach Mr. Butler. What do you want me to do, just keep trying?"

"I guess that's all we can do," Pete replied.

Pete was feeling a little bit concerned, and also slightly guilty. Pete also thought about Emily's comments. He thought not only about missing an opportunity to solve the terrorist crime of the century, but he also thought about being accused of negligence if he failed to take advantage of the opportunity.

Pete decided to call the local sheriff. After identifying himself as an FBI agent, it didn't take long to get the sheriff on the phone. "I have been trying to get in touch with a Mr. Jack Butler. He hasn't answered his phone, and I'm sure he was expecting my call. He doesn't have an answering machine either. He lives on the outskirts of your town. Perhaps you could contact him for me, and have him call me this afternoon. I'll be in the office all day."

Officer Coulter was generally suspicious of cold calls like that, and hesitated for a moment before responding. "Are you talking about Jack Butler, the nice old guy up on Warren Street? Friendly guy, guy who dresses like he sleeps in his clothes. Is he the one?"

"Yeah, that's the gentleman."

"Well, Mr. Vangard, that isn't much of a problem. I know Jack Butler quite well. He was a friend of my fathers, and before my father died, I used to sit in his kitchen and read magazines while the two of them reminisced about the olden days. I know exactly where he lives, and, in fact, I have to go out near his place sometime this afternoon. If I can't reach him by phone before then, I'll zip over and tell him to call you. It's not too far out of my way. You say he will know who you are?"

"He'll know. I'm actually returning his call."

"Okay, I'll give him a call right away."

Officer Coulter tried to reach Jack Butler on the phone several times. No answer. *I guess I'll have to swing out there to see what is going on*, he thought.

Jack Butler heard the phone ring each and every time, but all he could do was stare at the ringing phone, longing to communicate telepathically with the person on the other end. *Help me. I'm a prisoner. Come rescue me.*

Jack Butler was panicking. In his whole life he had never been threatened like Sun Lee was threatening him now. Pete Vangard hadn't told him what crime Sun Lee was involved in, but Jack Butler intuitively knew it wasn't a minor crime. He was facing a real criminal. Jack Butler responded to Sun Lee, "I haven't given any information to anyone. I don't even know what type of business you're in, and I don't care. All I care about is getting my rent check every month. Take the papers. I don't want them."

Sun Lee grabbed Jack's arm. "You're coming with me. I'll decide what to do with you later." Sun Lee thought to himself, *There are reports on television all the time where old men wander from their homestead and die for various reasons. Jack Butler could always wander on to a highway, or he possibly could drown. One of those scenarios wouldn't be too hard to arrange.*

Suddenly Sun Lee released Jack Butler from his grip. "Wait a minute," Sun Lee blurted out. "What are we doing? This is nonsense. What do I care if some landlord wants to write down what his tenants do? Let's have a cup of coffee and discuss this sensibly."

"Good idea," Jack Butler replied. "A cup of coffee sounds great, and you're right Dr. Lee. We can work this out." He thought to himself, *The cup of coffee will at least give me some time.*

The two men were both calm as Sun Lee helped Jack prepare the coffee. Sun Lee carried the two cups to the table, sat down and addressed Jack. "Okay Mr. Butler, what is happening here? What are you doing?"

Jack Butler took a big gulp of coffee before answering, all the while hoping he would give an acceptable response.

Sun Lee also took a drink of coffee, and then spoke again before Jack had a chance to answer. "Let's settle this like reasonable men. It sounds to me like you need money. I need privacy—that's the type of business I'm in. What do you think?"

Jack was nervously sipping his coffee the entire time Sun Lee was speaking, but now he had to respond. "I believe that you and I can…" Then it started. There was a little twinge in Jack Butler's face, and then a gasp for air. He desperately looked to Sun Lee for assistance. "I can't breathe. Help me. Please. I need an ambulance." Sun Lee stepped back and watched. He watched as if he were a scientist observing a helpless lab animal dying in a failed medical experiment.

The phone rang again, and both Jack Butler and Sun Lee fixated on the beckoning sound. Jack realized that getting to the phone was his only hope of survival, but Sun Lee blocked his pathway. Jack Butler thought to himself, *All I have to do is knock the receiver off the hook and yell. I don't even need to talk.* He lunged toward the phone, bumping the surprised Sun Lee to the side. Jack strained, and squirmed, but Lee recovered quickly, and dove at Jack Butler's legs, causing them to crumple under him. Luckily the fall brought Jack even closer to the phone. Now his possible link to freedom was just a few fingers beyond his grasp. Jack Butler rose to one knee and desperately flailed at the receiver as Sun Lee tugged and pulled at Jack's slowly advancing body. Suddenly a burst of energy from Sun Lee caused Jack's knee to buckle under him, and Jack's face and body crashed solidly to the floor. Jack pulled himself up once again and attempted to crawl the remaining short distance, but his drugged and feeble body was becoming helpless against the strength of the younger Sun Lee. He was overmatched to begin with, and now he was weakened further by a decreasing heart rate and a lack of oxygen. Jack Butler was fading rapidly. His efforts were dwindling, and his muscles were becoming relaxed. He slumped into Sun Lee's arms. It was over. Jack Butler was dead.

Sun Lee thought to himself, *I spent four years in premed, four years in medical school, and four years in residency training, and my most important medical decision was killing someone by poisoning his coffee.* It was just a bland thought. There was no guilt attached, and there may even have been a wry smile over his sick humor.

Sun Lee placed Jack Butler's body neatly on the floor, and then cleaned up what minor disturbance had occurred in the kitchen. He gathered all the incriminating papers, both cups of coffee, both spoons, and all the other evidence that would indicate there had been another person in the room. He calmly walked to the waiting truck and his waiting companion. A truck was driven to Jack Butler's residence, where Sun Lee continued to give orders to his companion. "Hurry up. We've got to get this body out of here."

Charlie Lai, Sun Lee's associate looked at Jack Butler's body and immediately exclaimed, "Good God, Sun Lee, what happened?"

Sun Lee exclaimed, "What happened? Why it's obvious, isn't it? I killed him. I had to. He was writing down everything we were doing: our actions, our descriptions, the license plate numbers, everything. I didn't have a choice. He wasn't gathering that information for himself. He was going to give it to the authorities."

"I don't like this." Charlie Lai replied. "It's also been rumored that you had a part in Professor Wadsworth's death. How do I know you're not going to kill me?"

Sun Lee replied, "With regard to Professor Wadsworth, it's not a rumor. I killed him. He was a threat to our program."

"Again, how do I know you're not going to kill me?"

Sun Lee responded, "Under the right circumstances, and if it was in the best interest of China, I might try to kill you, but those conditions don't exist right now. Right now it is in the best interest of China that you and I work together to complete this last Ovamort delivery. I had to kill Kirby Wadsworth and Jack Butler because they were a threat to our program. You're not a threat to the program, and, in fact, you are now a major indispensable ingredient to its success. You have nothing to fear."

Charlie Lai replied, "That isn't the most comforting answer I've ever received, so I think you better explain a few more things. Tell me how you killed him. I don't see any blood or anything, and it looks like he just passed away in his sleep."

"That's the way it's supposed to look," Sun Lee replied. "You don't want to kill anyone in a manner that's going to attract attention. I killed him the same way I killed Professor Wadsworth. I figured the time would come when somebody would have to be eliminated, so I prepared for it. I decided there would be no guns or knives, and there would be no evidence of violence. I am a medical doctor and my weapons consist of a complete arsenal of drugs, poisons and mislabeled medicines from International Pharmaceutical. With unsuspecting persons and with an unsuspecting police force, a planned death can be accomplished very efficiently and very secretively." Sun Lee stopped for a moment and pulled a small pill from his pocket. "This pill is just as deadly as any bullet, and it is certainly less conspicuous." He then produced a small needle and syringe from his pocket. "This is my knife. It is much more lethal, and the puncture site is certainly less detectable than a regular knife wound. Less bloody, less messy. I would say it would not be detected unless specifically looked for. If no crime is suspected, there is no investigation. Of course we need guns for long distance problems, but I hope they do not become necessary. We are to accomplish our mission without any violence, or at least without any evidence of violence. Professor Wadsworth and Jack Butler were interfering with our mission, so they had to be killed."

Charlie Lai responded, "That's very interesting, and it explains the deaths, but it doesn't explain what we're doing here. I just spent a considerable amount of time exchanging the boxes of one truck with the boxes of the other truck, and the boxes in the two trucks were exactly the same, right down to the serial numbers. It didn't make sense. What is happening here?"

"We're helping our homeland China?"

Charlie Lai replied, "Sun Lee, that's garbage. Because my life seems to depend upon your whim, I need to know what's happening. Give me the specifics, everything."

"Alright," Sun Lee replied. "I'm not sure how much time we have, but listen closely, and I'll go as fast as I can."

The whole narrative was given quickly, efficiently and without hesitation. When it was over Charlie Lai replied, "Sun Lee, that's an amazing story and it also sounds plausible. It's also very patriotic, and in your mind I suppose it justifies killing two people, but what do we do now? We have a corpse on our hands."

Sun Lee replied, "I'm not sure what I'm going to do, but Charlie Lai, you're going to dispose of the body. I'm a government official assigned to the Chinese Embassy, and I don't think it would look very good if I was caught driving up and down the highway with a dead body in the back of my truck. I'd also love to get the Ovamort delivered, but someone let Jack Butler's phone ring an awfully long time. Somebody was trying extremely hard to get in touch with him, and I wouldn't be surprised if it was a return call from the police, and if it were the police, we don't have much time. What is ironic is that I killed Professor Wadsworth, the one man who would be capable of supplying me with the answer I need right now. Professor Wadsworth always talked about "critical mass," and how it was necessary to drive the number of pregnancies below a certain critical mass level in order to achieve success. Maybe we've already reached that level, and we don't need this Ovamort delivery, but on the other hand this last Ovamort delivery would definitely drive the number of pregnancies below the critical mass level, and China would definitely succeed. Maybe it would be better to err on that side. I'm going to make a few phone calls, and then I'll decide what to do. Now you better get out of here."

After his unsuccessful attempts to contact Jack Butler by phone, Officer Coulter decided to swing by Mr. Butler's place. He was surprised to find Jack Butler was not at home, but perhaps Jack was visiting someone for the day.

Nothing seemed unusual, so after leaving a note for Jack to call him, Officer Coulter embarked on the remainder of his afternoon duties. He tried to call Jack Butler several more times. No answer.

He called Agent Vangard. "This is Officer Coulter. There is no sign of Jack Butler out at his place. I don't know where he is, but there was nothing out of the ordinary, and he is probably just out visiting. I'll check tomorrow, and I'll give you another call."

CHAPTER 38

An hour went by, and then two hours, and still Pete Vangard hadn't called Emily Chandler to tell her he was unable to reach Jack Butler. Emily couldn't remain passive any longer, and called Pete Vangard's secretary. "Catherine, this is Emily Chandler. Has Agent Vangard contacted Jack Butler yet?"

She politely replied, "No, Ms. Chandler, I don't believe he has, but I think he's still trying. I'm sure he will keep you informed."

Emily thought to herself, *Catherine "thinks" Pete Vangard is still trying to contact Jack Butler. That's not good enough. Catherine should "know" whether Pete Vangard is trying to call Jack Butler. I'm going over there and ask him myself.*

Emily found Pete sitting in his chair, gazing out the window, and fidgeting with his tie. She stared at Pete for just a second and then spoke. "Well, what's going on? Did you ever talk to Jack Butler?"

Pete turned around and looked directly at Emily's face. "I was never able to contact him, so I ended up calling the local sheriff, an Officer Coulter. Officer Coulter couldn't find Jack. He made numerous phone calls, drove out there twice, and still there was no sign of Mr. Butler. He said he would investigate further and if Jack didn't turn up soon, or if he found any evidence of wrongdoing, he would call me. So far I haven't heard from him, but then again I haven't heard from Jack Butler either."

Emily spoke again. "Pete, maybe Jack did have some real information for us, and I'm worried about him. It seems too much of a coincidence that Jack Butler calls an FBI office one minute, and the next minute, not only does he not answer the phone, but he's unable to be located. Don't you think that's kind of suspicious? I'm going up there, and I'm going up there right now. Unless I go and see for myself, I'll wonder about it for the rest of my life. Are you coming, or am I going alone?"

"Emily, I couldn't possibly let you go alone. You're starting to act too much like a loose cannon, but we'll talk about that later. Now let's get going."

"Good. I'm glad you're coming. I'll call Coulter and ask him to meet us. I'll ask him to get a search warrant for both the warehouse and the apartment. Just in case everything is not exactly kosher, I'll tell Officer Coulter to meet us at his office. We don't want any country bumpkin disturbing any evidence."

Pete, Emily and Officer Coulter all arrived at Officer Coulter's office right on time, and after some brief introductions they were all on their way to Jack Butler's place. Officer Coulter drove the sheriff's car while Emily and Pete drove together in an FBI vehicle. After the relatively short ride they all parked a short distance from the warehouse and walked the rest of the way.

Both Pete and Emily immediately noticed that the appearance of the warehouse was different. The papers and leaves were no longer resting against the door, and there were tire tracks in the dust around the building. Somebody had used the warehouse. Pete questioned Officer Coulter about any unusual activity in the area recently, but Officer Coulter couldn't remember any, and offered to check with some of the locals.

All three went to the apartment. Quietly but efficiently they pushed the door open, and quickly gave a superficial glance over the entire kitchen area. Whether anything had been disturbed or not was impossible to tell. The place was a mess. The apartment was just as unkempt as Jack Butler himself. They investigated further, and soon Officer Coulter intuitively began to sense there was something wrong. Something is not right here, he thought. Suddenly it struck him. Officer Coulter looked directly at the kitchen table and uttered. "That's strange. Jack always kept a notebook right there. There were always papers right on this end of the table." He repeated the sentence, only now with more emphasis. "There were ALWAYS papers there. His notebook was ALWAYS there. All those times I came out here with my father, and more recently when I came out here when Jack was having some heart problems, the notebook and the papers were always there. I remember he used to write down the license plate numbers of some of the trucks that came in here, and we used to kid him about what he was doing, and about how somebody was going to bomb his warehouse way out here in the middle of nowhere."

Pete Vangard responded, "You're right Officer. The notebook was right there when Emily and I were here before."

Officer Coulter spoke, "You've got to tell me what's happening here. Why are two FBI officers up in my sleepy old town investigating some old man who hasn't bothered anybody for years, and who now has completely disappeared?"

Pete answered, "We'll tell you everything, but first let's see if we can figure out what happened in this sleepy old town of yours."

Pete walked pensively around the room and tried to imagine what had happened. He imagined Jack writing down what was happening at the warehouse, and being surprised by the perpetrators. He pictured Jack being overpowered, or being kidnapped, or possibly even murdered.

Pete's expression suddenly changed, and he quickly and enthusiastically exclaimed to Emily, "Emily, I think we have a chance. This whole episode started this morning, and I doubt if it's complete. If we get moving right away, I think we can catch them. Let's start by contacting the Ryder truck people."

Pete then stopped for an instant, "Emily, congratulations on being right."

CHAPTER 39

Emily Chandler was immediately on the phone trying to reach either Joe Fleming or Alice Jones at the Ryder truck agency.

"Good evening, Ryder Truck Agency."

Emily felt an optimistic warm sensation surge throughout her entire body. "Alice, thank goodness you're there. This is Emily Chandler from the FBI. Remember me? I need your help, and I need it right away. I need a list of all the Chinese people who rented any of your trucks in the last month and I need ..."

Emily was abruptly interrupted. "I'm sorry ma'am. This is the answering service. No one is in the office at this time. Do you want to leave a message?"

Exasperated, Emily replied, "Lady, I need either Joe Fleming's or Alice Jone's phone number right now. This is an emergency, and I need to talk to one of them immediately."

"I'm sorry ma'am. We're not allowed to give out those numbers. If you want to leave a message and your phone number, maybe one of them can call you back."

Emily replied again, "Listen lady, I need to contact one of them right away. It is an emergency. Give me the phone numbers."

"I'm sorry ma'am. I can't do that. Policy dictates that I contact my supervisor in all emergencies. Now what is your name and what is your phone number? Some one will call you back as soon as possible."

Realizing her anger was getting her no place, Emily took a deep breath and responded in a calm clear voice. "My name is Emily Chandler from the Federal Bureau of Investigation. My number is 555, and this is a real emergency. Now get moving."

It wasn't long before Emily received a response. She roughly grabbed the ringing phone and hoisted it to her ear. "Emily Chandler here."

"Good evening Ms. Chandler, I'm Kathy Dalton with Acme Answering Service. I'm Stephanie's supervisor. May I help you?"

Emily was ready to explode, but controlled herself admirably. She spoke very clearly and very slowly. "My name is Emily Chandler. I am an FBI agent and this is an emergency. I need to speak to Joe Fleming or Alice Jones from the Ryder Truck Agency, and I need to speak to them immediately. Now what are their phone numbers?"

Kathy Dalton hesitated only briefly, but even that response time was too long for Agent Chandler. Emily screamed into the phone. "Lady, give me those numbers. This is the FBI and this is an emergency."

Kathy was flustered and acquiesced.

"Thank you Ms. Dalton, you have been a big help."

As soon as she hung up, Emily was back on the phone dialing Joe Fleming's number. "Joe, this is Emily Chandler from the FBI. I need your help right away. I need a list of all the Chinese people who rented any of your trucks in the last month, and I need it now."

Joe stared through the surrounding darkness and barked into the phone. "Are you kidding me? It's the middle of the night, and besides it's a weekend."

"Mr. Fleming, this is an emergency. Pete Vangard and I are on our way to your office. We'll meet you there. Contact Alice Jones and have her there too."

Joe rolled his eyes and shook his head in exasperation. "Is this for real, or am I dreaming? How often am I going to have the pleasure of talking to you or your friend Pete? Our company is barely surviving, and you are making it even more difficult. After the last time you were in our office I didn't read about any large Chinese crime ring being broken. I didn't even hear about one single Chinese person being arrested. Have my competitors given you their lists yet?"

Emily screamed, "Joe, this is an emergency. You and Alice be at your office as soon as possible, or you will charged with obstructing the investigation of a crime."

Both Alice and Joe were already there when Pete and Emily arrived. No one extended any social courtesies, and there was an uncomfortable silence until Pete spoke. "Have you found anything yet?"

Considering the circumstances, Joe Fleming's responding voice was not openly angry. It was better described as a combination of irritation and anger. "Yes, we've got what you want. Here."

It only took a short time for Pete and Emily to go through the lists. There were exactly four Chinese people who had rented Ryder trucks during that time period. What a surprise!" exclaimed Pete, "Anyone want to bet that I can predict the total mileage on those trucks." Pete's attitude changed to complete determination. "Okay Emily, let's get moving. Write down their names, addresses and phone numbers. We'll track down the one in Frederick. Officers Jordan and Wiley can take the one in Philadelphia, and we'll need additional help for the other two. Call our central office and have Agent Dunlop assign four special agents to track down those other two. Tell him also to call ahead and inform the local police so we can expedite our search. An escort would be helpful. Now let's go. I don't want these guys to have even the slightest chance of getting out of here."

The drive to Frederick took about forty five minutes, and then the two of them were directed to the exact apartment complex which was already surrounded and secured by a waiting police entourage. As swiftly and quietly as they could, they approached apartment number thirty two and knocked on the apartment door. No answer. Pete spoke, "Why doesn't anyone want to speak to me? I'm not a bad guy." They waited. Still no answer. "Okay, let's check with the neighbors." It was the same old response. "Yeah, a Chinese man lived up there. No, I didn't really know him. He didn't seem to socialize at all. Haven't seen him in a couple of days though. As a matter of fact, I haven't seen him since last Friday."

The next day Agents Chandler and Vangard met with the other six agents, all of whom looked equally downcast. None of them had found any of the suspects. Agent Wiley spoke, "We didn't have much success, and the best we did was to speak to one upset landlord. The landlord noticed that one of the Chinese gentlemen was leaving one day with a suitcase. To be social the landlord asked him if he was going on vacation, and the Chinese guy replied that he was not going on vacation, but that he was going home. He was going to China, and he wouldn't be back."

Pete Vangard slumped in his chair. He knew exactly what had happened. Just like before, all four perpetrators had returned to China. He addressed no one in particular. "This is great. It certainly is convenient to be able to commit a crime and then hop a plane to China. I would say that going to China decreases the chances of being prosecuted. What do we do now?"

Emily Chandler was the only one who responded. "We don't just sit here and do nothing. We go get Sun Lee at the Chinese Embassy. I realize he has diplomatic immunity, but we don't have any choice. We at least have to question him."

Pete Vangard immediately tried to arrange a meeting with Sun Lee. He explained to Sun Lee's secretary that he wanted to meet with Sun Lee and ask him some background questions about a case he was working on. The secretary replied, "Sun Lee has gone to China for a few days. He's going to receive a humanitarian award over there, and he will be back at the beginning of next week. When he returns, I will tell him what you want, and I will call you."

Pete tried to act unconcerned as he conveyed the secretary's message to his waiting associates, but Agent Chandler knew what Pete was thinking. Sun Lee was returning to China, because his mission in the United States was complete. The terrorist activity was successful again.

Pete Vangard avoided any eye contact with Agent Chandler, who by this time was slowly and rather aimlessly heading towards the exit. Trancelike, Emily walked to her office, plopped herself down at her desk, and folded her head in her hands. *I've failed,* she thought to herself. *I've failed not only in my personal life, but also in my professional life. I've failed the millions of American women who were counting on me. Maybe Pete is right. Maybe I should consult a psychiatrist, but, then again, what's a psychiatrist going to say? He can't restore my ovaries. He can't catch Sun Lee. He can't do anything.* She thought about Kirby Wadsworth, and she thought about Sun Lee. They both had beaten her. The world had beaten her. She thought about her future without any children to comfort her. *What else can go wrong,* she thought. *My professional and personal lives are a disaster.*

CHAPTER 40

Mrs. Rosenbloom and Carol were sitting at the kitchen table waiting for John. They had been crying already, but the tears flowed a little faster when John entered the room.

John suddenly stopped when he realized both of them were crying. Exasperated he flapped his hands against his thighs and whined, "God, can't I ever come into this house without finding somebody crying? Mom, I don't know how your parents put up with you two. I'm only here part of the time and I can't take it. You must be driving them crazy."

Mrs. Rosenbloom rose from her chair, and slammed both fists down on the table. "Stop it! Stop it!"

There was silence except for the soft sniffling sounds of Carol crying. Mrs. Rosenbloom had stopped crying and was now speaking to her son in a voice that was a mixture of anger and sympathy. "John, you had some visitors while you were gone, a Detective Collins and his partner, Detective Howard. I asked them what they wanted, but they wouldn't say. All they would say is that they wanted to speak to you for a few minutes. I told them I didn't know where you were, or when you would be back, and they requested that I have you contact them as soon as possible.

What do they want with you John? Are you in trouble?"

When Detective Collins hadn't returned to the house for such a long time, even though the purpose of his original visit pertained to Jack Holder, John illogically concluded he was free and clear. John stood there in a trance like state, unable to speak or move. Mrs. Rosenbloom wasn't sure John could hear her anymore, and she walked over to her son and gently held his arm. "John, we can go down to the police station together if you want. Detective Collins seemed like a reasonable man, and I'm sure you can explain everything satisfactorily."

John lashed back at her, "I'm not going to any police station. I'm getting out of here."

His mother grabbed his arm more securely. "You're not leaving. You are going to the police station, and you are going to talk to Detective Collins. You're going to straighten this out right now. If you run now, your life will be ruined."

John pulled his arm away. "You can't tell me what to do. I'll do what I want, and I'll do it when I want to."

"John, don't you dare speak to me like that. I'm your mother, and I will always be able to tell you what to do, and right now you are acting like a stupid, naïve young man. You are not going to run from this." She repeated her offer. "If you want, I will go with you."

John felt better. At least he wasn't being abandoned. He knew his mother was right. "No, I'll go myself. I'll go right now and get it over with."

"John Rosenbloom," Detective Collins said in a friendly voice, "I'm glad you came. We didn't want to drag you in here; we wanted to give you a chance to come by yourself." Detective Collins didn't waste any more time. "John, we've been watching what you and your associates have been doing recently, and we're not too pleased. We know there are several problems, but we think we can help you out of your mess without any permanent scars. We have a file on you already and I want you to listen to what it says. 'Intelligent, has common sense, comes from a good family, never been involved in violence, so far essentially plays minor part in operation, but starting to get more involved.' Under recommendations it says, 'Talk to him, maybe can help us if he cooperates, maybe can save himself if puts his mind to it. Work with him.'"

John just sat there. Not only did he not speak, he was absolutely motionless.

Detective Collins continued, "How about demonstrating some of that intelligence you are supposed to have. Help us. Give us the information we need, and you can probably go free. Show us how dumb you are, and you wind up in jail, and that's a place where you don't want to be."

Detective Howard chimed in, "Who do you think you're going to meet if you go to jail? Do you think you're going to meet people like your pansy friends from Clancy Prep? Going to jail is not like going up to Pleasant Street to meet Dick and Jane and Sally. It's more like meeting the murderers and rapists of Dick and Jane and Sally."

Detective Collins and Detective Howard stopped speaking in order to let their words sink in. Absolutely silent they both stood directly behind John in order to emphasize John's complete isolation, and also to intensify his growing discomfort.

John broke the silence. "I want to talk to my mother."

The two detectives burst out laughing. Finally Detective Howard scornfully spoke while Detective Howard continued to laugh. "My God son, do you know how ludicrous you sound? We're talking about prison here, and you want to talk to your mother. You wouldn't make it through one night in prison. In fact you wouldn't survive two minutes."

"I want a lawyer," John quickly responded.

The two detectives continued to laugh until Detective Collins walked around the table and positioned his face six inches from John's nose. "Go on home, and get a lawyer. Talk to your mother. Do whatever you want, but I want you back here the first of next week and you be ready to talk to us. Now get out of here."

John's journey home was filled with relief, and apprehension. He was relieved that he was no longer a captive, but fearful that he now had to face his mother. He knew he would not be able to avoid an explosive confrontation unless he told her the truth. He could always bolt, but that wouldn't be a satisfactory solution. It wouldn't even be a conclusion. It would just be a postponement.

With his mother there would be some blood sympathy, and she was also a reasonable person who had managed to survive since his father's suicide.

As expected, Joan Rosenbloom was waiting for her son. "John, how did it go?'

"Not too bad. They just want me to help out on a case."

The slap came too swiftly for John to defend himself. "John, don't lie. The detectives know you're involved in something, and I know it too. How else would you be getting the money that you have? Now we're going to get you a lawyer, and we're going to get you out of this predicament with as little damage as possible. To do that you've got to be truthful. Tell me exactly what you have been doing."

John hesitated and then spoke in a clear definitive voice. "Mom, I can't. I can't tell you anything. There is no confidentiality privilege between a mother and her son like there is for a husband and wife. The court could subpoena you to testify against me, and you would have to repeat everything I told you. Don't get involved. I'll get myself a lawyer. Besides, there's no hurry. Detective Collins said I had until next week."

"Now aren't you cute?" his mother replied. "You know the law and everything else about what you can or can not say and do. Your new friends have certainly taught you well. They have taught you how to think and act like a criminal. Your father and I certainly didn't teach you that stuff. Go to your room. We'll talk tomorrow."

Mrs. Rosenbloom answered the front door and cordially invited Detective Collins and Detective Howard into the living room.

Mrs. Rosenbloom was somewhat anxious when she and John returned to the two detectives. On the other hand John was completely relaxed and completely upbeat.

John spoke, "Good afternoon Detectives. I'm surprised to see you. I understood I had until next week to reply."

"You did John, but things change, and unfortunately there has been a catastrophic change for the worse. We have to bring you down to the station and book you. Put your hands behind your back. You're under arrest. Detective Howard, read John his rights."

Detective Collins approached John with handcuffs, but Mrs. Rosenbloom jumped between the two of them.

"Don't interfere, Mrs. Rosenbloom. It will only make matters worse."

"What did my son do? I am sure what he did doesn't warrant being dragged off to jail in handcuffs. Please, no handcuffs. The neighbors will think he's a real criminal."

"Mrs. Rosenbloom, you don't need to worry about what your friends or neighbors think any more. You need to worry about what a judge and jury think. Didn't you read in the paper about that young woman who died over in the town of Oxdale? Well, she died of a drug overdose, a drug overdose from drugs that have been traced to your son. Your son is going to be booked for murder, and I hope he is convicted, and I am going to use my entire armamentarium to see that he is. Maybe if he has a super lawyer, and he cooperates completely, he'll get off with a lesser sentence, but I am going to do my best to make sure he spends time in prison. I'm going to encourage the district attorney to push for it. Now don't make this worse Mrs. Rosenbloom. Out of the way."

Mrs. Rosenbloom quickly spoke, "William Fisher is John's lawyer. Can't John speak to Fisher before you take him to the police station? My son's not going to run away or hurt anybody, and I don't want him to say anything foolish before consulting with a lawyer."

Detective Collins coldly responded, "You tell Attorney Fisher to either call me at the station house, or come down in person. He can meet with your son down there."

Attorney Fisher walked swiftly down the prison corridor to the jail cell where John Rosenbloom was being held prisoner. He hated walking down that corridor—it was dark and depressing. The corridor walls were plain, and there were absolutely no decorations. There were four cells in this section of the prison—all had a very strong, locked, metal door with only a small unbreakable glass window in its upper portion. The window itself was covered with iron bars. Each cell housed one prisoner.

Attorney Fisher and the accompanying guard peered in. "That's him," the guard said. "Do you want me to stay around, or are you alright?"

"I'll be alright," Fisher responded. "Just let me in. I won't be long."

"Hi John, I'm Bill Fisher, your attorney. I've known your family for years, and your mother wants me to help you. The detectives say they have you cold, and they are going to charge you with some pretty serious crimes. Why don't you just tell me what happened, and we'll see what we can do? Start anyplace you want."

John consciously knew his best option was to cooperate completely, but he hesitated briefly and Bill Fisher spoke again.

"John, I just finished talking to the detectives, and they know you're involved, and they have solid evidence to prove it. However, the district attorney is willing to offer you minimum jail time in a minimum security prison in exchange for your cooperation and information. In particular they want Mr. Moran and Dr. Frank Rush convicted. Those associates of yours were involved in quite a few illegal activities, and the police need as much information as possible. I believe you should take the offer. Otherwise, you may be facing a long jail sentence, and I believe they've got you. You're partly responsible for the death of a young woman, and that's serious business. I think you should cooperate. What do you say?"

John responded, "Jail time, even minimum time in minimum security makes it a tough decision."

"No John, it doesn't, not when one of the other possibilities is twenty years to life at hard time, and that is a very strong possibility. The district attorney is promising minimum jail time, and possibly only probation, depending on the evidence you provide. I think you should take it."

"Mr. Fisher, are you sure? Remember, it's me who's going to prison, not you."

Bill Fisher replied, "A person's never sure when talking about the future, and trying to figure out what a jury will do is almost impossible, but I'm pretty close to being sure right now, and in situations like this, I'm not wrong very often. I can make the arrangements right now if you want."

For John it was a momentary yet eternal silence.

"Well John, What's your decision?"

"Okay, I'll cooperate. I'll make sure they get Mr. Moran and Dr. Rush."

"John, I believe that's the correct decision. If everything goes well, you'll be out in less than eighteen months, and probably sooner, and if we can get a little sympathy for you, maybe you'll only get probation. Now let's get Detective Collins and Detective Howard back in here, and you can begin being a good citizen again."

John began slowly in a soft quiet voice. "My involvement began with a meeting with Dr. Frank Rush. He recognized me one day as I was walking down the street, and he initiated a conversation."

'John, John Rosenbloom, I thought that was you. Dr. Rush said. You're Dr. Rosenbloom's son, aren't you? I'm Dr. Rush, one of your father's classmates. How are you doing?'

"I'm doing fine, thank you."

"Good John, I'm glad to hear that. You know, I was just talking about you the other day with Joseph Moran, my business manager, and we both agreed that you would be the perfect person to assist us in some of our new endeavors. We can really use you, and if you're interested, we would be glad to have you on our team."

"What will I be doing?" I replied.

MIKE HOGAN

Dr. Rush answered, "I tell you what. I will pick you up in this exact same location next Tuesday, and you can watch what we do. You'll never see such joy as you'll see then. You'll love it, and you'll make good money, but don't tell your mother quite yet, because if it doesn't work out, I don't want her to experience any more disappointments. Heaven knows she's suffered enough this year."

"I loved that first afternoon with Dr. Rush. I followed him into the room where the expectant couple was waiting. Dr. Rush spoke, 'Good afternoon, Mr. and Mrs. Brody. Your baby will be here shortly. We're just finishing some paperwork in the other room.'"

Mrs. Brody responded, "Thank you Doctor, thank you. I didn't think this would ever happen, and I can't express how much my husband and I appreciate what you are doing for us."

After a few more polite niceties Dr. Rush spoke again, "Mr. and Mrs. Brody, are you ready for me to bring your baby in?"

"We're ready," Mrs. Brody responded. "We've been ready for a long time." "Just a minute, and I'll be right back," Dr. Rush said.

Dr. Rush was only gone a few minutes before he returned with a newborn baby boy.

"Here you are, Mr. and Mrs. Brody, the new addition to the Brody family, a beautiful baby boy. Congratulations."

"That man and woman stared at that baby for what I thought was an eternity. They smiled at him; they poked him; they hugged him; and they were absolutely in heaven."

Finally Mr. Brody spoke, "The baby's perfect. You're right. He's beautiful."

"Mrs. Brody was unable to speak, and she buried her face in the baby's chest and cried uncontrollably. Mr. Brody also cried as he clutched his wife in his arms. Dr. Rush was right. I never saw such joy in all my life, and I joined Dr.

Rush and Mr. Moran immediately. How could something that produced so much happiness be illegal? Dr. Rush told me it made him feel like he did in the good old days, when he delivered healthy babies to parents who really wanted a baby. He said everybody involved was happy. The people who received the baby were ecstatic, and the woman who provided the baby was also happy, not only because of the money she received, but mainly because her baby was joining an affluent family that would provide for him for the rest of his life. It was a win-win situation, and I couldn't imagine participating in any project more satisfying. I was hooked."

Detective Collins spoke, "John, that story temporarily had a happy ending, and I strongly emphasize *temporarily*, because that baby now has to be taken from the so-called adoptive parents, and returned to the natural birth mother, or placed in an institution. Can you imagine the anguish those people are going to experience when that happens? I also heard there were instances in which the outcome was painful and even cruel. You must have been aware of some of those cases, or did they only let you participate when a happy result was guaranteed."

"No," John replied. "I knew several cases where there was a tremendous amount of mental suffering. I wasn't a direct participant in those cases, but as I was given more freedom around the office, I often overheard different transactions taking place, and my first experience with Mr. Moran was just as revolting as my first session with Dr. Rush was joyous."

Mr. Moran spoke to the expectant couple, "Mr. Webster, look at your wife. She wants this baby, and surely you can afford the extra five thousand dollars we need in order to consummate this deal."

MIKE HOGAN

Mr. Webster looked over at his sobbing wife and agonizingly replied, "Mr. Moran, we scraped together as much money as we possibly could, and we can not afford to go any higher. You have to stick with your original price."

"I'm sorry Mr. Webster, but we have a couple who wants this baby more than you do."

Mr. Webster cried out, "Don't say that Mr. Moran. There's no couple on this whole earth who wants this baby more than we do. We'd be the perfect parents."

"Mr. Webster, business is business, and the other couple is simply willing to pay more than you are. This particular baby is the product of a father who is both intelligent and athletic, and the mother even more so. The medical history is superb. There is no congenital or hereditary illness going back at least three generations, and this baby commands an extra high premium. If you can't afford it, I'll put you on the list for a future offering."

"I'll never forget the despair on that woman's face as she walked out of the office. She was embracing an empty yellow baby blanket, and her husband had to struggle to keep her upright. It was one of the most pitiful sights I had ever seen. I ended up vomiting."

"Another time one of the providers (that's what they called the young girls who produced the babies for Mr. Moran and Dr. Rush), refused to relinquish her baby. At the last minute the provider decided she wanted to keep the baby herself, but Mr. Moran eventually convinced her otherwise. He threatened the provider with a lawsuit, and financial damages, and possibly even physical harm if she didn't surrender the baby. I thought the mother was going to have a nervous breakdown right there in the office, but Mr. Moran didn't care. He was completely unsympathetic and completely emotionless throughout the entire episode. He wanted that baby, and he didn't care about that mother one bit. She was a provider and nothing else. It was repulsive."

Detective Collins spoke again, "Do you have the name of that woman?"

John replied, "Her name was Beth Wilson, and I'll never forget her. She lived in Eastside, about sixty miles from here."

Detective Collins spoke, "This information, particularly with the names attached, will help a great deal. Now tell us about the drugs."

John responded, "That also started in a rather benign fashion. I thought I was providing an innocent messenger service for Dr. Rush and Mr. Moran and their clients. I didn't know drugs were involved until I heard Dr. Rush explain to Mr. Moran how he obtained the drugs without attracting the attention of the narcotics squad. Then I knew. Dr. Rush would do a history and a physical on a patient, and then order some lab tests. He would then write a prescription for a narcotic, and then instruct the patient to return in about two days, when supposedly Dr. Rush and the patient would then discuss the completed results of the history, physical and lab tests. Of course, the patient was instructed to bring all his medications with him. When the patient returned, Dr. Rush would say the prescribed medicine wasn't appropriate for that particular ailment, and he would throw the narcotics in the trash. When the patient left, Dr. Rush would retrieve the narcotics from the waste basket, and deliver them to Mr. Moran, who, in turn, would distribute them to his clients. That story should be easy to verify. Check with the patients and check with the pharmacy."

Detective Collins replied, "Don't worry, we will. Now is there anything else you want to tell us?"

"Yes, there is," John replied. "One of my jobs was to go through my father's medical records, and determine which women were not affected by the infertility epidemic. I was to ascertain which of his patients were still capable of having children. All I had to do was determine which girls were still having their periods. I gave the list to Mr. Moran, who in some way directed those women to Dr. Rush. I think some of them are now pregnant, and are on the provider list."

Detective Howard spoke, "You will testify to all this?"

"Yes sir, I will," John replied.

"Good, now is there anything else?" Detective Collins said.

"No, that's it," John replied.

Detective Collins spoke, "What about all the foreigners who went in and out of the office?"

"I saw them there, but I didn't pay much attention to them. They were always over by the treatment room."

"Didn't you speak to them?"

"No, I didn't. Most of them were Latinos who spoke Spanish, and the others spoke a variety of different languages. I couldn't understand a word they said."

"What do you think they were doing there?"

"I have no idea. I just thought they were getting a physical, or were being treated for some illness or something. I know they weren't pregnant."

"No, they weren't pregnant. Most of them were unwilling egg donors, and they were also illegal aliens. Your bosses contracted with certain "businessmen" who transported these women across the border illegally. These women were guaranteed safe passage into the United States and a cash payment of one hundred dollars, provided they would then subject themselves to an egg donor procedure. Your bosses, after obtaining the eggs, would then sell the eggs for ten thousand dollars or more. The entire operation netted millions of dollars, and you say you had no knowledge of any part of it."

"That's right. I never did, but now it makes sense to me. Mr. Moran was very polite, and even obsequious to these women when they first arrived in the office, but as soon as they left the treatment room, he was as mean as he could be. I couldn't figure it out then, but I guess that once he had the eggs, he didn't need those women anymore and they were on their own."

"You got it son. Nice guys, huh? That's who you worked for, and now you're going to help us put them in prison, right?"

"Right."

Detective Collins hesitated for a short while and then spoke, "John, I can understand what you were going through, but you were peripherally involved in some pretty heinous crimes. You should have known better, and you should have alerted the police. However, I do believe you told us the complete truth, and you certainly provided us with some corroborating evidence which will help us convict Dr. Rush and Mr. Moran. I will ask the prosecutor to recommend to the judge that you get six months in a minimum security prison, and then probation. We all generally agree on cases like this, so I would say you can count on it. You're a lucky young man, John Rosenbloom, and I believe you still have your whole life ahead of you. Make the most of it."

CHAPTER 41

Joan Rosenbloom knocked on Carol's bedroom door, and knowing there wouldn't be an answer, immediately pushed the door open. As Mrs. Rosenbloom expected, Carol was still in bed. "Come on Carol. Up and at em. It's a new day, and it's time to move on. Your days of sleeping and moping around the house all day are over."

"Mother, do you have to be so loud?" Carol moaned.

Mrs. Rosenbloom replied, "If getting you to be part of the world again requires me to be loud, I'll be loud. Now get up."

"Mother, please, give me a minute."

"No, I won't. I'm not giving you any more time to lie around here and feel sorry for yourself. I know what's going through your mind, and I know you're disappointed your business failed, but that's what happens in life, and be thankful that's all that happened. Now out of bed. Get yourself a good breakfast, and get your body and brain working again. Start living your life again."

"Mother, I don't believe this is happening. How can you be so cold?"

"It's not being cold Carol; it's being realistic. You can call it "tough love" if you want, but nothing else has worked, and it's my responsibility to make sure this family survives. I've got to survive, and you've got to survive, and you're not going to do it by lying in bed all day. That's bad for you physically, and it's bad for you mentally. Now get up. Right now."

"Mother, you don't understand."

"Yes Carol, I do understand. I was a young girl once, and I had my share of disappointments and failures, but my parents taught me to struggle forward, and to learn from the past."

"Mother, that's nice and easy for you to say, but everything has gone wrong: my business failed, dad's gone, I can't go to Clancy anymore, I can't go shopping anymore, everything's wrong. You want me to learn from the past? What can I possibly learn from dad's suicide?"

Mrs. Rosenbloom responded, "Everything is not wrong. You're here, you're young, you're healthy, and you've got your whole future ahead of you. I would consider you blessed, and what can you learn from your father's death. I hope you learned that suicide is not a good way out, and that you should consult a psychiatrist if you're ever severely depressed.

"Now I want you to set one goal for yourself every single day. It can be minor, or it can be major, and you may not achieve it every day, but you can't achieve anything unless you try. After you get dressed and you have your breakfast, why don't you go for a walk and think for a while. That can be your first goal—to think positively for fifteen minutes. See you downstairs."

It was almost noontime when Carol left the house, and she did so with little enthusiasm and absolutely no direction. She meandered to the center of town, sat herself down on the park bench, and watched as Crossville's residents engaged in their daily activities. She watched while the majority of the citizens shuffled monotonously from street corner to street corner, and she watched as the rare

267

affluent soul moved nonchalantly from building to building, as if completely unaware there was a severe recession.

Officer Collins, the police officer who arrested John, walked by, and Carol hatefully glared as he entered the police station and its adjacent jail. Tears welled up in her eyes.

Sporadically there was the happy and uplifting laughter of children as they scampered carefree over the park lawns and recreation fields. At the same time the accompanying parents maintained their plain but troubled expression of worry. *Oh, the beauty and happiness of innocence*, Carol thought to herself.

Suddenly her daydreams were interrupted by the sound of a pleasant voice. "Good afternoon miss, how are you today?" the good looking gentleman asked. "My name is Peter Leonard and I just couldn't help myself. I just had to speak to you. You look so peaceful and refreshing sitting there. Do you live around here?"

Carol looked at the well dressed man that had spoken to her. "Thank you sir, and yes, I do live around here. I live about four blocks from here."

Mr. Leonard responded, "I thought so," Mr. Leonard responded, "the way you're sitting there, so relaxed and comfortable. You look like you're part of this town, and most assuredly the town is lucky to have you. I'm sure the town is proud of you, with your good looks and everything."

Carol blushed and beamed simultaneously as she sat there quietly as Mr. Leonard continued, "And I'm sure you're a good student too."

"You're right. I am a good student, thank you, but how did you know that?"

"I just know," Mr. Leonard replied. "And I bet you have a part time job, and I bet you're just as successful in your work as you are in school. Am I right again?"

Carol started to laugh sarcastically. "You're wrong this time Mr. Leonard. I don't even have a job."

"Gee, that's too bad," Mr. Leonard responded. "A lot of young women feel having a job is very gratifying. It gives them extra spending money, and often times provides them with the opportunity to assist their family financially, and that's a very rewarding experience. Would you like to have a job? If you do, maybe I can help. I've helped many girls like you over the past few months, and I believe a girl like you could make a good income for herself. You're good looking, you speak well, you seem to have a pleasant personality, and you have a lot of class."

Carol blushed, "How do you know all that about me? You just met me. You don't know what I'm like."

'Yes I do miss; I can just tell, and I believe you just need a little encouragement to start you on your way."

Carol perked up, "What kind of a job is it?"

"Well, you will be doing a lot of freelance work. All you have to do is be nice to some of my gentleman friends, accompany them to some parties, and make sure they have a good time."

"I don't understand," Carol replied. "Why would someone want to pay me to go to a party? It doesn't make sense." Suddenly it hit her, and Carol glared hard at Mr. Leonard. "Are you saying what I think you're saying? If you are, you better get out of here. You're disgusting."

Mr. Leonard replied "Don't get so upset. It's just like any new job. You'll be nervous at first, but after a while you'll adjust, and you'll become perfectly comfortable in your work. I believe you will do very well. And think about all the money you can make, and all the clothes and jewelry you can buy, but most of all think about how you can help out your family."

Carol jumped from her bench, and with her nails fully extended she lunged at Mr. Leonard's face and neck. "How dare you? Get away from me! I'm going to report you to the police," Carol screamed as she flailed wildly at Mr. Leonard's head and neck, but Mr. Leonard calmly and deftly repulsed her attack. Repulsing such attacks was a common part of his occupation. He then calmly spoke, "I'm sorry I offended you miss, and I'm always disappointed when a young girl says she's not interested, but on the other hand, the next girl I speak to may very well say yes, and that's how I make my living. And as far as the police are concerned, it's my word against yours, and because I'm leaving town right this minute, they will completely ignore you."

"No they won't ignore me. They will track you down, and they will put you in prison."

"No miss, you're wrong, and if they don't ignore you, they will consider you a nuisance, because you will have wasted a considerable amount of their time. They will have to fill out a considerable amount of paperwork; then they will have to go through the motions of an investigation, and then they will have to fill out more paperwork. Finally, they will have to file an unproductive and unrewarding report, and during all this process, I'll be long gone. They may even think you fabricated the whole event just to attract some attention."

And Mr. Leonard was gone, leaving Carol amazed at the speed with which he had vanished. Of course vanishing quickly was also a common and necessary part of Mr. Leonard's occupation.

After an initial hesitation Carol moved almost as fast as Mr. Leonard. She didn't even reflect on what had just happened. Instinctively she wanted to get out of the park and into the comfort and security of her own home. Her adrenaline propelled her from block to block, up her walk-way and into her home where her loud and sudden closure of the door startled her mother.

She confronted her mother immediately. "Mom, look at me. How do I look? Do I look like a tramp?"

"Carol, what are you talking about? You look lovely. You don't look like a tramp at all. Why? What happened?"

"As I was sitting on the park bench minding my own business, this evil man approached me and wanted me to become a prostitute."

Mrs. Rosenbloom gasped. "He didn't hurt you, did he?"

"No, he didn't hurt me."

"Did he threaten you?"

"No, he didn't threaten me. He was very polite, very well dressed and acted very much like a gentleman but he made me feel dirty. I'm going up and take a shower. I need it."

"Carol, wait. Maybe we should report this to the police."

"No mom, it won't do any good. He said he was leaving town immediately, and he also said it would be my word against his."

Mrs. Rosenbloom walked over to her daughter and tried to comfort her. "Carol, there is no reason for you to feel dirty. What happened today was not your fault, and it would have happened no matter how you were dressed, and no matter how you acted. Carol, you're still young, and you're inexperienced, and you have to realize that you're going to have a lot of crude and uncouth men approach you during your lifetime. You just have to realize that's the way some men are."

"Mom, they are not just crude and uncouth, they are evil, and I'm not going to put up with it. I failed in one business, but starting today I'm going to start working on another, and if that doesn't work, I'll try another, and if that doesn't work, I'll try another. I'll keep working until I succeed."

Mrs. Rosenbloom's feelings turned from sadness to joy. "Carol, I believe you. I believe you will succeed. It's amazing how God works, isn't it? I believe this hideous event has awakened you from your coma, and I believe you'll be leaving Crossville before too long. Now go upstairs, and take your shower. Change your clothes, and then come back down. We'll talk some more. You sound like the Carol Rosenbloom of old."

Carol turned and started towards the stairway when Mrs. Rosenbloom spoke again. "And one more thing. Remember your mother when you come into your riches."

"Don't worry mom," Carol replied. "We'll leave Crossville together."

CHAPTER 42

B efore the group meeting was to begin, Chou Chang
summoned Sun Lee to his office. Chou Chang greeted
Sun Lee warmly, and courteously offered him a seat. Chou
himself then rose from his chair and talked directly to Sun
Lee. "Sun Lee, you have performed superbly, and you have
been very effective, but I believe it is time for a change. Back
in the United States FBI Agents Pete Vangard and Emily Chandler are looking for you. Your secretary informed
us—although, actually, she is our secretary. In addition, our
sources in the FBI and CIA have informed us of numerous
communications and e-mail traffic pertaining to Mr. Jack
Butler. Many FBI and CIA agents are involved in this case,
and eight of our own people have been mentioned as suspects. Most importantly, they are focusing on you. The death
of Kirby Wadsworth is also being questioned. I have my suspicions about Professor Wadsworth's death, but no matter,
the officials in the United States think there was foul play,
and an investigation into his death is underway. You cannot
return to the United States. We will always be indebted to
you, and I am sure we will always need your advice. Feel free
to offer your opinion at any time, but please don't interfere
with your successor. He has already been chosen, and, as we
speak, he is on his way to the United States."

Sun Lee was stunned and speechless. He started to speak and beg for a chance to complete his work, but he realized that getting reinstated as the chief architect of the Ovamort program was unachievable, and he politely replied, "I did the best I could, and I believe the program is a success. Ovamort has been delivered successfully on two occasions, and I do not think a third delivery will be necessary. Taiwan will definitely fall, and I believe Taiwan will soon be a part of China. As for the United States, I believe that in not too long a time period it will be tremendously weakened, and its supremacy as the only world power can certainly be challenged. Who knows what will happen in a year or so?"

Chou Chang responded, "I believe you're right and thank you once again. Now let's get ready for the meeting."

Chou Chang was at the head of the table and began the discussion.

"Thank you all for coming, and thank you all for your dedication and service to your beloved native homeland of China, and particularly for your dedication and service to Project Mao. I would like to thank Mei Lee for all her financial help, and Yu Chen for bringing the proposal to me. In particular I would like to thank Dr. Sun Lee for leading the entire project. Sun Lee, you were superb. I am sorry you won't be continuing your work on the Ovamort program in the United States, but I can understand why you submitted your resignation. I am sure you will enjoy your retirement here in China, and I hope you will continue to advise us in the years ahead. With the generous stipend granted to you by our government, you should be very comfortable.

"Now I would like to thank those of the original group who are not here today. I would like to thank Chin Dong, now deceased, for developing Ovamort, our ultimate weapon. Lastly I would like to thank Kirby Wadsworth, our former American partner, who, more than any one else, was responsible for this project.

"Because of the great work of Sun Lee, pregnancies in the United States will continue to decrease. Almost the entire female population in the United States will have been affected by Ovamort, and the total population will fall drastically. I believe the United States will enter a great depression, and I believe economic ruin will follow.

"Project Mao will soon be a complete success. I believe that in the near future it is possible we will be holding this meeting in the United States, and instead of being served Western-style coffee, everybody will be drinking tea. It will not be high tea served at four o'clock in the afternoon like the English, but good old Chinese tea served all day long."

The meeting was actually quite short for the monumental achievement they were celebrating, but everyone was emotionally drained and ready to retire. Sun Lee left particularly early, because of his disappointment at being relieved of his position. Residing in China, and being promised a comfortable life style for the rest of his life did not bring him much solace.

Chou Chang and Yu Chen were the last to leave, neither of whom was very euphoric. Yu Chen spoke to Chou Chang, "It sounds like Sun Lee gave you a very favorable report."

Chou Chang replied, "He gave me and excellent report. There was one rather major unavoidable complication, but the delivery of the Ovamort was a complete success. Sun Lee performed in his usual stellar manner, and all the Ovamort trucks reached their destination. We have succeeded.

Yu Chen lowered his eyes and spoke again, "When's it going to happen?"

Chou Chang replied, "It's already over. I have already been notified, and I think Sun Lee expected it. He certainly would have agreed that a person in his situation was expendable, and that he was too much of a liability to be allowed to remain alive. The United States was making too many inquires about Sun Lee's role in certain activities related to the Ovamort project. Our government was receiving too much official correspondence and too many official communications for us to completely ignore the situation. You know, I can actually picture Sun Lee making the presentation, and hearing him conclude that in the best interest of China, his own death was the only option. He was a true Chinese hero.

"Yu Chen, go on home and relax. There is nothing we can do but wait and see. It has been a long process and I am sure you have your own thoughts and memories. Enjoy them. You deserve them, and bring them with you to our next meeting. Sun Lee told me we will love New York."

Pete Vangard had only taken a few steps towards Emily's office before his concentration was suddenly interrupted by the ring of his land line. Agent Jordan was the closest, but didn't make any attempt to respond until Pete finally yelled, "Jordan, answer the phone. The last time somebody didn't answer a ringing phone, he wound up missing."

"Okay, Okay, don't be so impatient," Agent Jordan said as he grabbed the receiver.

"Agent Jordan here."

"Agent Jordan, this is Catherine, Agent Vangard's secretary. I need to speak to Agent Vangard immediately. It's very important."

"Pete, don't leave. It's your secretary. She says she needs you right away."

'Okay, I'll take it. Thank you."

"Agent Vangard, this is Catherine. Do I ever have fabulous news for you? Listen carefully because you're not going to believe your ears."

Agent Vangard remained silent as Catherine continued speaking.

Finally he responded, "Catherine, are you sure?"

"Yes, I'm sure. I just received notification."

Agent Vangard spoke, "Catherine, thank you. You made my day, my week, my year. I'll tell Agent Chandler right away. I was on my way to her office when you called."

Pete gushed with excitement as he quickly walked towards Emily's office. Emily, he thought, *you're finally going to get some good news*. Without knocking, he barged into her office and found Emily sitting motionless in her chair staring at the papers on her desk.

"Emily, thank goodness you're okay. I was worried about you."

"You needn't have worried, Pete. I'm not the suicide type. Yes, I was depressed, and thinking about an unhappy future, but at least I was thinking about the future. That's always healthy. I was always taught that a person will go to hell if he commits suicide, and living on earth is certainly better than that. Besides I'm chicken."

"Emily, you don't need to torment yourself anymore. One of Sun Lee's lieutenants just drove one of those elusive Ryder trucks right up to a nearby police station and gave himself up. The police have already transferred him to F.B.I. headquarters, and you and I are to report to the interrogation room to interview him. Let's go. I'll let you do the honors."

Agents Chandler and Vangard walked to the interrogation room quickly. They were promptly briefed by the awaiting senior personnel, and then entered the interrogation room ready to begin their inquisition.

"Good day sir, I'm Agent Chandler, and this is my partner Agent Vangard. I understand you have some information for us. Why don't you begin by telling us your name?"

"My name is Charlie Lai."

"Okay Charlie Lai, why did you drive that truck up to the police station and turn yourself in?"

"Because I know too much, and I was afraid I would be murdered."

"Why don't you explain that?"

"I was afraid I would be killed by Sun Lee, my past immediate boss. Sun Lee told me he had already killed two people because they "had" to be killed, and I figured I was next. I knew too much not only about the murders, but also about Project Mao and a drug called Ovamort."

Emily questioned him, "What are Project Mao and this drug called Ovamort, and how do you know about them?"

"I know about them because Sun Lee told me everything. He had to tell me or else I wouldn't have helped him with his last delivery. I figured he thought he could tell me everything, because I was a dead man. That's why I'm here, for protection."

Emily spoke, "Tell us the whole story from the beginning, and tell it any way you want. We'll interrupt if we think it's necessary."

"Alright, I'll tell you just the way Sun Lee told me."

"Project Mao is the name of the project in which Ovamort, an ovary destroying drug, was developed, tested in experimental field trials in China, and then disseminated throughout the entire United States. The purpose was to sterilize as many American women as possible so that they would be unable to bear children. Sun Lee speculated that this would cause an economic collapse in the United States."

Pete Vangard spoke, "I'm curious about that economic collapse. We live in a global economy, so why wouldn't there be an economic collapse in China?"

"Because our officials in China prepared for it. It hurt, but they were ready, and they also had the psychological advantage of knowing what was happening, and how it was going to benefit the people of China."

Agent Chandler spoke, "How did they spread the Ovamort throughout the United States?"

Charlie Lai responded, "They spread it through salt, common table salt. Look at the labels on the foods you buy. Salt is always one of the main ingredients. That's how they did it, through common table salt."

Agent Chandler interrupted, "Wouldn't that take a tremendous amount of salt to accomplish that?"

"Not really," Charlie Lai replied. "Remember, we had four transfer stations distributing the salt and it took only three truckloads from each station to supply the entire United States for two months. Even that gave us plenty of room for error."

Charlie Lai continued, "Ovamort is a chemical compound that consists of two parts. One part is the active ovary killing part. The other part is normal food salt. These two parts were chemically joined together to form Ovamort, the pharmaceutical compound that chemically sterilized the young Chinese women during the experimental field trials in China.

"During the experiment, Ovamort was placed directly in the food. It was simply sprinkled in the food before the lunches were distributed. It functioned like salt, and was the finishing touch ingredient that made the food delicious.

"Distributing the Ovamort nationwide in the United States had all been worked out during the research and development phase of Project Mao. In fact easy distribution and undetectability had been part of the Chinese medical researchers' mission. The researchers had developed Ovamort so that it had the same texture and appearance of normal salt. It was odorless. It had the same color as salt, and it tasted like salt.

"With the open business policy between the United States and China, China had acquired Kleins Salt Company, the company which supplied eighty-five percent of the consumable food salt in the United States. Kleins reputation and the reputation of its salt were excellent. Kleins brand name was part of the American culture. The Chinese continued to operate Kleins in the same highly professional manner as before the acquisition. The only change was the hiring of some new loyal Chinese personnel, and even this was minimal.

"Kleins had four production centers and ten supply terminals nationwide. At the production centers the salt was produced, packaged in one pound containers, and then boxed in bulk for distribution. Each of these one pound containers was the easily recognized bright orange container known throughout the United States

"After the food salt was packaged and boxed at each of the four production centers, it was then trucked to two or three different Kleins' supply terminals. In this way all ten supply terminals received the salt. From the supply terminals the salt was then distributed to restaurant supply houses, grocery store supply stations, food producers, hotels, hospitals, etc. These businesses and organizations would then use the salt as intended. The salt would be placed on French fries, on restaurant tables, and on grocery store shelves. It would be put in the canned foods, in the packaged foods, and in the frozen foods. Salt is an amazingly large ingredient in almost all foods.

"The delivery system for Ovamort required only a minor modification from that already established and used by Kleins. After being packaged the Ovamort left International Pharmaceutical and was transported in Ryder trucks to four secret transfer stations that the Chinese government had set up. The transfer stations consisted of only a small warehouse, but more importantly, they were in close proximity to Kleins' four salt production centers.

"When the time came for the Ovamort to be substituted for Kleins'salt, the trucks filled with salt made a detour from the production centers. Instead of going directly to the supply terminals, they went to the closest secret transfer station. At the transfer stations, each truck unloaded its salt cargo, picked up a shipment of Ovamort, and then left for the supply terminals. The switch at the transfer stations took only a minimal amount of time. The salt that had been unloaded and left at the transfer stations was then trucked to the research wing of International Pharmaceutical. International Pharmaceutical then chemically changed the salt into Ovamort and the cycle would begin again.

"Sun Lee, M.D. followed the manufacture of Ovamort from beginning to end. He saw the process begin, and he saw the final packaging and boxing of the Ovamort. He watched as a random container was chosen for inspection. He saw the Ovamort loaded onto the Ryder tricks, and he himself drove the Ovamort laden truck to the transfer station. Sun Lee watched intently as the normal food salt was unloaded, and the Ovamort was substituted. The truck was then on its way to one of Kleins' supply stations. Sun Lee once again drove the truck carrying the Ovamort. The lost time was completely regained during the transportation, and the Ovamort was successfully delivered to the terminal supply station. The process was complete and it was successful.

"There was no increase in salt volume as there was always just an exchange of the salt for the Ovamort, or the Ovamort for the salt. There was never any excess storage or accumulation.

"An inspection of the salt took place randomly just before the salt left Kleins' production facilities. It always passed. Why wouldn't it? It was pure normal salt, all packaged and ready for distribution.

"After leaving Kleins' production facilities very rarely did any other inspections take place. The FDA didn't inspect. The military occasionally had inspections on their bases, where meats were inspected routinely, but that was about it. These areas received normal food salt without the stop at the transfer stations. This was very easily computer controlled, and it was also accomplished with the long time usual truck drivers.

"Once delivered to a grocery store no inspections took place. The same for the fast food restaurants and hotels. No inspection took place. It was just a matter of time before Ovamort reached the dinner table and the French fries.

"The whole distribution process of the Ovamort took a relatively short time period. It only took a single distribution to the respective end terminals for it to be distributed nationwide. It was consumed. It destroyed the ovaries, and then it was excreted. And one of the strong points of the plan was that its effect took place several months later. By that time the routine was back to normal, and only normal food salt was being delivered. There was no trace of Ovamort in the production facilities, in the trucks, at International

Pharmaceutical, or anyplace in the United States. And that's my whole story."

There was a short silence before Pete turned to Emily and hurriedly spoke. "Emily, the Ovamort can't be too far disseminated at this point. It's only been a couple of days. Maybe we can stop it."

"Don't worry," Charles Lai said. "Sun Lee only distributed pure salt for his last delivery. While Sun Lee was busy with Jack Butler, I never made the exchange of the Ovamort for the salt. As I told Sun Lee, everything was the same in both trucks, right down to the color of the boxes, the position of the boxes, and even the same serial numbers. You don't need to worry about Ovamort affecting any more of your young women. The last delivery of Ovamort was never made. As I said before, only pure salt was delivered. I knew that Sun Lee had killed Professor Wadsworth, and I wasn't going to let that happen to me. As far as I was concerned, it was more important that I keep an eye on Sun Lee than it was to exchange the contents of the two trucks. I wanted to remain alive, and guess what—here I am, alive, and seeking political asylum."

Pete and Emily gasped, and Emily even smiled a little bit, something she hadn't done in a long time. Emily said. "You stay here, Mr. Lai, and I'll get you a pen and paper so you can write it all down. Write it down clearly, because I'm going to read your report again, and again, and again."

"Well Emily, how do you feel now?" Pete said as they exited the interrogation room.

"Pete, you know how I feel. I've been redeemed. We stopped Professor Wadsworth; we stopped Sun Lee, and we stopped the entire Mao Project. We got them all. Personally, I'll always be disappointed about not being able to have children, but as my husband said, we'll get by, and besides, families without children are now the norm. I just have to face reality, and accept it. I can do that. Hatefully and grudgingly, I'll probably also end up accepting Professor Wadsworth's opinion that not having children is good for the country. And how about you Pete? How do you feel?"

"I feel great. I just participated in one of the most important investigations this country has ever seen, and we were victorious. What a glorious feeling!"

"That's not what I mean Pete, and you know it."

"I know what you mean Emily, and truthfully I feel pretty good. I told you before that both the CT scan and the ultrasound exam revealed a mass in my pancreas, but I don't think I told you about my needle biopsy. The results were inconclusive so we still don't have a definite diagnosis, although my surgeon told me he isn't very optimistic. He said that statistically most masses like mine are malignant, but anyway, we'll know soon. Now that this case is over, I'm going to have surgery as soon as possible. If you get a chance, come visit me in the hospital."

Emily peered slowly around the hospital door to see if Pete was awake.

"Come on in Emily," Pete said. "I'm awake."

Emily spoke, "I didn't want to disturb you if you were sleeping, but I just had to see you. How are you doing?"

"I'm doing great. The surgeon says he got it all, and there was no evidence of cancer. The mass was completely benign, and I'll be going home in a few days. He doesn't expect my symptoms to recur, and he expects a full recovery. I'll be back to work in about five weeks."

"That's great news Pete. I'm happy for you."

"Thanks Emily, I appreciate that, but hold on. I've got more good news."

"What is it?" Emily said.

"I got a promotion. I'm going to be in charge of the western half of the entire district. I'm to have three weeks of intensive training, and then I will assume my new position as soon as I'm physically able. What do you think of that?"

"That's fantastic Pete. Congratulations. You deserve it."

"And you Emily. I want you to join me. Come with me. We're a great team." Emily paused briefly as a tear welled up in her eye. "Thank you Pete, but you're going to need a new partner."

"What do you mean?" Pete said.

"My husband and I won the lottery," Emily replied.

Pete exclaimed, "You won the lottery. You're awfully calm for having won the lottery, but I guess I missed all the excitement because of my surgery. Congratulations! That's great. But hey, what about me? You're rich and now you're going to abandon me."

"No, I'll never abandon you Pete, but now I've got other interests. Yes, my husband and I are rich, but not financially rich. We got a baby---from overseas. Remember, the blight never hit over there. Well, we entered a baby lottery over there, and we won. My husband did it. He persisted, and persisted and persisted. All that time we were working on the case, Dave was trying to get us a baby, and we finally got one. It's a boy, and we're going to Ireland in two weeks to pick him up. I can't wait."

Emily leaned down and gave Pete a hug."

"Stop!" Pete squealed. "That hurts my incision. Besides physical contact like that is against organizational guidelines. I'll have to report you."

Emily stepped back and defiantly spoke, "Agent Peter Vangard, go ahead and report me. I'm not even on the payroll anymore. I have completely resigned from the FBI. I've got a new boss, and with all due respect, he's going to be smarter and better looking than my previous boss, and he'll certainly have a better disposition. When we get him back from Ireland, come see him anytime. You'll love him."

CHAPTER 43

President Freeman immediately assembled the inner circle of his most trusted advisors to discuss the crisis. He spoke with a clear and sharp voice, "I have already talked to each of you individually and you all know that it was the Chinese who attacked us. It was the Chinese who perpetrated this heinous crime on the United States. They purposely disseminated their ovary killing agent Ovamort throughout the entire United States in order to cause the infertility catastrophe we are now facing. What are we going to do?"

Don Hudson, the White House Chief of Staff answered, "Where's the rest of the staff? Are they coming, or is this the entire brain trust?"

President Freeman responded, "This is it. At this point in time I don't want too many people involved. The more people you include, the greater the chance of an accidental disclosure, or even a deliberate leak, and we certainly don't want that."

Don Hudson replied, "I understand that, and I also understand how tough this is going to be. This is a very delicate and complex situation, and it is going to require a very diplomatic response."

The President replied, "Let's discuss some possible options for a while, and if it seems like we're hitting a brick wall, we can always expand our task force later."

John Watkins, the Director of Homeland Security, spoke, "When Charlie Lai was interrogated, I believe he told the truth, and I believe this particular Chinese plot is over. That Ryder truck that Charlie Lai so politely delivered to us contained the whole last shipment of Ovamort. At this time there is not an imminent security risk on that front, and we have tried to minimize any future Ovamort effects by recalling every single Klein's salt container still on the market."

President Freeman spoke, "Thank you John. I agree with you in that regard, but how are we going to retaliate against the Chinese?"

General Arnold, the Chairman of the Joint Chiefs of Staff replied, "Retaliating against China would be a formidable, if not impossible, assignment."

"Why is that?" the President said.

General Arnold answered, "Because China is a powerful country that's a long distance away; it has a large land mass, and it has over a billion people. It would be extremely difficult to retaliate successfully."

Don Hudson spoke, "I believe it will also bring down your presidency. Look what happened in Viet Nam and Iraq, both of which are small countries compared to China. With China you would have to magnify your commitment in money, men and other resources a zillion times. The United States can not afford to enter into any type of military conflict with China. The United States will lose, and you will lose your presidency."

General Arnold spoke again, "Before everyone becomes too pessimistic, I want to remind everyone that the United States possesses some very powerful weapons."

President Freeman responded, "So do the Chinese. They have weapons that are just as powerful as ours, and I don't think those weapons should be used. Those weapons that constitute such a marvelous scientific and military achievement are so destructive, that they simultaneously represent a tremendous engineering feat of our modern technological world, but they also represent an anachronism in that same modern world because of their same destructive capability. I firmly believe that the old time direct confrontational wars are becoming obsolete. Wars are questionably alright for small countries with limited firepower, but the major destruction, devastation and loss of life caused by major wars using almost unlimited weaponry are unconscionable. Even excluding nuclear weapons, if we fought an old-fashioned conventional military war, there would be monumental damage to both countries. We cannot do that."

General Arnold spoke, "How about a single limited strike aimed at a particular target?"

President Freeman replied, "There is no such thing as a limited single strike. The Chinese would be forced to strike back, and then we would have to do the same, and so on into infinity."

Don Hudson spoke, "I thought you were going to say 'and so on into' World War Three."

"Believe me, I've agonized over that consequence, and if I thought it was even a remote possibility, I wouldn't retaliate at all," the President said.

"Since you mentioned it, why do we need to retaliate?" Don Hudson said.

The president replied, "In order to protect and maintain our strong image in the eyes of the Chinese, and also to prevent possible future attacks. The Chinese have to know we retaliated, and at the same time our retaliation has to be concealed from the rest of the world. The Chinese have to be able to save face, so that they are not required to retaliate against us."

General Arnold spoke, "Are you considering economic sanctions?"

President Freeman responded, "For effective economic sanctions we would need a multinational agreement, and in this day and age we can't get it. Too many countries derive a tremendous economic benefit from their trade with China."

General Arnold responded, "If we can't use economic sanctions and we can't use our military might, what do we do, just sit here and pretend nothing happened?"

Don Hudson replied, "I think that may be a prudent choice. Only a limited number of people are aware that the Chinese used their Ovamort to cause this catastrophe, and we could always deny that we ever discovered the cause of the infertility crisis. Then there would be no reason to retaliate. According to our experts our country is going to recover, and like all major crises of the past, the United States will come back stronger and better. I think a complete profession of ignorance is a reasonable possibility. Don't let the American people know it was the Chinese. Let them think it was some unexplained natural phenomenon that was self limited, and that has now passed. Mr. President, the American people will never know the true cause, and they will thank you for leading them out of this crisis."

President Freeman spoke, "That's an interesting concept, and I would consider some variation of that theme as a temporary delaying tactic, but we can't let the Chinese think they got away with this heinous plot. Otherwise, they may attack again. We have to retaliate in some way, and I believe we have to do what the Chinese did. We have to produce a bloodless, non-lethal, non destructive method of retaliation. That's the way the new wars will be fought. In the future, non destructive methods will be used to achieve international superiority, and I want the United States to be preeminent in this field."

General Arnold spoke, "And how do we accomplish that?"

President Freeman replied, "We assemble our research physicists, and our research chemists, and our research biologists, and any other intelligentsia we need and we put them to work. If we are to become the dominant world leader in this new type of warfare, we need to develop our own disaster producing agents. The main research thrust of the entire United States should be geared to discovering the "silent killers" that will serve as our future weaponry. When we have developed those weapons, then we will retaliate with an attack."

"Do you have any ideas?" John Watkins said.

"Of course I do," President Freeman replied, "If Kirby Wadsworth were still alive, I would have him in my office this afternoon, but because he's dead, I'll settle for a few of his colleagues who have the same determination and mind set that he did. We need to get a few of those brainy guys from the Institute of Population Demographics, and have them develop a product that can affect China like Ovamort affected the United States. Of course, all of this has to be off the record, and if by accident we are discovered, we can always justify our actions by saying we were trying to solve the world population problem. We can say we were acting on the conclusions of the late and world famous population control expert, Professor Kirby Wadsworth."

CHAPTER 44

Fertility Crisis Hits China blared the newspaper headlines. The unexplained exponential increase in the number of multiple pregnancies (twin, triple, and even quadruple pregnancies) was putting a marked strain on Chinese society, and was actually starting to precipitate a crisis. In addition to the human pregnancies, the same unexplained increase was occurring in the country's dogs and cats. More animal pregnancies were occurring, the litters were bigger, and the dog and cat population was exploding.

The Chinese spokesperson had no explanation for the precipitous increase in these multiple pregnancies. He only verified that they were occurring throughout the entire country, and he pessimistically stated that no one had any idea as to how or why they were happening.

LaVergne, TN USA
16 April 2010
179501LV00001B/3/P